Motel California

Michael Carlon

ISBN-10:0-9979839-7-3
ISBN-13:978-0-9979839-7-5

Praise for Uncorking a Murder Farrah Graham Book 1

"It is a real page turner murder mystery with so many interesting plot twists. The best part of the book is how the mystery gets solved - it brings a whole new level of excitement to the storyline. Michael is a fun and creative writer." —Tracy, 5 Star Review on Amazon.com

"Whoever likes Patterson, Harlan Coben or Patricia Cornwell, you need to check out Michael Carlon's book Uncorking a Murder! Just finished reading it and I love it. Can't wait for more! Michael Carlon, you better hurry up with your next book!" —Monika, 5 Star review on Amazon.com

"Uncorking a Murder had interesting characters, plot twists and of course a good old mystery to keep you guessing. Kept my interest and found it hard to put down. Can't wait to read the next book in the series and see how the characters develop." —Susan, 5 Star review on Amazon.com

"Wow, I had fun reading this book and can't wait for the next one! I looked forward to turning the page as I enjoyed picking up on all of the clues and finding the humorous references." —Laurie, 5 Star review on Amazon.com

Praise for The Last Homily Farrah Graham Book 2

"The plot of this book is something you don't read every day. You never see the twists coming, which makes this a hard book to put down. Once again Michael Carlon has created complex characters and a story that keeps you intrigued from the very beginning. Buy this book now! You won't regret it."
— Layla, 5 Star Review on Amazon.com

"Another awesome read. This time, Mr Carlon touches upon very sensitive, but very real subject matter; he subtly weaves it into the story so as not to shock the reader, but only as a reminder of what's out there, often right in front of us. Farrah and Jimmy bring it all together, but not without a little humor in the midst of a rather serious story. Michael really knows how to twist a plot so engaging than when the big reveal happens, one is left stunned." — Cecilia, 5 Star review on Amazon.com

"Once again Mr. Carlon did not disappoint! This was a great read that I would recommend to anyone. Anxiously waiting for the next installment." — Jennifer, 5 Star review on Amazon.com

For Diane O'Connell—the heart and soul of Trinity Catholic High School

CHAPTER ONE

Peaceful Easy Feeling

Joe Feld was disgusted by the fat man's use of bread to sop up the remaining Francaise sauce from his plate, an action which was accompanied by a slurping sound that Feld found both unnerving and distasteful. Ordinarily, the topic of breaking a man's legs isn't usually discussed over a plate of Chicken Francaise. Conventional mob wisdom dictates that such a discussion be held over something with a red sauce such as Chicken Parmigiana or, better yet, Cacciatore, but this was south Florida and that meant conventional thinking could be thrown out the window.

A graduate of MIT, Joe Feld just inked a deal to sell his tech company, Fast Lane, for twenty-five million dollars to an LA-based conglomerate looking to the mobile sector as a path to growth. While the money wasn't yet in his account, he had plans to invest in a new venture, one closely tied to a childhood dream. To realize it, though, he needed the fat man's help and that's what brought him down to Pompano Beach.

Gianni's restaurant is a Pompano staple, a town where

the fat man, mob boss Anthony Carbona, spent the winter months. At sixty-six years old, Carbona's blood was thinner than it used to be and he simply couldn't take the New York winters any longer. The fact that the mercury in the thermometer had only climbed to the fifty-six degree mark had him in an extraordinarily foul mood.

The restaurant was named after his oldest son, who had an important role to play in the family business. Carbona was involved in racketeering, loan sharking, and illegal gambling and needed a way to clean his money. A cash-only restaurant was perfect for that purpose and the oldest Carbona boy was more than happy to help his father wash his cash. He couldn't be any more different than his younger brother Michael, whose proficiency in math and science propelled him to the halls of the Massachusetts Institute of Technology and a degree in Astrophysics. Michael was the reason Anthony was having the discussion he was having over a plate of lightly pan-fried chicken in a lemon and white wine reduction.

"Let me ask youse something," the mob boss said with a mouth full of food, "how comes you scientist types keep talking about global warming and it's not even sixty degrees in south Florider."

Even if he wanted to hide his New York accent, Anthony couldn't. It was as much a part of him as his pinky, which was adorned by a diamond encrusted ring commemorating his April birthday (though Anthony privately wished he was born one month later as he felt emerald green was more his color).

"Personally, I think global warming is a hoax created by and for the Chinese in order to make U.S. manufacturing non-competitive."

Joe Feld didn't believe the words that just came out of his mouth. In fact, they were posted on social media by the current president of the United States back in 2012 when he was still a reality TV star. Feld said it because he thought it's what the mobster wanted to hear; he had a knack for telling people exactly what they wanted to hear.

"Smart answer, kid," Anthony said while tearing a piece of bread in half. Joe noticed the man had hands like baseball mitts and didn't have a hard time believing they could pulverize another man's bones.

"My son Mikey tells me you are about to sell your company for a mint, so why is it some soon to be Internet rich guy is having lunch with a guy like me at a restaurant in Pompano Beach that is technically closed on Mondays?"

Joe was a classmate of Michael's. After graduating, Michael went on to further his education in a doctoral program while Joe started Fast Lane. They graduated number 1 and number 2 in their class, respectively.

On the surface, Fast Lane was similar to ride share competitors Uber and Lyft—people used the app to arrange rides from other users willing to turn their cars into taxis. While Joe majored in computer science and engineering, he minored in behavioral psychology and built operant conditioning principles into the app as a way of differentiating it from the competition. Software randomly gave users free rides—a feature that explained its growth trajectory, but that's not all. It also doubled or tripled the fee paid to drivers on a random basis (at the company's expense). This led to a glut of drivers eager to service the fast-growing user base. Anthony took the meeting with Joe as a favor to his youngest son.

"Mr. Carbona, I have a business proposition for you."

Carbona put down the piece of bread he was using to clean his plate of the last remnants of sauce and stared Feld right in the eyes.

"I don't know what Mikey has told you about the family business kid, but I ain't what youse might call a traditional businessman."

"Let me explain," Joe said smugly, clearly not intimidated by Carbona's change in tone. "I'm looking to take some of my money and fund a comeback tour for a band I loved when I was a kid."

"Good for youse kid, but I ain't exactly the Make-a-Wish foundation."

"I'm not asking for your money Mr. Carbona, but I do need a man with your type of connections to see that the deal goes through."

"Explain."

"The band I want to bring on tour was very popular in the 90's. There were four members; Glenn, Donnie, Randy, and Bernie..."

"Sounds like a fuckin' boy band," Carbona interrupted.

"Not quite," Joe replied, but held back the true nature of the band. "When they disbanded twenty years ago, they signed a contract stipulating they could never tour again unless they all agreed to it. Three of the guys are on board, but one is refusing to participate."

"Let me guess, you need my help in getting one of these pussies to see the light."

"Bernie was their guitarist and wrote all of their songs. He's reinvented himself and has a new album to promote. He's adamant about keeping as far a distance as he can from the old days."

"I gotta ask, kid, why do you give a shit? Find another band or something else to invest in."

"Mr. Carbona, nostalgic acts like theirs pulled in tens of millions of dollars on tour last year and every other band is already doing something. I've been in discussions with their former manager and I'm pretty sure I can double my investment. It's a license to print money."

Carbona contemplated what Feld just told him. The mob boss could certainly empathize with wanting to make some quick cash and, given the kid was a friend of his son's, decided to help him out. Plus, Carbona had his own connections in the music business and knew that what Feld said about nostalgia acts was true.

"Whadya need from me?"

Joe smiled. "Bernie is going to be in LA this week promoting his new album. On Thursday night, he'll be attending a party at a suite in the Hotel Palomino..."

Carbona interrupted, "How come youse know so much about his schedule?"

"Because I arranged the party and hired him to make an appearance."

Carbona was satisfied with Feld's answer. "Continue."

"I just need you to send a guy over to the hotel to have a chat with Bernie and tell him it's cool if he doesn't want to reunite with his former band, but that it would be in his best interest if he allows them to tour with a new guitarist."

"And if he turns my guy's offer down?"

Feld looked at the mob boss square in his eyes. "Your guy breaks his fucking legs."

"You've seen way too many movies kid. How's about you leave the method of convincing to me." It was a statement, not a question.

"You're the boss," Feld said.

"Now there's another matter we need to come to an agreement on," Carbona let his last word hang until Feld caught his drift.

"How much?"

"Fifty large aughtta do it."

When Feld didn't blink at the number, Carbona countered his own offer. "Make that seventy-five. Yeah, dat sounds better. Now I usually ask for half now and half after the job is done, but since youse friends with Mikey you can pay me afterwards. Deal?" Carbona extended his hand across the table. Feld shook it.

"Deal."

Carbona started to relax. "Gianni," he shouted, "I'm done. Take my plate and bring me an espresso."

Almost immediately, a tall and painfully thin man with shoulder length hair and a beard came and removed a plate.

"Joe, you ever meet Mikey's brother Gianni?"

"Can't say that I have."

"Gianni, Joe here went to college with your brother. In my day, college meant something else." Carbona laughed. Old time gangsters like him referred to doing time as going to college.

"Nice to meet you," Gianni said, avoiding eye contact.

"You want espresso too?" Gianni asked.

"No thank you."

"I don't trust a man who doesn't drink espresso," Gianni said to his father.

"That's enough, Gianni," his father said. "Joe's a friend of mine now."

Gianni left and Anthony looked Joe in the eyes. "You seem awfully comfortable for a man that just asked me to potentially break another man's legs."

"I gotta peaceful easy feeling about it, Mr. Carbona."

In Feld's mind, he was a master of the universe and was in complete control over his destiny. Nothing could go wrong with a plan that someone with his brains and talents concocted. He wasn't blinded by hubris, he bathed in it.

CHAPTER TWO

Bringing on the Heartbreak

Farrah Graham, the creator and host of the Uncorking a Murder podcast, was waiting in Adam Kimmel's green room when a producer dressed in black entered looking both nervous and disheveled with an earpiece dangling from her ear.

"Ms. Graham, you're on in sixty seconds. Where's your partner?"

Jimmy Rella, whom Farrah nicknamed Jimmy Doubts due to his nervous tendencies, left the green room five minutes earlier to find a men's room. While only twenty-seven, his bladder mistook him for a much older man.

Farrah reached into her purse to grab her phone and text him when the door swung open.

"You like to keep me guessing don't you, Doubts?"

"Sorry, pardner," Jimmy said in a western twang, "I got a little turned around. It was like playing a level of Pac-Man to get back here."

Farrah rolled her eyes. It wasn't the first time Jimmy's need for a men's room came at an inopportune moment, and it certainly wouldn't be the last.

The producer stuffed the earpiece back into place and spoke with someone in a remote part of the studio.

"Ready to rock," she confirmed to the voice on the other end.

"Ms. Graham, Mr. Doubts, please follow me."

They followed the producer through a dark maze as the sound of Adam Kimmel's voice grew louder.

They were in Los Angeles on the first stop on their press tour to promote the third season of their podcast, which takes a serialized deep dive into interesting murder cases. For four years running, Uncorking a Murder has been the number one downloaded podcast in the United States, a fact that brought them financial comfort along with the envy of other podcasters – not to mention those in traditional media who considered podcasters below stand-up comedians in the show-biz caste system.

The two were now standing behind the curtain, waiting for Adam to introduce them.

"Sixty seconds till pullback," the producer said.

Farrah looked at Jimmy, who was breathing deeply.

"You look nervous, Doubts," she whispered.

"Comes with the name."

Four years earlier, Jimmy was interning for Uncorking a Murder when he took a call from a retired police detective in Florida who was looking for Farrah's help on an old case. Farrah was intrigued, so she and Jimmy followed their curiosity to south Florida where they unraveled a case featuring a wrongly imprisoned man, a corrupt senator, and a narcissistic Romanian CEO who thought he was a vampire. The subsequent season of Uncorking a Murder broke download records on iTunes and Google

Play and thrust both Farrah and Jimmy into the limelight.

The host's voice boomed in front of them. "You know our next guests from the wildly successful Uncorking a Murder podcast. I hope they don't ever make a season about me. Please welcome Farrah Graham and Jimmy Doubts!"

The curtain pulled back and the house band played a jazz version of Iron Maiden's Murder in the Rue Morgue while Farrah and Jimmy walked on stage. They approached Adam's desk, where he was waiting to greet them. After shaking hands, they took their seats on the couch adjacent to the desk. Once the applause died down, Adam began his interview.

"First off, let me just say that I love your podcast. The only problem is, whenever you release a new season, I lose an entire day of my life. The storytelling is so good I just can't stop listening."

"Thank you for saying that, Adam," Farrah said. "Who would have thought a former patent attorney from New York could hold anyone's attention for ten minutes let alone ten hours a season?"

Her wisecrack earned a laugh from the studio audience.

Five years ago, Farrah was a workaholic partner in a high-powered Manhattan law firm when Melody, her girlfriend at the time, gave her an ultimatum—the job or me. Farrah quit her job and the two sold their SoHo loft and bought a place in Connecticut. Not content to sit idly at home, Farrah started the podcast as a way to keep busy and never dreamed of the success that followed. Her relationship with Melody fizzled after Farrah's workaholic tendencies returned following the unintended popularity of the show. She's recently adjusted to being single and has dated both men and women while navigating the complicated world of being a celebrity dating in her forties.

"I just finished the last season this morning," Adam continued, "not to give anything away but my wife had to pick my jaw off the floor at the end of it."

"It was a surreal experience. I was just trying to enjoy my vacation when this case literally landed in my lap."

The previous summer, Farrah was vacationing on Cape Cod when she went to Mass one Sunday morning and saw the priest collapse near the altar while attempting to say the closing prayer. The medical examiner pronounced him dead and would later rule poisoning as the cause. Farrah and Jimmy got involved in the investigation and were able to prevent another murder.

"And Jimmy, do I understand correctly that you were interning at a law firm last summer when Farrah asked you to help her in this investigation?"

"That's right," Jimmy said. "I had just completed my first year as a law student and was interning in New York when Farrah saved me."

"Saved you? Was it that bad?" Adam asked while laughing.

"Let's just say I wasn't up for playing the game," Jimmy said.

The day Farrah called Jimmy to ask for his help last summer he was berated by the director of human resources for not telling her about his lunch with one of the firm's partners. She then sexually harassed him by asking that he bartend a party she was hosting—he was to wear nothing but a black bow tie and tight black pants. He walked out of the firm that day and never turned back, slamming the door closed on his nascent legal career.

"Well it seems as if your decision paid off. If I'm to read these numbers correctly, Uncorking a Murder has over two hundred million downloads. I'm no math genius, but that must translate to some pretty significant advertising revenue."

"We are not going to starve anytime soon," Farrah said.

"It begs the question, what's season four looking like?"

"Well, to be honest, I'm not sure if there is ever going to be a season four."

The studio audience gasped collectively at Farrah's admission and Kimmel was caught off guard. "Wait, what?"

"At the risk of boring your audience, there's a patent troll coming after successful podcasters."

"I'm sorry, but what does the term patent troll even mean? Sounds like a character in some kind of legal fairy tale penned by the Brothers Grimm, Esquire."

Adam's joke earned a laugh from the audience.

"A patent troll is basically what we'd call a person or company that holds a patent and sues businesses that they believe infringe on their intellectual property."

Adam saw an opportunity for another joke and cut Farrah off. "You weren't kidding when you said being a patent attorney was boring."

The studio audience laughed at the host's joke.

"Our syndicator, Pro Cast, doesn't want to cough up the fees that this Troll is demanding so the future of our show, and others on our network, is in jeopardy until we come to a legal solution."

"You're bringing on the heartbreak here, Farrah," Adam said, quoting a song from his favorite band, Def

Leppard. He tried to fit a Leppard reference in every show and was pleased to keep his streak going. "Does this troll have a name? Do you want my viewers to harass him?"

The studio audience cheered at this suggestion.

"We actually don't know if it is a he or a she," Jimmy piped up. "The suit was filed by an LLC named Interpersonal Audio. We can't find any names attached to that organization. Whoever set it up was very clever."

"So, what are you doing to fight this?"

"At the request of Pro Cast, I'm actually meeting with some other podcasters this week here in LA to discuss a plan of attack, but it would be premature to discuss at this juncture."

Part of the reason Farrah started their media tour on Kimmel's show was to make it more convenient to meet with the two other top podcasters on her network, Drew Baron and Tommy Tercel, whose shows were both based out of Southern California; Baron's from his garage in Highland Park, Tercel's from his studio in Glendale.

Adam rolled his eyes at Farrah's sudden switch back to formal legal speak and the audience responded with laughter.

"Well I hope you kick his ass!" Adam proclaimed, leading to cheers from the audience. "So, do you have any time to have fun here in LA? You know what they say about all work and no play."

"Well Adam, tomorrow Jimmy and I are going to wake up at 3am and do a media tour from the Beverly Hills Hotel."

"An ungodly hour. Why so early?"

"East Coast radio," Jimmy piped in. "We have to start recording spots for the morning drive."

"Oh yes, I remember my morning radio days. Brutal." Adam got his start doing 'morning zoo' radio shows in markets all over the country.

"It pays the bills," Farrah added.

"Well I wish you the best in your tour and especially in your fight against the troll," Adam said. "Can you guys stick around for our musical guest?"

"Absolutely," Farrah and Jimmy said simultaneously.

"Excellent," Adam said and then turned to look into a different camera. "Ladies and gentlemen, we have a special treat from you when we return. You may remember him as Bernie Beagle, but these days he's playing to a more mature crowd. When we come back, Bernie Deville will sing his new single *I Only Drink When I Smoke*.

The camera zoomed in on Farrah and Jimmy; viewers were treated to a close up of Doubt's mouth agape before the cut to commercial. While Jimmy was aware that Bernie Deville was the musical guest, due to a name change, he didn't connect the dots that the musical guest was actually one of his childhood heroes.

The band began playing and Farrah turned to Jimmy. "You look like you're in shock, Doubts."

"Years ago, I was literally the world's biggest fan of Bernie's old band. I saw them live once, and up until recently, it was one of the best days of my life."

"I wouldn't bring that up if you meet him," Adam advised. "He doesn't like to talk about his Beagle days."

"Yeah, I once ran into Debbie Gibson at a charity event and she corrected me by asking me to call her Deborah," Farrah added. "They are so eager to run away from the fame that made them rich."

"If he's so sore about his earlier stuff, why did you mention it in your teaser?" Jimmy asked.

"We cleared that with him. Without the teaser, I was afraid no one would tune in."

A producer came to the desk along with a makeup artist to touch up Adam's foundation—the show's director noticed he was looking a bit shiny during Farrah's segment.

"Everything okay in the dressing room, Annabelle?" Adam asked, wondering why his music segment producer was on stage when she was supposed to be escorting Bernie to the stage in two minutes.

"It sounds like World War 3 back there. This Bernie guy is pissed about something."

"Great," Adam replied. "Just great. Can you fix it? Adam asked. "You always have a way of taming the beasts that come into this place."

"I'm on it," Annabelle replied cheerily, then turned and muttered, "they don't pay me enough for this shit," as she walked off stage.

CHAPTER THREE

Desperado

While Farrah and Jimmy were being interviewed by Kimmel, Bernie Deville was tuning his guitar while arguing with his long-time manager, George Martini.

"No fucking way!" Bernie shouted.

"It's just twenty dates and the money is obscene!" Martini protested. He had not aged well over the past two decades. His face was blotchy with broken blood vessels and his stomach was distended, telltale signs of his constant overindulgence of alcohol. For the past month he'd been in negotiations with a potential promoter looking to reunite Bernie's old band in a tour that could bring in big bucks for all parties involved. Martini was aware that nostalgia acts were hot and when a well-financed old fan came along looking to capitalize on that trend, Martini reached out to Bernie's old bandmates to pitch them the idea. Due to their personal circumstances, all three practically salivated at the opportunity and now it was Martini's job to try and convince Bernie to join in.

"I don't need the fucking money. Why are you

buggering me to do this?"

His working-class British accent always came out when he was upset. He grabbed his cross necklace and unscrewed the bottom. It concealed a coke spoon, which he put to his nose for a toot.

"You better watch that," Martini protested. "We don't need an episode like The Canyon Club."

Last month, Bernie played a gig at a well-known club in Agoura Hills, CA. He had been up for three nights and passed out in the middle of a guitar solo.

"Have another drink, you fucking lush," Bernie said while wiping his nose.

"I know you don't need the money, but the other guys do," Martini argued picking the argument back up.

His former bandmates had either run out of money or were about to. Because Bernie was the lead songwriter, he still made a decent income on publishing and royalties, as their music was still in rotation on stations targeting younger listeners.

"It would mean a lot to them."

"Let me say it more clearly, no fucking way," Bernie screamed.

"Would you at least consider allowing them to tour under the name with another guitar player?" It was Martini's plan-b, while having all four original members together was preferable, touring with three-quarters of the original band would still lead to a payday.

"The only way they can do that is if I'm taking a dirt nap, and I got news for you, Martini old boy, I ain't dyin anytime soon."

So long as Bernie was alive, there would be no reunion.

Hearing the argument intensify, Annabelle went in and

asked Bernie if he needed anything.

"What I fucking need is the door to the past to be closed once and for all," Bernie screamed, then looked the producer up and down.

"Sorry for losing my temper, love," Bernie said in a kinder voice—seeing a beautiful woman had that effect on him. "Georgie old boy, how about you leave me alone with..."

"Annabelle," the producer piped up.

"...Annabelle over here, so we can get better acquainted."

"I'm flattered," she said, "but sixty seconds to air."

"I only need thirty, baby."

Christ, Annabelle thought, they *really* don't pay me enough for this shit.

"Follow me, please."

Bernie picked up his guitar and followed her out the door.

"Would you at least think about it?" Martini asked one last time.

His request was met with a two-word answer: "Wank off."

Adam checked himself out in a handheld mirror he kept in his desk drawer.

"Adam, does the microphone on your desk work?"

Jimmy had been eyeing the old-fashioned microphone on Adam's desk since he came onto the stage.

"Just for show, Doubts."

"Ten seconds to air," the director said. The house band began to wind down the number it was playing.

Adam put the mirror away and turned his attention to camera two. When the last note rang out, he said, "Ladies and gentlemen, here to perform his new song *I Only Drink When I Smoke*, please welcome country music's newest desperado, Bernie Deville."

Bernie had conceived of positioning himself as an outlaw country type as a way of further distancing himself from his past and being introduced as the world's newest desperado was a condition of his performing on the show.

The audience erupted in applause as Bernie began playing the opening chords to his new song. It was a standard blues progression with a country twang; his gravelly voice did give it a bit of an outlaw feel.

They say it's going to kill me
Before it's my time to die
Old No. 7's my only companion
And on him I can rely
Unlike all my exes
Who'd pay to see me fry
And that ain't no joke but

I only drink when I smoke
Drink when I smoke
Drink when I smoke
I only drink when I smoke
And
I smoke all the time

While Bernie was singing about drinking and smoking, his manager had a call to make. He knew Glenn and Donnie were eager to hear from him, but Bernie hadn't given him a free moment to reach out and touch someone, so to speak.

"Where have you been, Martini? Donnie and I have been waiting all god damn day."

Glen's voice had all the anxiousness of a man who could no longer afford his rent, which, of course, he couldn't. He squandered the millions he made in his younger years on three divorces and a collection of Italian sports cars, the last of which was for sale.

"This is the first chance I've had. Is Donnie with you?"

"Yep. I'll put you on speaker."

"Please tell me some good news, Martini. Is the fucker going to play ball or no?"

"Let's just say he hasn't seen the light yet. How's Randy?"

Randy, their old bass player, was at the Henley Center, an inpatient facility for sex addicts in Winslow, Arizona. Randy admitted himself after hitting rock bottom on the day of his granddaughter's fourth birthday party. He was supposed to entertain her friends by playing guitar and singing songs; when he didn't show up, his daughter went looking and found him hanging buck naked from a doorpost in his bathroom, penis in hand. It was the first time he'd explored his curiosity for sexual asphyxiation — bad luck followed Randy like a newly hatched baby duck.

"He's doing well at the center. Should be ready to tour in a month."

"Guys, it's not looking good with Bernie, but have no fear, Martini is here."

"What the fuck does that mean?" Donnie spoke for the first time since being put on speaker.

"I don't want you boys to worry so let's just say I got a plan to help your former guitar player see the light."

"Oh, that's much clearer," Glenn quipped.

"Listen, you guys worry about getting in shape for a tour. It might behoove you to lay off the weed for a bit and actually relearn your old songs."

"Warning, warning, fun police," Donnie said, disguising his voice like Robbie the Robot from Lost in Space—a phrase that could also be used to describe Donnie's present state of mind.

"You make fun of me now, but you'll miss me when I'm gone," Martini replied, using a phrase his grandmother used to mutter regularly when she was alive. "And listen, it may be that you need to find a new lead guitar player."

"What are you going to do Martini, Hans Gruber his ass?" Glenn's question threw Donnie into a fit of hysterics. The two made it a point of watching Die Hard together every Christmas Day. They once got baked out of their skulls and video recorded themselves jumping off a couch making the face actor Alan Rickman made when falling from Nakatomi Plaza.

"If it comes to it, the promoter I've been talking to is a really good guitar player himself."

"Whoa, whoa, whoa Martini. You manage the business and leave the creative decisions to us. That's is and always has been our deal, world without end, Amen!" Donnie protested.

"Listen boys, this guy who's going to be fronting the money wants in on your band then he'll get in your band unless you are still content living in your parent's basement, Donnie."

Glenn, always the voice of reason, tried to calm the

situation down, "Let's just cross that bridge when we come to it. This guy got a name so we can at least look him up?"

Joe Feld was very clear with Martini that his real name should never be given to the guys in the band for fear that it might hurt his credibility in the two worlds he wanted to live in; the world of high tech and the world of music. "Yeah, he goes by the name of Max Ruby. I've got a demo video of his playing some of your songs which I'll send along if it comes to that."

Glenn and Donnie were mollified by this and nodded to each other. "Fine," Glenn said, once the voice of the band, always the voice of the band.

Martini ended the call. He walked over to the dressing room bar and poured himself a tall glass of vodka, which he drank as if it were water. The music business had changed so much in the last twenty years and he found it harder and harder to make any money in it. He only made money when his clients toured and right now he only had one working artist, Bernie. Unfortunately, since he was staging a comeback, most of his gigs were to support other acts, a reality that led to smaller pay-days. Martini needed the reunion tour just as much as Bernie's bandmates.

The crowd was silent as Bernie started singing the last verse. They were clearly caught off guard, expecting to hear the soft pop and easy listening sounds his old band was once known for. Instead, they were treated to something that could have been written by a lesser Merle Haggard.

With one foot in the grave
Can my soul even be saved?
With one hand on the bottle
And the other on the throttle
But I won't go down without a fight
And will grasp that bottle tight
But
I only drink when I smoke
Drink when I smoke
Drink when I smoke
I only drink when I smoke
And
I smoke all the time
All the fucking time!

Bernie then proceeded to smash his guitar on the stage floor, a move designed to earn headlines. After the performance, Kimmel was caught off guard and stared blankly until the director got his attention.

"That's all the show for you we have tonight, ladies and gentlemen," Adam said, looking a bit stupefied. "Be sure to tune in tomorrow night when our guests will be actor Blaze Hazlewood and author Hunter Carson. Musical guest Sammy Hagar will round out the show. Thank you and goodnight."

It was customary for Adam to walk over and thank his musical guest, but luckily, Bernie had already left the stage.

A product assistant came over to lead Farrah and Jimmy off stage. "Do you guys need anything from the green room? Because there might be kind of a scene in there."

They decided to steer clear of it.

"That was different," Farrah said to Jimmy.

"I feel as if a bit of my childhood just died."

"Your own personal American Pie?"

"What?"

"Don McClain? Chevy to the levee? About the death of Buddy Holly. Come on Doubts, look me in the eyes and tell me you don't know that song."

Jimmy smiled, "I gotcha!"

Farrah punched him in the arm, "I hate to split on you, but I'm due in Malibu in ninety minutes."

While mile wise Malibu wasn't all that far from the studio in downtown LA where Kimmel's show was recorded, rush hour LA traffic required that Farrah leave an inordinate amount of time to make her dinner meeting on time.

"I'm still jealous that you are getting to meet with those guys. Is it true that the brass at our network didn't want me there?"

"Don't take it personally Doubts." While Farrah referred to Jimmy as her partner in the podcast, that was in title only – it was her baby. Still, she paid him very well and felt bad that he felt left out. "Look, these things are a lot more boring than they sound. Why don't you go out and have some fun tonight, but not too much fun since we have a very early day tomorrow."

"I'll probably just go back to the hotel and chill."

Jimmy wasn't exactly the adventurous type. When Jimmy told Farrah he was going to try online dating she suggested the following profile description, *attractive podcaster with limited sense of adventure seeks woman to watch Hallmark movies with.*

"Live a little Doubts. You are young, this is LA. Let

loose."

Jimmy looked at his watch, "Shit!"

"What's the matter?"

"I forgot to call my mom."

Jimmy and his mother, Diane, were very close and made a point of speaking daily.

"Do me a favor Doubts, in the event that you go out on the town tonight, don't use that as a pickup line."

"How are you getting to Malibu?" Jimmy wanted to change the subject.

"Kimmel's staff arranged for a ride."

Jimmy rolled his eyes at Farrah. "Must be nice."

Farrah couldn't help but let out a little smile, she was starting to enjoy the benefits that came with her growing celebrity.

"You want to see if they could get you a ride back to the hotel?"

Jimmy shook his head. "I'll take a Fast Lane car. Throw a little love to my cousin's business."

Jimmy and Joe Feld's mothers were sisters, though they weren't all that close.

"Hey, he lives out here in LA, right? Why don't you try and see him?"

"I called him right before we left New York. He was in Florida earlier this week and that set him back a bit with work. He's back in town but I'm not sure if he could spare the time."

"Sarcastic much Doubts?"

"It's just that he and I were never really that close. I'm just going to stick to my plan of going back to the hotel."

"Maybe there's a good Hallmark movie on."

"Enough with the Hallmark!" Jimmy protested. "A guy

mentions one thing about enjoying a Hallmark Hall of Fame movie and he never lives it down."

"Alright Doubts, then I don't have to say what I usually say."

"I know, I know, stay out of trouble."

Farrah left and Jimmy had to adhere to the call of nature. Once in the men's room he heard the unmistakable sound of sniffing coming from the stall. A flush later, Bernie Deville exited. While Jimmy's bladder was screaming to be emptied, coming this close to one of his childhood idols gave him a severe case of stage fright.

"You okay there, fella? Looks like you are struggling to pee. Your face is as red as a tomato." Bernie walked to the sink and started washing his hands, the sound of the water didn't even help Jimmy evacuate his bladder so, after an uncomfortable moment, he zipped up his pants and flushed the toilet.

"What are you and that blond piece of ass doing tonight?"

In his wildest dreams Jimmy would never have imagined discussing his evening plans with a celebrity of Bernie's caliber.

"Cat got your tongue pip?"

Jimmy snapped out of the trance he was in. "Farrah's got a business dinner in Malibu. I think I'm going to head back to our hotel. Early day tomorrow."

"Young fella like you should be dining on some good ole fashioned tuna taco. I've got an appearance at a hotel on the Sunset Strip tonight, why don't you tag along? We'll go beaver hunting together."

In his twenty-seven years on the planet, Jimmy had never hunted anything, including women. His inexperience, though, wasn't enough to overcome the excitement he felt by Bernie's suggestion.

"Where's the hunt?"

"Ahh, that's the spirit mate! The Hotel Palomino, seedy no questions asked kind of place. Right near the Chateau Marmont on Sunset. See you there around 8?

"I'll be there."

"Brilliant."

Bernie left and Jimmy walked back to the urinal after he realized he still had to go.

CHAPTER FOUR

Fallen Angel

Jimmy hailed a Fast Lane car using his cousin's app and plugged in the address for the Hotel Palomino so the driver knew where to take him. When the car arrived, Jimmy decided to call his cousin.

"This is Joe," Jimmy heard on the other end of the line.

"Joe, it's Jimmy. This a bad time?"

Joe was sitting behind the desk of his home office in Manhattan Beach. He was eager to hear from Carbona to see how the events of the night unfolded and didn't look at the clock to see what time it was or the caller ID to see who was calling. Had he known it was his cousin, Joe would have let it go to voicemail.

"I may have to jump off if I get another call but what's up?"

"You'll never believe who I'm going to hang out with tonight?"

Joe assumed it was going to be some celebrity he'd never heard of. Since the podcast Jimmy joined took off, he resented his cousin's success and the fact that it provided him with access to A-Listers. Success always landed in Jimmy's lap with little effort whereas Joe had to work his ass off; though his cousin's seemingly perfect life bothered him more before he inked a deal to become twenty-five million dollars richer.

"Who?"

"Bernie fucking Beagle." Jimmy rarely swore but his excitement got the better of him.

The blood rushed from Joe's face and he remained silent.

"Remember when we were kids and our moms took us to that concert? Remember Bernie calling me on stage to help them sing their closing song?"

"How could I forget?" Jimmy's cousin said sarcastically. The memory was one that pained Joe for multiple reasons, although he wasn't about to divulge that to Jimmy.

"How did this come about?"

"Farrah and I taped Kimmel's show today and Bernie was the musical guest. He's staging a comeback as an outlaw country type."

"So I've heard." In Joe's mind, it wasn't a coincidence that Jimmy shared the stage with Bernie, it was a result of the cosmic forces that worked in unison to make Jimmy's life a charmed one.

"Hey, I think the appearance was one of our best. You should stay up to watch it tonight."

Hearing these words made Joe's blood rush to his face. Why did Jimmy always have to rub his success in his face?

"Where are you going?" Joe was nervous that Bernie was going to flake out on the appearance he had been paid to make at the Hotel Palomino.

"The Hotel Palomino, ever hear of it?"

"Rings a bell." Joe relaxed once again knowing that his plan was still in effect. He picked the hotel as it was popular with rockers, and for the fact that he knew all of the hotel's security cameras were inoperable.

"Well you sound busy so I'll let you go. Good to catch up."

"Word of advice Jimmy," Joe said. "They don't call the Palomino the Motel California for nothing. It's a seedy place so watch your back."

"Will do."

The line went dead and Jimmy stared out the car window while the car drove up the 101 on its way towards Hollywood. This was the most exciting thing he'd done in a very long time, and he had to admit it felt kind of good to go out on, what his mother would call, a school night.

Jenny Slade sat at the bar inside the Hotel Palomino drowning her sorrows with her third gin and tonic. The bar was aptly named The Pulled Plug – urban legend has it the hotel stood on the former grounds of an old Hospice center and the current owner has a twisted sense of humor. At the moment, Jenny was reflecting on all the wrong turns she made on the way from her small town in Ft. Wayne, Indiana to the bright lights of LA, the majority of which were made in the last five miles of that journey.

Seven years ago, she left her parent's Indiana home seeking fame and fortune and everything that goes with it. At the time, she was known as Michelle Davies and had just graduated from Bishop Luers High School where she wasn't only a scholar, but excelled in the Catholic school's theatre arts program, having played Dorothy in The Wizard of Oz, Nellie in South Pacific, and Guinevere in

Camelot — three starring roles in her three years on stage; and to imagine she only volunteered for stage crew her freshman year thinking she wasn't good enough for the front of the house. It was this success that prompted her to go against her parent's wishes and put off college for a long shot in Hollywood.

Things didn't pan out the way she intended.

Her misadventures started on the bus leaving Fort Wayne. Michelle wanted to head to California on the road to experience the different personalities of America; saving a few hundred dollars by taking a Greyhound instead of an airplane informed her decision as well. In total, her journey to LA took her across eight states in just under 60 hours, during which she was pick pocketed once, sexually harassed twice, and offered drugs three times — her sacraments of initiation into the religion of show business were complete.

Then as soon as she stepped off the bus in Downtown LA, she was immediately intercepted by a fast-talking guy named Eddie Costello who preyed on the horde of young and beautiful girls who arrived in LA via bus multiple times a day. For $250, he promised her a professional headshot, five guaranteed auditions, and help finding housing — he even offered to give her a ride to his "studio." Later on, she would come to know the evil that was "Fast" Eddie Costello.

Two hundred and fifty dollars lighter – pretty much all the money she'd saved by taking the bus – Michelle got into Eddie's car, a flashy Jaguar, and drove with him to his place in North Hollywood. Once there, he asked her to pose in a variety of outfits that got skimpier and skimpier as the "photoshoot" went on. She was so green that she didn't understand what was going on — though in a short amount of time, it would become clear to her.

At the end of the shoot, Eddie asked Michelle to take some nudes, arguing they'd make the difference for the independent, art house producers looking for fearless actresses. Sensing her trepidation, Eddie offered her a drink to calm her nerves — he didn't care that she was underage.

After some convincing, Michelle had her first taste of liquor in the form of a hard iced tea. That brought her defenses down enough to strip for good ol' Fast Eddie; and that was about it for the innocent Catholic girl from the Midwest.

Eddie made good on his promise to find her housing, setting her up with eight of his other "clients" in a two-bedroom bungalow in Van Nuys, a town in the San Fernando Valley — nicknamed the San Pornando Valley for reasons that would soon become clear to her. All of her new roommates were all young and beautiful and the green girl from Fort Wayne really thought she was actually on her way to making it in show business.

Eddie also made good on his promise to set her up on an audition, or at least what she thought was an audition. Within a few days of arriving in Southern California, Michelle found herself in a Sun Valley office where she was asked to run lines with a casting agent. The lines read like they'd been written by someone with an eighth-grade education but Michelle chalked that up to paying her dues — hey, you have to start somewhere, right? When she was asked to remove her top while sitting on the casting agent's couch, she did so with a little less hesitation than when Eddie asked her a few days before. Unlike Eddie, though, this agent sat down beside her and copped a feel. Michelle slapped him and the guy acted as though he was the one who'd been wronged. He screamed that he was doing his friend a favor by running lines with a non-represented actress and threw her out — after calling her a bitch, of course.

What happened next could only be described as sinful.

When she arrived back at the house, Eddie verbally assaulted her, claiming she'd ruined his reputation with the casting agent. He then grabbed her by the throat and demanded fifteen hundred dollars in rent money while tightening his grip. The decision to empty her savings account at the small credit union in Fort Wayne with the intent of depositing the cash in an LA bank was one she was about to regret. Michelle went over to where she kept her bags and rifled through them only to find her money was gone. She would later find out from the other girls that this was simply a matter of history repeating itself.

Eddie threatened more harm unless she could make rent by the end of the week and underscored that threat with a slap to her face. Too proud to go to her parents for help after being in LA for just a few days, Michelle turned to her roommates. One of them, Cassandra, told her how she could make fast money doing webcam chats with lonely guys, arguing she was pretty enough to command a high per-minute fee. Of course, Michelle was hesitant at first but found a little alcohol took away her jitters. While her first show was awkward, she was relieved it lasted all of five minutes — and she made fifty dollars. That she could make a rate of six hundred dollars an hour left her speechless.

Upon Cassandra's advice, Michelle worked under a

stage name and quickly rose to being one of the cam service's top earners; she had no idea her time on camera was also making Eddie Costello a few dollars, as he owned the site. Gone was Michelle Davies from Fort Wayne, Indiana. In her place: cam-ster Jenny Slade from Los Angeles, California. Jenny promised herself she'd only do it until she saved up enough to rent her own place and get free of Fast Eddie Costello's grasp. Of course, it didn't work out that way.

Another roommate asked if she wanted to earn more money in less time, and Jenny wound up in another casting director's office, this time one for hardcore adult films. At this point, cocaine had replaced alcohol as Jenny's barrier reducer, and after a few lines of b-grade Columbian, Jenny "auditioned" by letting the agent have sex with her on his desk; according to him, the casting couch was so cliché. From there, it was a rocket ride up the ladder at Peach Productions, where she would eventually earn up to fifteen-hundred dollars per scene. Had she read her contract fully, she'd have realized she was agreeing to be represented by one Eddie Costello, who was entitled to twenty percent of her earnings. He had her by the short and curlies, both figuratively and literally.

Resigned to working for someone she hated, she was able to buy a small apartment in Culver City where she could escape from her days in Silicone Valley, as she came to call it.

Recently, Jenny tried to get out of the business altogether by attempting to leave LA and driving home to Indiana. When Fast Eddie got wind of this, he tracked her down using a GPS transmitter he'd hid in her car and took her forcibly back to LA. Wanting to protect the cash flow Jenny provided him, Costello assigned what he called a bodyguard to her; in reality Greg Page was a muscle head chaperone paid to use any means necessary to keep her in line. He was sitting next to Jenny in The Pulled Plug to make sure she completed tonight's assignment.

Eddie Costello was more than just a talent manager, he was also an entrepreneur in the Adult Film industry and was looking to pioneer a new genre called Reality Porn. As such, he conceived of a web series called Fantasy First Dates.

The concept is that his girls would go to seedy hotels like the Hotel Palomino and come on to middle of the road guys who would lose the ability to reason after being hit on by women well out of their league. They'd record the setup in a small video camera hidden in their eye glasses and, when the moment was right, would offer to take their mark to a room at the hotel, where additional hidden cameras would capture their sexual escapades.

Afterwards, for legal reasons, the guys would be let in that they were filmed and offered cash to sign a release. If they refused, Eddie would use their footage as blackmail until they signed. Once they agreed, an editor would block out their faces to make the series appear that much more authentic. Eddie knew that there were still a lot of holes in his idea, but was eager to test it out and assigned Jenny to film his "pilot." When Jimmy Doubts walked into the bar, Jenny knew she found her man.

Jimmy's Fast Lane car left him in front of a five-story art deco hotel that would look more at home on Miami Beach than in Hollywood. He walked into the Hotel Palomino's lobby and immediately felt out of his element; he was dressed in a preppy button-down shirt with a whale logo on it while everyone else looked like an extra from an 80s hair metal music video. He looked around and, failing to see Bernie or his manager, decided to take a seat at the bar.

"Welcome to the Motel California," the bartender said. "What are you drinking?"

"You got light beer on draft?"

"You got a vagina?" The bartender retorted.

Jimmy was taken aback by his response, "IPA?"

"Be right back," The bartender said and then muttered to a colleague, "you know the fucking strip is going to shit when the Vineyard Vines crew arrives."

Focused entirely on his insecurities, Jimmy didn't even notice the brunette wearing a super tight red dress sit down next to him at the bar.

"Excuse me," she said in a playful voice while gently touching his shoulder, "do you have the time?"

Jimmy looked at her and was speechless, which was his typical response when in the presence of a beautiful woman — he was Farrah's intern for three days before he could actually hold a conversation with her. In this case, his eyes feasted on a stunning young woman in a red dress so tight he thought it could be painted on. The fact that it was cut a good five inches above the knee and that she was clearly not wearing a bra made his eyes practically bulge from his head.

"The time?" She reiterated.

Jimmy shook his head, "Oh, sorry," and then looked at his watch, "Ten after eight."

"Ugh, thanks," She said. "I was supposed to meet a

blind date here at seven thirty, but I guess I got stood up."

The bartender arrived with Jimmy's beer. He was thankful for the distraction and took a long pull on the bottle.

"Thirsty?"

"Yeah, kind of," Jimmy said nervously.

"Hey, I have an idea," Jenny said while seducing Jimmy with her eyes, "you could be my date tonight."

Jimmy coughed up his beer and, while reaching for a cocktail napkin, knocked over a small bowl of cocktail peanuts on the bar. This led to a menacing stare from the bartender.

"Let's take it slow," Jenny said and extended her hand. "Hi, my name is Jenny and I work in the entertainment industry."

Jimmy shook her hand and held onto it a little too long without saying anything.

"And your name is?"

"Oh, sorry," Jimmy replied by taking his hand back. "Jimmy Doubts." Over the past two years he quit using his real last name, since everyone else had.

"Sounds like a dangerous name. I like dangerous. What do you do Jimmy Doubts?"

"I am the co-host of a podcast. Ever hear of Uncorking a Murder?"

"I'm sorry baby, I'm not familiar with it. I'm an old-fashioned girl and stick to FM radio." She was telling the truth, Jenny was one of a dying breed of people who still listened to the actual radio.

"What do you do in the entertainment industry?"

"Actress. You can say that I'm working on a pilot right now," Jenny winked to underscore the words 'right now.'

Jimmy's eyes lit up, one of the reasons he was excited to be in LA was that he crafted an idea for a game show and was eager to pitch it to anyone in the industry who might listen. "I have an idea for a gameshow pilot," he said.

Jenny moved in a little closer and started rubbing his knee. "Don't hold out, give it to me Jimmy Doubts," her hand massaging his inner thigh.

After another long pull on his beer, Jimmy realized that an idea wasn't all that he was pitching, and adjusted himself accordingly. "Okay, it's called Reasonable Doubts. Picture this, a courtroom setting where the studio audience shouts out ideas for a court case. These are taken up by two trained Improv actors, one who acts as the defense attorney and the other as a prosecutor. They then present a case to a jury made up of real trial lawyers. At the end of the show, the jury votes on who presented the most compelling argument."

Jenny's mouth dropped open, "That's actually fucking brilliant." She was being honest, in her mind the idea was original and had the potential for big laughs.

"Really?" Jimmy sounded surprised.

"One hundred percent," Jenny confirmed.

Jimmy's eyes lit up like a little kid's on Christmas morning. "That was the first time I ever pitched the idea, I thought it would be harder."

Jenny's hand was now moving up his while her lips went to his ear. "Things can get as hard as you want them, Jimmy Doubts."

CHAPTER FIVE

For Whom the Bell Tolls

Looking around the Mastro's, Farrah didn't know what looked more beautiful, the spectacular views of the Pacific at sunset or the near perfect looking patrons at the bar enjoying cocktails. To Farrah, each and every one of them looked as if they'd feel right at home in front of a camera. This is not to say Farrah isn't attractive – she was often hit on by both men and women — but everyone at the bar looked made for the movies, and they knew it.

Farrah looked for her dinner companions and, failing to spot them, took a seat among the gorgeous people at the bar and ordered a glass of wine. In any other town, the men would be on her in a feeding frenzy, but this was LA and most men were too self-involved to notice a beautiful woman in their midst. One of these nights, I'm going to feel like I fit in at a place like this, Farrah thought to herself.

To pass the time, she tapped a note to Jimmy saying, "Just reminding you we have an early morning tomorrow." Jimmy was one of the most responsible people she knew and she wasn't really worried he'd be late, but that didn't stop her from riding him a little bit.

While she waited, Farrah entertained the possibility of Uncorking a Murder going away as a result of the patent troll. She was confident that the podcasting industry could put up a solid fight, but it would cost a lot of money. While she was now comfortable financially, she didn't want to invest any of her own in defending the suit and her syndicator was notoriously cheap. Besides, would it really be the worst thing in the world if the show ended? She could do the things she never got to do working as a lawyer all those years — travel, get married, start a family.

Who am I kidding? Farrah asked herself — she was only happy when she had something interesting to work on and loved the podcast because it scratched her itch for solving puzzles. Plus, she felt responsible for Jimmy — he gave up law school to help her and while money was fine now, he was still in his mid-twenties and what he had now wasn't enough to live on for the rest of his life.

Farrah was thinking about Doubts when she felt a tap on her shoulder. She turned around to see podcaster Drew Baron clad in his leather jacket and form fitting jeans. His long hair fell to his shoulders and his Frank Zappa facial hair screamed aging 70s rocker more than successful podcaster. A standup comedian by trade, Drew had the third most downloaded podcast on the network Farrah was syndicated on—he had been number two until Uncorking a Murder was released.

"You just leave Joe's garage?" Farrah asked, referencing one of the late Frank Zappa's more popular hits.

"I'll take that as a compliment coming from a woman who glamorizes murder."

"Can't we all just get along? Drink?"

"I've been sober for two decades, but I'll let you buy me a club soda."

Two decades ago Drew's drinking had gotten to the point where his anger alienated those closest to him and caused him to "lose his funny," as he tells it. Sober now, he's still angry as hell, and many people still don't like him, but his stand-up career has never been stronger, thanks in no small part to his podcast. The drinking and rage cost him his marriages and now he lives with four feral cats, and the occasional girlfriend.

"Where's Brillo?" Baron asked. Brillo was Baron's nickname for Tommy Tercel, the carpenter turned radio personality turned TV host turned podcaster. He had short, wiry hair, much like a Brillo pad. Hence the nickname.

"I thought you were coming together." She laughed as she said it. It was well known that Drew and Tommy were on opposite sides of the political spectrum and wouldn't last five minutes in a car together, let alone the seventy minutes it would take to get from Tommy's house in Glendale to Mastro's in Malibu in the thick of LA traffic.

"He's probably working on one of his goddam cars. Seriously, why does somebody need so many cars?"

Striking it big in the entertainment industry allowed Tommy to indulge in many expensive hobbies, with collecting classic race cars at the top of his list. As a matter of fact, his podcasting studio was built on the second floor of a custom garage housing ten of his twenty automobiles.

"Want to get a table?" Farrah asked.

"Why not. If I have to stare at any of these women any longer, I might start drinking again," Baron quipped.

Farrah walked over to the hostess and asked for a table overlooking the water. After they were seated, she told the hostess to be on the lookout for a tall man with wiry hair.

"So, is it over? Have we had our run? Am I going to have to go back to doing 50 weeks on the road doing standup? First Trump becomes president and now this."

Drew was staring blankly at the ocean and oblivious to the fact that Farrah had stopped listening to him.

The top brass at Pro Cast, the company that syndicated Farrah, Drew, and Tommy's podcasts, wanted Farrah to pitch an idea to her fellow podcasters thinking that if the idea appeared to come from one of their own they'd be more likely to agree to it. "I have some thoughts about it but don't want to get into them until Tommy is here."

They heard a commotion at the door and turned to see Tommy arguing with the hostess. Farrah got up to investigate while Drew stayed at the table and popped a nicotine lozenge; he quit smoking a decade ago but still used the lozenges because they helped calm his nerves.

"That car is priceless," Tommy shouted. "I'm not going to hand it over to some undocumented valet."

Just about every restaurant in LA required valet parking. Mastro's was no different.

"Sir, I understand..."

"I don't think you do. That car once belonged to Paul Newman!"

Tommy was fascinated by the late actor turned racing champion — so much so that he collected his old Datsun race cars. Why he drove one to a restaurant in Malibu was anyone's guess.

"Who's Paul Newman?"

Tommy's draw dropped. "I am afraid for your

generation."

By this time, Farrah was standing beside Tommy.

"Tommy, we've got bigger problems to discuss than who parks your car."

Tommy turned to Farrah wild-eyed. "Not to me we don't!"

"The valet will do his best to park it without damaging it," the hostess said, trying to reassure him.

"I don't want him to do HIS best," Tommy quipped. "I want him to do MY best!"

The restaurant's manager now joined in. "Sir, would you like to park your car yourself?" The scene Tommy was causing could be bad for business and the manager was happy to relax the parking policy.

"That's what I've been saying this whole time!" Tommy said, exasperated, hands flailing in the air.

Tommy ran back outside and looked his car over as if he suspected someone had keyed it in the few moments he'd been inside. He jumped in and Farrah watched him whip the car around. His license plate read PODFATHER.

Tommy was the first celebrity to make a significant amount of money in the world of podcasting, and he didn't hesitate to let everyone know it.

Farrah made her way back to the table where Drew looked deep in thought.

"I don't know, Farrah. If it's all over, I'm quitting show business and moving to Laurel Canyon to live like a hippie."

"That should do wonders for your sobriety."

"To hell with it all. This business is a young man's game anyway."

"We can't just lay down without a fight," Farrah argued.

"You want to fight this thing? Come on, they got lawyers and patents and shit. All I have is a studio in the garage of a two-bedroom, one-bath bungalow in Highland Park."

"I thought you were in Silver Lake."

"I moved! Too many goddamn hipsters in Silver Lake, may as well be Brooklyn with all the food trucks and farmer's markets and shit. I can't stand seeing men wearing hats everywhere I fucking go. Seriously, who brought the fedora back?"

Farrah and Drew turned around when they heard a loud sniff. It was Tommy's trademark sound effect — the all-knowing, self-assured, sniff. He used it to announce his presence.

"What did I miss?"

"Get your car parked okay there, Tercel?"

Drew knew Tommy hated being called by his last name. The general consensus was, as a car guy, Tommy resented his paternal lineage that he shared a name with a low-end Toyota. He had the choice to change his name, as many celebrities do, but didn't do it because he wanted to rub his success in the faces of those he went to high school with in North Hollywood. For senior superlatives, his classmates voted him most likely to wind up in a gutter. Now he paid more in yearly income taxes than most of them made in a decade, a fact he reminded his listeners of regularly.

Tommy, though, never let a snide remark go unanswered. "I'm surprised you could make it today, Baron. I figured there was a leftist rally somewhere in LA.

You know, the ones where you liberal types argue about global warming while all your hot air burns a hole in the ozone."

"Boys, come on now..."

"That's okay," Drew said. "I can take it. Listen, my belief in climate change means I'm on the right side of history. I heard your rant about street congestion the other day, Tercel. Do you think that will make a difference to the greater good?"

"In Los Angeles? Hells yeah. How long did it take you to get here from Silver Lake, Baron?"

The Zappa-esque podcaster looked at him blankly and said "Highland Park," and then added, "point taken."

The exchange was interrupted by a waitress looking to take a drink order. The men looked at Farrah first. She ordered another wine. Drew ordered another club soda with lime. Tommy, of course, had to be difficult.

"Do you have Forever Rant IPA?" He'd developed the India Pale Ale with a local craft brewery.

"I'm sorry, we don't carry that."

"Guygria?" Another Tercel product, which tasted nothing like Sangria.

"Strike two."

"Do you have any Zima?" Tommy knew they wouldn't have a beverage that had been off the shelves in the US for almost 20 years; now he was just being difficult to be difficult.

"Not since 1997, sir, I'm sorry. Would you like me to bring back Oasis and The Cranberries too?"

"Feisty, I like that! How about an old-fashioned?"

"That I can do. I'll come back with your drinks and tell you the specials."

"Now if your little pissing contest is done, boys," Farrah said, "we can discuss some things that actually matter."

"Look, I'm just a carpenter from the valley," Tommy said. "I was hoping you could take the lead on this, Farrah. I don't have time for Pro Cast's bullshit."

"For once, I agree with Tercel over here," Drew said. "The only thing I'm qualified to do is tell jokes. This legal shit is over my head, unless its divorce law."

Farrah anticipated this and was prepared. "We have three options. One, we can roll over, stop doing what we're doing, and leave the troll with no way to make money."

The vast majority of podcasters don't make a living through their podcasts, but rather use it as a promotional vehicle for their other activities. That Farrah, Drew, and Tommy earned a good living through their shows was the exception, not the rule.

"I don't think any of us wants to stop," Tommy said. Drew nodded his agreement. "What's option 2?"

"We fight the troll in court. I think we can win it, but it will be very expensive."

"How much are we talking here?" Drew piped up.

"Easily in the millions."

"I imagine the cheap fucks we work for want us to help fund the defense. I don't think I can do that," Drew said. This time Tommy nodded his agreement — it would leave significantly less play money for his sports car habit.

"Those seem pretty mutually exclusive to me, Farrah. What's option three?"

Farrah knew it was time to setup the idea that Pro Cast's executives came up with. "How many unique listeners do you have, Drew?"

"Weekly? A few million."

"And you Tommy?"

"3.6 million unique downloads every day of the week."

"Why am I not surprised you know that number off the top of your head?" Drew asked, not hiding his sarcasm.

"Each ten-episode season of Uncorking a Murder gets about 50 million downloads domestically and double that globally."

"Is the point for you to rub our noses in your audience numbers?" Drew asked.

He released two episodes a week and Tommy put out five. That Farrah's ten-episode serials beat their numbers was a bone of contention. She did a fraction of the work, yet she earned more advertising revenue on a per-episode basis.

"Relax, I'm going somewhere with this. What if we crowdfunded our defense? It's safe to say our audiences don't overlap. It's equally safe to say that they love what we do. If they all pledged a dollar to the cause, that's our defense fund right there."

The waitress came back with their drinks.

"Just in time," Tommy said. "I do believe we have something to celebrate." He raised his glass and tried to think of something noble to say but all he could come up with was, "Time marches on, for whom the bell tolls."

"I didn't take you for a Hemingway guy," Baron said.

"Hemingway? That's all Hetfield, baby. Saw Metallica last night and they closed with that tune."

CHAPTER SIX

Fight for your Right to Party

Bernie and his manager got out of a cab in front of the Hotel Palomino. Joe Feld worked with Martini to arrange an appearance at the Palomino as a way of getting Carbona's guy to Bernie. There weren't going to be any fans at the hotel, just a mob enforcer with a lesson to teach Bernie Deville.

"It's bad enough I have to do an appearance at this glorified Motel," Bernie said before lighting a cigarette. "Remind me why we're staying in this fucking place when my rider specifically states I must be put up in the Marmont."

The Chateau Marmont had a reputation for attracting those who took it to the limit, and then some. While notable past residents include Hunter S. Thompson and Jim Morrison, actor John Belushi's death there in 1982 sealed the hotel's reputation with those who live life in the fast lane.

"It was oversold," Martini lied. He put Bernie up at the Hotel Palomino per instructions from Joe Feld, who knew that the video surveillance system at the Palomino was just for show. "Plus, have you seen your rider lately?"

Rock stars are known for some pretty unreasonable requests in their contracts. For example, Van Halen forbade brown M&Ms from their candy bowls, punk rocker Iggy Pop required that seven dwarfs greet him in his dressing room, and metal god Nikki Sixx demanded his dressing room include a boa constrictor of no less than fifteen feet. Bernie Deville's topped them all — he demanded that anyone wearing red be turned away at the venue gate unless they agreed to change. While other bands drafted their riders to ensure a venue owner paid attention to detail, Bernie's was strictly out of vanity – he had to wear red on stage with his old band and, since then, he tried to stay the hell away from the color. His craziness had an ancillary benefit, it helped to spur tee shirt sales in the lobby.

"Fuck it. Let's go inside and get this appearance over with," Bernie said. "You want a drink? What am I stupid, of course you do. First one's on you, Martini."

Bernie took a drag and turned to go in.

"You can't go in there with that," Martini said.

Bernie spat on the ground and flicked the lit cigarette at his manager. Then he went inside, his manager following immediately behind.

Jimmy was downing his third beer when Bernie Deville walked into The Pulled Plug. The musician looked extraordinarily pissed as he walked in Jimmy's general direction.

"What's the matter, Jimmy?" Jenny asked. "You look concerned."

"How old are you?"

"You never ask a girl her age!"

"I'm guessing twenty-seven."

"Twenty-six and a half. Why?"

"Do you remember..." Jimmy whispered the name of Bernie's old band into her ear.

Jenny began singing one of their songs, "I got an easy, peasey feeling..."

Jimmy made a slashing motion across his neck.

"What's wrong?"

"I'm supposed to meet their former guitar player here tonight and he's coming this way."

Jenny looked over Jimmy's shoulder. "Shit, there he is, he looks pissed."

"Aye ya fucker!" Bernie said to Jimmy. I see you've already done some hunting without me."

"Ah-hem," Jenny coughed to indicate introductions were in order.

"An who do we ave here?" Bernie asked and looked her over. Seeing the red dress he said, "Dreadful color."

While Bernie hated the color, he was willing to overlook it dreaming about what was underneath.

"Excuse me?" Jenny asked.

"Never mind him," Martini butted in. "He's off the rails on a crazy train."

Bernie turned to his manager, "Martini, make yourself useful and get us some shots."

"Say, Red, you look like a girl who likes to party. You wearing your snow shoes tonight?" Bernie used a cocaine reference he learned from watching a biopic on Robin Williams.

The singer had caught Jenny's interest and she pivoted

to make him her mark. Nothing against Jimmy, but she thought the pilot of Fantasy First Dates might get more traction with the aging singer than with a milquetoast podcaster.

"I'm always up for some skiing. In fact, I have some fresh powder in my room. Care to join me?

While Jimmy was oblivious to all this code, he had the feeling that Bernie just cock-blocked him and was about to call the singer out on it. Just as he was about to confront Deville, Martini came back with four double shot glasses filled with a greenish liquid.

"Bottoms up, fuckers!" Bernie said and threw his shot back. Martini, Jimmy, and Jenny followed. Jimmy had to concentrate on his breathing to prevent him from throwing up all over the bar; Doubts wasn't a hardcore drinker and shots typically invoked his gag reflex.

"Ahhh!" Bernie said pounding on his chest like Tarzan.

"Apologies gents, but the lady and I have to see a man about a mountain." Bernie extended his hand towards Jenny as if he were a gentleman and she took it.

"Hey, Jenny..." Jimmy said but was cut off by Bernie.

"Sorry mate," Bernie said while getting directly between Jimmy and the girl. "This is a hunter's game and you, my friend, are a farmer." Bernie accentuated his point by poking Jimmy in the chest.

Jimmy felt belittled and, ordinarily, would have let it go but whatever was in that shot altered his personality enough to stand up for himself.

"Are you really going to go upstairs with a guy who wrote a song parody called We Can Walk it Out?"

As the words left Jimmy's lips he felt as if he was having an out of body experience.

Bernie looked shocked. "What the fuck did you just say you little shit?"

"Don't poke the bear kid," Martini warned. "You don't know what he's capable of."

"Go home to your mum," Bernie said. "How old is she anyway? Mid-fifties? Ask her if she knows me. I fucked half the east coast twenty years ago."

"Excuse me?" Jimmy said loud enough to gain the attention of other people, some of whom, in anticipation of a fight, started recording the confrontation on their phones. Jimmy was very protective of his mother, whose struggles as a single parent were never far from his mind.

"Bugger off, you glorified DJ," the singer said to Jimmy and then turned his attention to the red-clad Jenny Slade. "Come on, luv, let's go climb Mount Columbia, preferably in our skivvies."

Jimmy's blood was starting to boil and began seeing Bernie-Beagle red. He knew he couldn't take the singer physically, but he didn't want to walk away either so he tried to get under Bernie's skin using the only weapons at his disposal, his words.

"I looked up to you as a kid. I mean, I considered Take it to the Hydrant a work of genius when I was six."

Bernie's eyes went wide. "Keep shooting your mouth off like that you little prick, and I'll bust it like your mother's pelvis."

Undeterred, Jimmy pushed forward with his verbal assault. "Do you still talk to the old band?" Jimmy said it loud enough to elicit laughter from the real rockers at the bar.

"You have five seconds before I beat the shit out of you."

Jimmy's pride wouldn't let him leave. If he had to take one to the face, so be it.

"He's not kidding, kid," Martini whispered in his ear. "I once saw him throat punch a Downs kid who asked for an autograph."

"Bartender, I'd like to buy this man a drink. Do you carry Screaming Beagle Cabernet at the bar?"

"That's it." Bernie raised his fist and threw a left jab at Jimmy's face. Jimmy weaved away from it but a follow-up cross from Bernie's strumming hand caught his left eye.

Greg Page, who nobody could have known was Jenny's handler, got up from where he was sitting and wedged himself between Bernie and Doubts. "Cut it the fuck out."

"It's cool," she said to her bodyguard. "Just a little misunderstanding."

Furious at the mess he found himself in, Jimmy wandered outside, used his cousin's app to arrange a ride, and waited for the car that would take him to The Beverly Hills Hotel, where he and Farrah were staying.

Jenny took Bernie by the hand, "About that mountain."

Bernie looked to his manager, "Martini old chap, why don't ya get us checked in."

"What about your appearance? We are supposed to be in a suite upstairs in twenty minutes."

I'll meet you there," Bernie paused while looking Jenny over, "when I'm done or fucking feel like it, whatever comes first."

Martini walked towards the front desk and shook his head while Jenny and Bernie walked towards the elevators.

CHAPTER SEVEN

Modern Day Cowboy

Former professional wrestler Greg Page waited a full three minutes after Jenny and Bernie went into the elevator before he got in one himself. Since he was Jenny's minder, he already knew her room number and parked himself on a chair he left outside her door earlier in the evening.

At six feet five inches tall, Page was hard to miss, but his height was only part of what made him unforgettable—the fact that he dressed like a cowboy added to what made him extraordinarily memorable.

Page grew up in a small town west of Ft. Lauderdale called Plantation. When he was a kid in the 70's, the town had more farmland than strip malls — that changed permanently during the economic boom of the 90's. While the President was getting his lollipop licked in the Oval Office, south Florida's developers were buying up all the open land they could find in Plantation and transforming it from farmland into shopping malls, condos, and office parks.

Long before Bill Clinton's presidency though, Greg's

father, Floyd, was an old-time cattleman who refused to let his family's ranch become part of the concrete jungle. It was during the Ford administration when the government claimed eminent domain on his property; he responded by barricading the family inside while simultaneously starting a standoff with authorities.

Floyd Page's stand lasted three days, ending on Easter Sunday in 1975. Unlike Jesus, there was no resurrecting Greg's dad after he made the mistake of walking in front of a window that a Swat Team sniper had his sights trained on. Young Greg saw his father's head explode like one of Gallagher's watermelons smashed by a sledgehammer. It's fair to say little Greg was never the same.

After that, he bounced around foster homes until he turned eighteen and decided to move west. Heavily influenced by the memory of his father, Greg adopted a cowboy persona and hitchhiked his way west until he found a place where his eccentricities weren't second guessed by anyone, Los Angeles.

He wasn't blessed with brains, but what he lacked between his ears, he made up in brute strength. A wrestling promoter by the name of Crisoph Hart spotted him bussing tables at Dan Tana's, Hollywood's standby for aging actors and future has-beens, and thought he had a look unique enough to make it in professional wrestling. But after just three months at a training camp for aspiring wrestlers, Greg Page, who then became known simply as The Cowboy, was let go, deemed too unstable for professional wrestling. When an industry with stars dressed like a cross between circus performers and carnies considers a guy unfit for their ranks, you know that fella has to be pretty screwed up.

The fact is, The Cowboy was a textbook sociopath – he didn't feel the least bit remorseful for any of the damage he left in his wake and wasn't going to feel bad after what he was about to do to Bernie Deville, which was all entirely avoidable had the singer been smart enough to keep his mouth shut.

Page didn't mind the assignment to keep an eye on Jenny, who was, by all accounts, a hot piece of ass. While many mistook The Cowboy to be a homosexual due to his over reliance on leather and under reliance on any other fabric, the fact was he was at least sixty-five percent heterosexual and he had a fondness for the girl even though she resented like hell the constant shadow he cast in her daily life.

While looking at his phone to pass the time, The Cowboy heard an argument start to break out in Jenny's room. When it sounded like the spat turned physical, The Cowboy took out his own key to the room and entered.

Minutes before The Cowboy parked himself outside of Jenny's room, Jenny cut some lines of coke on a glossy magazine that was provided courtesy of the hotel. While she was taking a razor to the rock and chopping it into fine rails, Bernie decided it would be a good time to relieve himself. When Jenny heard the sound of the shower start, she was grateful for the added time she had to check on the small wireless video cameras she set up earlier to record the multiple angles required to pull off a good sex scene.

Bernie came out of the bathroom wearing nothing but a towel. When he saw that Jenny was still wearing the red dress he walked over and attempted to rip it off her.

"Hey!" she protested loudly, "this is my nicest dress. Careful."

"It would look better on the floor, luv," Bernie said but gave up when he spotted the blow on the magazine. "Hold that thought," he said.

Jenny realized she made a mistake in choosing Bernie. While she knew it would be good for the pilot of Fantasy First Dates, there was something about this guy that wasn't right. It's not that he simply wasn't nice, he seemed like a complete creep.

After taking both lines for himself, he looked at Jenny in euphoric bliss and removed his towel. "Say hello to my little friend," he said in a terrible Cuban accent.

Jenny looked down and giggled, Bernie was right about the little part.

"Are you laughing at me, bitch?"

Bernie's sudden mood swing caught her off guard.

"What? No." She cowered on the bed.

"You fucking giggled you little twat, what were you laughing at?"

"Nothing, I swear."

"What the fuck is that?"

Bernie saw one of the small cameras Jenny had set up earlier. "Are you trying to film me you little cunt?" His anger rose to a level so high that he tried to release it by throwing one of the empty glasses from the desk across the room.

"Calm down!"

"You want me to fucking calm down you little whore..."

Before Bernie could finish his sentence the door to the room opened and he came face to face with The Cowboy.

"He hurt you?"

"Not yet, but he's crazy."

"Who in the fuck are you, some Judas Priest fan boy? Mind your own fucking business."

Greg responded with a quick punch to Bernie's nose, which popped and gushed blood. The rocker went down hard.

"Was that necessary?" Bernie asked.

Greg responded with a kick to Bernie's midsection, which seemed to send another gush of blood from his busted nose. The Cowboy then turned his attention back to Jenny, "I think it's time to go."

"The hell it is, fella." That Bernie was able to stand and charge The Cowboy was testament to how powerful of a drug Cocaine really is. After such a beating, most guys not under the influence would simply take a knee. Bernie, however, had some serious coke muscles to flex proving that what Rick James once proclaimed is true, cocaine is a hell of a drug.

There was no way of knowing that The Cowboy had trained to be a professional wrestler so it caught Bernie off guard when Page slipped to the side and grabbed the singer by the wrist and used his own momentum to thrust him against the sliding door leading onto the balcony, the glass cracking upon impact.

The Cowboy looked outside and saw that Jenny's room was right above the hotel's swimming pool just one floor below. This gave him an idea – Bernie was about to take a swim. He slid the door open and the cool night air felt good on his face. Page grabbed the singer.

"What's your name?"

"Bernie Deville."

"Well Bernie, it looks like you like to get high," The Cowboy said while picking up the rocker as if he was about to body slam him. "Let's see if you can fly."

The Cowboy tried to aim the rocker toward the pool, but the singer was heavier than Page thought and his aim was a little off. Bernie's naked body landed head first on the concrete patio. The awkward landing suggested that Bernie wouldn't be playing any more gigs. He turned to Jenny who was about to make a beeline for the door.

"Not so fast." The Cowboy blocked her exit.

In that moment, Jenny realized how much of a train wreck her life had become. She tried to leave the business before, but Fast Eddie had found her and forced her back in; for her, there was only one way out. She ran to the balcony and, before The Cowboy could react, was standing on the three foot high protective railing.

"Do you think you can fly too?" The Cowboy asked.

"No," Jenny replied. "But I can swim."

She then jumped off the balcony and landed square in the deep end of the pool where she sank to the bottom but wasn't hurt; she quickly swam to the shallow end. Fearing for her life, Jenny sprinted out of the pool, re-entered the hotel through the door on the patio, and ran down the steps toward the lobby.

Later on, witnesses would tell stories about a crazy woman running for her life through the lobby, but the retellings didn't seem to captivate. This was LA, after all. Many had seen much weirder stuff than that.

Meanwhile, the cowboy chose not to pursue Jenny, reasoning he'd call too much attention to himself. Instead, he decided to exit the hotel quietly, taking the stairs and ducking through the lobby. He had some unfortunate news to break to Fast Eddie Costello, and time was of the essence.

CHAPTER EIGHT

Free Falling

Terry Tomasulo, a foot soldier in Carbona's crime family, always dreamed of becoming a screenwriter. While one of his screenplays, *The Sons of my Bitches*, received a little interest in Hollywood, it was clear to everybody but Terry that he was never going to make his living as a writer. Carbona kept him in LA, though, because he was a reliable enforcer in a town where people try to talk their way out of everything from parking tickets to gambling debts. If Terry had a twenty for every time he heard someone ask, "Do you know who I am?" he'd be a rich man. Well, maybe not rich, but he'd certainly have enough scratch for dinner at Lawry's.

Before getting involved with the Carbona family, Terry was just another artistic kid in The Bronx who was routinely picked on by other kids who didn't share an appreciation for his command of the written word. One day, after a particularly hard beating, Terry decided he wanted to change the ending of his story so he got up and cracked the lead attacker over the head with a rock that he grabbed while on the ground. The kid dropped and his friends, instead of running to their buddy's aid, hightailed it in the other direction. Mob boss Tony Carbona saw everything, from Terry's initial beating through his resurrection and moment of triumph, from his perch on the corner.

After that, Carbona took Terry under his wing and treated him as if he were Carbona's third son, making him untouchable to anyone who valued keeping his bones intact. After some tutelage, Terry became the enforcer for the Carbona crime family, and when the family business extended west to California, Tony set his surrogate child up with a place to live and a steady flow of people to shake down. Celebrities liked to gamble but weren't always quick to pay their debts; Terry made sure they did, even if that meant visiting a set or two.

He was sitting on a stool at The Pulled Plug when he saw Bernie Deville walk in with his manager and then join a couple at the bar. Carbona had given Terry a copy of Bernie's picture and told him where the singer could be found that evening; Terry was supposed to have a one-on-one conversation with the singer at a suite in the hotel, a plan he assumed went sideways once he saw the singer head upstairs with a very attractive woman.

Terry's creative mind kicked in and he started to imagine a damsel in distress scenario as Bernie led her into the elevator but, instead of following his curiosity towards the elevator, Terry decided to check in with the singer's manager, who was waiting in line to check into the hotel. Carbona let Terry know that Martini would be the one to let him into the suite at the appropriate time and Terry wanted to make sure they were still on for a sit down.

"Excuse me, do you represent Bernie Deville?" Terry asked after walking up to Martini.

Martini looked Terry up and down, "Who wants to know?"

"My name is Terry Tomasulo. Mr. Carbona sent me to talk to Bernie."

Martini looked the enforcer over, "I thought you'd be younger and more...brutish."

"You've been watching too many movies. Are we still on for a sit down?"

"Bernie is powdering his nose and entertaining a new fan at the moment. You can stick with me until he's done."

"Hey," Terry said. "I know this is a bit unorthodox, but I'm looking for some new representation." Terry handed Martini his business card and the fat manager looked it over.

"BreakaLeg.com? Is this some kind of joke?"

"Clever, isn't it? That website has a sample of all my best writing. I'd appreciate it if you could..."

Before Terry could finish his sentence, a soaking wet woman in a red dress ran through the lobby and out the front door.

"That ain't good," Bernie said.

A moment later, an alarm sounded in the hotel and rumors spread throughout the lobby about a jumper who was now sprawled on the pool deck.

Fearing the worst, Martini and Terri went toward the pool, along with just about everyone else in the lobby.

CHAPTER NINE

Running Down a Dream

Complete with shoulder length blond hair and matching guitars, identical twins Murray and Jeff Nelson came to LA in 1987 to pursue their dream of making it big in the glam metal scene. They had peaked in their hometown of Minneapolis and knew they had to head west to make it big. They spent four years playing places like The Troubadour, the Roxy, and The Whiskey before their dreams came crashing down in 1991 when the grunge movement, led by bands like Nirvana and Pearl Jam, put the final nails in the coffin that was glam rock and heavy metal.

Coming from a police family (their father was a captain in the Minneapolis PD), the twins traded in their blond locks for crew cuts and entered the LA police academy. Fast forward a quarter of a century and the two were now homicide detectives with blond hair just past their shoulders — they never fully let go of their rock & roll past and spent most of their non-investigatory time arguing about metal bands. They were cruising near their old stomping grounds on the Sunset Strip when the call about a potential wrongful death at the Hotel Palomino came in.

"On it," Jeff said into his two-way radio while Murray continued to drive. He then returned to the conversation he was having with his brother.

"I'm just saying no one really gave Gary Cherone a chance. Was he as good as Hagar? No, but he was better than Roth."

"What are you smoking?" Murray retorted. "Roth was the original front man, which makes him the best."

"What, because he could do high kicks?" Jeff said, sarcastically referencing the original singer's propensity to show off his dexterity on stage.

The only thing they argued about more than who was the better leader of Van Halen was whether Kiss was better with or without Ace Frehely. Murray was in the original Spaceman's camp while Jeff argued that Bruce Kulick was a superior axeman. Regarding Kiss, the only thing they agreed on was that, regardless of lineup, Kiss was better in makeup than without — no one in the band was destined to grace the cover of GQ.

"When was the last time we went to Motel California?" Murray asked his brother.

"Not since '89, after that night with the guys from Warrant at the Rainbow Room."

"That was a great night. Do you remember anything about it?"

"Nope."

"Me either."

While the Palomino was known as a place to party for the pharmaceutical set, it had never been the scene of a homicide. There's a first time for everything.

The brothers pulled up and parked out front, much to the ire of the bellman waiting to help a new guest with his bags, and probably sell him some uppers, downers, or weed.

"You can't just park here," the bellman protested. The brothers responded by showing him their badges.

"Shit," the bellman said.

"Don't worry, we are homicide, not vice."

"Phew. Wait, what?" Apparently, news of the third-floor jumper didn't reach the bell stand.

The brothers ran inside and left the bellman and his imagination to figure out what was going on. They raced to the second floor and entered the pool deck, where onlookers were staring at the naked body of Bernie Deville. A man in a suit introduced himself as the hotel manager after the brothers flashed their badges and told everyone to clear the scene.

Bernie was lying face down, except for his face, which was turned all the way around as if he were imitating Linda Blair in The Exorcist. The trauma it sustained would have made it hard for anyone to identify him, which was fortunate for the detectives who wanted to keep any murder victim's identity under wraps for as long as possible. They got enough heat from their Captain to solve cases, they didn't need any added pressure from the public.

"Any reason to think he didn't jump?"

"One of our guests was having a smoke on the patio and says she saw someone throw him out that balcony." The manger pointed toward the balcony of room 310. Two minutes later, she saw a woman jump off the balcony and land in the pool. Other guests saw her dart through the lobby and out the door. Good thing she did that tonight."

"Why's that?" Jeff asked.

"We are draining the pool tomorrow," the manager replied.

"Where's the smoker?"

"Sitting over there on a chaise lounge with a towel around her. I think she's in shock."

The brothers walked over to a blond woman with black lipstick and heavy eye shadow. She looked like a goth Taylor Swift.

"My name is Detective Murray Nelson, and this is my brother, Detective Jeff Nelson. Can we ask you a few questions?"

The blond's eyes darted between the brothers multiple times. "Am I seeing double or are you guys twins or something?"

"Same father, different mothers," Jeff said.

"What?" the woman asked.

"Don't mind my brother," Murray spoke up. "He's got a sick sense of humor. Comes with the job. Can you start by telling us your name?"

"Chrissy Snow."

"Do you still live with Jack and Janet?" Jeff asked.

"Not the first time I've heard that one. What can I say, my parents were fans of Three's Company. Tell me I was conceived while they were watching an episode."

"What did you see tonight, Ms. Snow?" Murray asked.

"I was out here having a smoke and all of a sudden I hear screaming coming from up there." She pointed toward the balcony where she thought the guy was thrown from. "And the next thing I know, I hear a crunch."

"Was anyone else out here?"

"No. It's cold out and I'm the only one of my friends who smokes cigarettes anymore."

The twins looked at each other and laughed. While sixty-nine degrees is cold by LA standards, it was nothing like what they were used to in Minnesota.

"I was about to run inside to get help and then saw some chick in a red dress jump from the balcony into the pool and then head inside."

"Any idea what she looked like?"

"White. Maybe about 5'5" but it was hard to notice anything besides the dress."

"Are you the one who called 911?"

"No. I ran inside to get the manager who wanted to see what happened before calling."

"So you deliberately delayed the start of a homicide investigation?" Murray said to the manager.

"I just wanted to see if I could help the guy, that's all. I was a lifeguard back in the day."

The brothers looked at each other. They had many ways of communicating nonverbally and this particular look suggested they thought the manager was full of shit.

"Did you see anyone else on the balcony? Jeff asked the witness.

"No. Too dark and too far."

"Let's take a look at the body," Murray said and the two walked over, the manager went with them but then threw up when he saw the state of the body.

"Lifeguard," Murray muttered and laughed.

The two looked over the body, "He remind you of anything?" Jeff asked.

"Yeah, a plate of spaghetti."

Turning toward the manager, Jeff asked, "What room does that balcony belong to."

"310."

"And who is staying in room 310?"

"Let's go to the front desk and ask."

"Jeff, you stay here with Ms. Snow and the paramedics. Call the crime scene team and have them do a workup of the room and the patio where the body landed. Maybe get the boys from the bus to put a sheet over that guy, huh?"

"Will do."

Murray followed the manager to the front desk, where he looked up the name of the recently deceased guest in room 310. After a series of seemingly never-ending keystrokes, the manager looked up and said, "That room is registered in the name of...," the clerk hesitated.

"The suspense is killing me."

"Jane Do."

"Let me guess, no card on file?"

"Paid cash."

"This place will never change," Murray muttered.

"Detective Nelson," the voice came from the bar. The bartender was waving his hands trying to get Murray's attention.

"Tommy Aldrich? I haven't seen you in twenty years." Tommy was a well-known drummer on the Sunset Strip. Like the Nelson twins, his career came to a halt in the days of grunge. He now tended bar at The Pulled Plug Thursday through Sunday.

"Hey, not sure if it's relevant, but there was a spat down here tonight."

"Between who?"

"See that fat guy over there?" Tommy pointed at Martini.

"Him?"

"Yes, guy he was with tonight and some young guy. I just saw that man come back from the pool deck really shaken up. On his second drink now. Maybe it's related, maybe it's not. Couldn't hurt to ask, right?"

"Thanks,"

"Your brother here?"

"Yeah, he's at the pool."

"He's right, you know?"

"About what?"

"Cherone."

Murray shook his head and approached Martini.

After seeing his one and only client smashed to smithereens on the pool deck, Martini went back to the bar and ordered a stiff drink and, after downing it, ordered another.

He remembered the conversation he had with Bernie earlier about how the only way the band could go on without him was if he was in the ground. The more Martini thought about it, the more Bernie's untimely death started to look like a true blessing; while the sit down that was supposed to have happened with Terry could have led to a positive outcome for everyone else involved with the band, this one was a definite. Martini started to feel a little bad about the way it all happened, but, let's face it, he really didn't like Bernie anyway.

Had Bernie had an actual appearance at the hotel tonight, there would have been a number of fans upset that he didn't show, but since the appearance was just a ploy to get him to the hotel, no one missed Bernie one bit and Martini started to relax. As he was beginning to calm down, he felt a tap on his shoulder and his nerves went through the roof again. He looked at the blond detective standing in front of him and tensed up.

"LAPD," Murray said flashing his badge. "And you are?"

"George Martini."

"I understand you might know a thing or two about the guy by the pool," Murray didn't know this but wanted to gauge Martini's reaction, and potentially save himself some time.

Martini's mouth went agape.

"Looks like I just won the lottery. What can you tell me about him?

"Name's Bernie Deville. My client. Last I saw him, before the pool deck, he was heading up an elevator with a girl." Martini was quick to give up information, if you were criminal he wasn't the guy you'd want as an associate.

"Red dress?"

"Yeah. Why?"

"I'll ask the questions," Murray said. "What do you mean client? What kind of work do you do?"

"I'm a talent manager. He's a singer."

"Was a singer," Murray clarified. "He say where he was going with the girl?"

"She propositioned him to go to her room."

"This girl have a name?"

"No clue." Martini went on to describe how Bernie met her in the bar and wooed her away from a dueling celebrity.

"Who's the celebrity?"

"The dude from Uncorking a Murder."

"Doubts?" Murray asked. Given their profession, he and his brother were familiar with Uncorking a Murder. They argued about it when they weren't arguing about Hair Metal bands.

"That's the guy. He and Bernie taped Adam Kimmel's show this afternoon and then got into it here in the lobby. Bernie got him pretty good in the face. Plenty of people got it on their phones. I'm sure it's on YouTube by now."

Murray wrote all the information down. "Any idea what your client and Doubts were arguing about?"

"I'll be the first to admit that Bernie was a Class A asshole. Jimmy was talking to a girl and Bernie moved in. Words were exchanged and it got a little heated. Happens all the time."

"I just have one more question for you Mr. Martini," Jeff said as if he were winding up for a pitch, "you see your client's body on the pool deck and your first response is to go to the bar. Isn't that odd?"

"What was I supposed to do? Stay at the pool and stare at the body? I'm a drunk, this is what I do."

"Do me a favor, stick around." Murray was never one to use the "here's my card, call if you think of anything else" line. He hated clichés nearly as much as ballads from his favorite bands. He long argued that ballads killed hair metal, not the grunge movement. Of course, his brother disagreed.

He left Martini and walked back to where the hotel manager was waiting. "Take me to room 310."

Jeff was waiting in the hallway outside the door. He'd followed the crime scene team up the stairs.

"What did you learn?" Jeff asked.

"Victim is Bernie Deville."

"The guy from The B..."

"Murray cut his brother off. "Yes."

"How'd you find out so quickly?"

"I just got lucky," Murray replied referencing a Dokken classic. "You know Jimmy Doubts?"

"Yeah. What's he got to do with this?"

"He and the victim had a bit of an altercation in the lobby. Search for Jimmy Doubts on YouTube and see if anyone uploaded it yet."

Jeff took out his phone and, sure enough, one of the first hits was the fresh clip of Jimmy's fight with Bernie. Jeff tapped play and saw Bernie poking his fingers into Jimmy's chest.

"You have five seconds before I beat the shit out of you," Bernie said.

"Bartender, I'd like to buy this man a drink. Do you carry Screaming Beagle Cabernet at the bar?"

The brothers watched as Jimmy blocked Bernie's first punch but then caught a second in his nose. The clip followed Bernie until the elevator doors closed on him and the woman in red.

"I'm guessing that's our lady diver. Wasn't that a song by Kiss?"

"No, that was Baby Driver from the Rock and Roll Over Album released in November 1976. Holy Diver, though, was a Dio classic." Between the two, Murray was the Kiss aficionado.

"Right. At least with this clip we know what the girl we're looking for looks like. You know what?"

"What?"

"She looks a bit like a short-haired Tawny Kitean." She was the ginger model/actress who starred in most Whitesnake videos from their eponymous 1987 release.

"A bit." It was a rare moment of agreement between the twins. "I think our first order of business is to track down Jimmy Doubts and see what he knows."

Murray checked his watch and saw it was close to midnight. "But before we do anything, let's catch a bit of TV. Trust me."

They entered room 310, and Murray flipped on Kimmel just in time to hear Farrah say they were doing a media tour at The Beverly Hills Hotel at three the following morning.

"How the hell did you..." Jeff started to ask.

"Bernie's manager said Doubts met him at a Kimmel taping earlier today."

"You know, if this mystery girl jumped off the balcony," Jeff said, "I'm guessing she was in a hurry."

"Clearly," his brother agreed. "So?"

"She probably left her purse here."

The two searched the room and found a red purse on the floor between the bed and the wall. Murray rifled through it and saw that it contained her phone and wallet.

"We got a name on the girl," Murray said while holding a driver's license in his hand. "Jenny Slade. Let's see what we can find on her."

"Things are really working out for us in here. You know, Farrah and Doubts are probably staying at The Beverly, too. Wanna take a ride down now?"

"No," Murray said. "We know where they are going to be tomorrow so let's catch Doubts off guard."

"Agreed. Why don't we pay a visit to Slade's place

tonight to see if she made it back there, there's questions only she can answer."

"Also," Murray said. "You, me, and Martini are the only people here who know the stiff is Bernie Deville. Let's keep it that way for as long as we can."

"Roger that," Jeff replied thus continuing a rare volley of agreement between the two. "Thankfully, his face resembles that of a pancake. The more attention this gets in the media, the harder it'll be for us to do our jobs though I'm guessing we only have until midday tomorrow before the cat is out of the bag."

CHAPTER TEN

Life in the Fast Lane

After seeing Bernie's body on the pool deck, Terry Tomasulo knew he had a call to make. With Martini back at the bar, Terry walked out into the cool LA night and dialed Tony Carbona's number.

"How'd it go?"

"Not so good."

"Waddya mean not so good? You're da best muscle I got."

"Someone got to our guy first. Bernie's dead."

"Dead?"

"Someone dropped him Suge Knight style." In addition to HGTV, Terry knew how much Carbona enjoyed VH1 and its documentary series Behind the Music. The one about Vanilla Ice was his favorite.

"Are you fucking kidding me?"

"Saw the body with my own eyes.

"Well how's about dat?"

"You seem surprised," Terry observed. "Maybe this guy had more than one enemy." In his experience, if one guy wanted someone hurt, chances are someone else did as well.

"All I know's that this guy was some kind of singer and our client needed him out of the way to make some tour happen."

"Think he hired more than one person for the job?"

"Nah, guy who arranged it was a friend of Mikey's. MIT type, real nerd."

Terry remembered the altercation between Bernie and a younger guy at the bar and relayed that to Carbona.

"Why didn't ya mention that in the first place? Classic crime of passion," Carbona reasoned. "I guess I better break da news to the guy who I set this up for. You're off the hook tonight. Try to stay out of trouble."

"I always do boss. Goodnight."

Terry hung up the phone and kept walking down Sunset when he came across a woman arguing with a cabbie. As he approached, he noticed she was wearing a red dress that looked painted on her body. As he got closer still, he saw that she was the girl who went streaking through the lobby not long before.

"Look, I don't have any money," he heard her say.

"No money, no ride!" the cabbie screamed as he pulled away.

Terry approached the woman. "Do you need some help?"

She looked him up and down. "I'm good."

"Really, because you don't look it."

"I can smell you mob types from a mile away."

Terry considered his outfit — black pants, black shirt, black leather jacket. When he got dressed that night, he was going for anguished writer, but he could see how she got the impression he was connected.

"Hey, I'm only a part-time gangster. I'm also a writer."

"Let me guess, you got a part for me?" the woman said angrily. "If you're a writer, you need to come up with a better pickup line than that."

"I don't have a part for you, but I do have a car. I'm happy to give you a ride."

Outside of breaking bones to collect money for his boss, Tomasulo was known as a guy with a big heart. Unfortunately, his soft side often led him into trouble and history was about to repeat itself.

"Without any money and looking like that, people are gonna think you're looking for a car date."

"I'll take my chances."

"Good luck with that," Terry said and walked away. This caused Jenny to reconsider her stance on Terry's offer.

"You really a writer?"

Terry turned around and pulled out the little notebook he carried to capture ideas whenever inspiration struck. "Been writing all night."

"Where's your car?"

"Around the corner behind the Vertigo." The club was one of the strip's hottest spots and run by a Carbona associate.

"How do I know you are not going to strangle me back there?"

"You've got an active imagination. We should be writing partners. You got a name?"

"Jenny Slade."

"Sounds like a rockstar."

"Actress, and don't judge the name. What's yours

anyway?"

"Terry Tomasulo."

"Sounds like a hit man," Jenny smirked. "You written anything I may have read?"

"You ever read The Sons of my Bitches?"

"Nah."

"Neither did 7 billion other people."

"Sounds like it could be a good name for a soap opera though."

Terry died a little bit inside. He remembered his grandmother watching daytime soaps — her stories. The writing was terrible and Terry didn't want to be lumped in with the hacks who penned them.

They got to Terry's car, a pale blue 1979 Cadillac Coup Deville.

"They didn't have anything older or bigger?"

"It was my grandmother's, and I love my grandma." He made the sign of the cross, kissed his pointer and middle fingers, and pointed to the sky. "If you prefer walking, let me know."

Jenny got into the car, fastened the lap belt – there wasn't a shoulder strap – and Terry pulled onto the strip.

"Where am I going anyway?"

"Culver City."

Terry breathed a sigh of relief, grateful she didn't live any further south or west. He lived in El Segundo and didn't want to be driving all over LA tonight.

"You want to tell me how you got yourself in this situation?"

Jenny was quiet for a minute, she wasn't proud of her association with the adult film industry and didn't feel the need to explain herself to a new acquaintance. "Let's just say my night went sideways."

Terry assumed she knew something about Bernie's death, but it really wasn't his problem anymore – though the writer in him wanted closure on the story. He decided to play the long game with her and push her for details if he got to know her a little better.

They drove in silence until they turned onto Jenny's street in Culver City. Terry could spot an unmarked police car a mile away and easily spotted the one parked across from Jenny's place. Two blond guys in suits were knocking on her door.

"Keep driving," Jenny said.

"Friends of yours?"

"Never seen them."

"Cops. Seems as if you are in a pickle, Jenny Slade."

"That's life in the fast lane."

Murray and Jeff were at Jenny Slade's door when they saw the blue Cadillac pass their standard issue Crown Victoria.

"There's something you don't see every day." Murray said. "78?"

"79. You can tell by the Cadillac script on the header above the grill."

"I hate the fact you have 20/20 vision. You should have written down the tag."

"California plates 8S75309."

Murray stared at his brother blankly. "Fuck you and your photographic memory. How come you got the superpowers?"

"Look at it this way, at least you got my good looks."

"Want me to run the plates?"

"Couldn't hurt."

"I don't think the girl's home."

"I wonder who she turned to for help. Couldn't have gone far without her purse and wallet."

"Run the tags. Maybe we'll find out."

Before Detectives Murray and Jeff Nelson left the Hotel Palomino and started discussing vintage Cadillacs on Jenny Slade's front porch, Joseph Feld was on the phone with Tony Carbona, who was giving him an earful about the continued cold spell in South Florida.

"They say da ice in da arctic is melting because of this global warming nonsense, but it ain't even 50 degrees here in Pompano."

Joe shook his head; why a mob boss was consumed with the temperature was beyond his comprehension.

"Have you heard from your guy in LA yet?"

"Yeah. That's why I'm calling. I got some unfortunate news about your friend Bernie."

The tech genius didn't know if that was code for Bernie being on his path to see the light or if something actually went wrong; mob lingo was a foreign language to him.

"What kind of bad news?"

"The kind where someone got to him before my guy did. Looks like he was Knight'ed."

"I'm not familiar with that term."

"Suge Knight?" Tony said, disappointed Feld didn't catch the reference. "Producer thug who held that Vanilla Icecream guy by his feet off a high rise, except Bernie's guy let go. Vanilla is now doin some home improvement show on HGTV. You ever watch that channel? Not bad what they can do with piece of crap houses."

In the history of mob bosses, Tony Carbona might be the first to admit to watching HGTV.

"And your guy had nothing to do with it?"

There was a pause on the other end of the line. All Feld heard was heavy breathing.

"Looks, I told ya some guy got to Bernie before my guy. To suggest otherwise would imply that I'm telling you a fallacy. Are you callin me a liar?"

For the first time in a long time, Joe felt afraid.

"No, Tony. I apologize."

"Good because, and listen to me carefully, no one calls me a liar. Got it?"

"Yes."

"I gotta tell you, kid. I'm already upset with myself for getting involved with ya."

Feld swallowed hard, wondering where this was going.

"My extended family runs all the limo businesses in New York. I did some digging on you. Your little app thingy is hurtin the Livery business everywhere it's allowed. Fortunately for you, you ain't in New York yet or else I'd send someone to help you see the light."

It's true, Tony Carbona's family controlled the entire Livery business on the East Coast and put the squeeze on anyone who attempted to cut into it.

Fast lane was still in its infancy and strictly a West Coast operation, which explained why it only sold for twenty-five million.

"Remind me to tell you the story about Sandy Greenfield someday."

"Okay," Joe said, haltingly.

"Now listen kid, even though things didn't work out as planned, you still owe me, capiche?" Carbona let his question hang a minute and doing so had its desired effect, Joe Feld was about to shit a brick at the prospect of spending seventy-five thousand dollars for nothing.

"Of course, I am a reasonable man so I wouldn't expect seventy-five large, but since you are a friend of Mikey's how's about this, you owe me a favor and when I need one from ya's? I'll let ya know should dat day ever come."

"What could I possibly be able to do for you Mr. Carbona?"

"Oh don't worry kid, I got an active imagination. In the meantime, stay outta trouble. This probably worked out for da best. Know what I mean?"

"Yes, I think I do." As this conversation was sinking in, Joe realized that, with Bernie permanently out of the picture, there were no more roadblocks to his getting Bernie's old band back together or his taking Bernie's spot on lead guitar.

"Now is there anything else I can help you with? It's after midnight here in Pompano and I need my beauty sleep."

With no response from Feld, Tony ended the call. While he thought he was no longer involved in Joseph Feld's mess, in actuality, he was just stepping into it.

CHAPTER ELEVEN

The Heat is On

Being a celebrity has many upsides, including access to hotels so luxurious they feel like an alternate reality where comfort and pampering are the norm and stress is a toxin eradicated by feather beds, in-room spa service, and exotic dining (organic, of course). But earning the star treatment comes at a price no one talks about — publicity tours.

Ever see a star on morning TV, then hear them on the radio during your drive to work, and then see them pop on whatever late-night show you watch before bed? That's not a coincidence. That's publicity, and while it's certainly not manual labor, it is exhausting to answer the same questions over and over and over. It takes an emotional toll, but marketing is a necessary evil.

The biggest downside to starting a media tour in California is that you have to wake up at an ungodly hour to hit the East Coast morning radio shows. Prime listening time is approximately 7:30am, but with so many stations in the large markets, it's impossible to be live on each and every one. The solution is to wake up super early, dial into a conference line, and then talk to hosts during commercial breaks who then play an interview as if it were live.

Once East Coast and Middle America interviews are complete, around 6:30 West Cost time, it's time to start all over again with West Coast DJs. By 9am, Farrah and Jimmy had appeared on more than 40 morning radio shows across broadcast, satellite, and Internet radio, with each host — or hosts, in the case of wacky morning zoos — asking them the same questions over and over:

"How did you get the idea for season 3?"

"What are your plans for season 4?"

"What's this about a patent troll?"

"How did you get the nickname 'Doubts?'"

"Have you heard from Melody?"

This last question really irked Farrah. She was loath to talk about her personal life, especially with radio hosts she didn't know — not to mention the millions of listeners who shouldn't care about her personal life. Even so, she always answered the question graciously — sounding like a bitch would get her painted as one by the media, and she was very careful to craft a likable image.

The last interview of the mid-morning, though, caught both Jimmy and Farrah off guard. It was being conducted by an Internet Radio host who thought he was the Howard Stern of the blogosphere. Farrah and Jimmy were only supposed to be doing morning and satellite radio during this part of the day, but Dirk Danger tricked his way into their morning radio queue. After asking some wildly inappropriate questions about Farrah's sex life, Dirk turned his attention towards Jimmy.

"So, Doubts, heard you got into it with Bernie Deville

last night. How does it feel to be trending on social media after getting beat up like a little bitch?"

Farrah looked at Jimmy who then began speaking into his microphone, "Just a minor disagreement. The story is pretty boring. Next question."

"Boring? Jesus Christ, an outlaw musician, with questionable interest in children mind you, stealing a pornstar from under your grasp is anything but boring. Come on, tell us what happened."

Farrah was utterly confused. Earlier that morning, the two went from barely awake to interview mode and had no time to catch up on the prior evening's events.

"What's this about a porn star Doubts?"

"This guy is insane, I wasn't with a porn star last night. I met a woman in the entertainment industry and we hit it off at the bar."

"Make that adult entertainment industry Jimbo. Her name is Jenny Slade and her latest film is Bitch Perfect 3. Farrah, I bet you didn't know that Jimmy Doubts was such a player!"

Farrah giggled. "LA is a funny town." Much to Jimmy's dismay, she was playing along to keep up her image.

"Did you hear about the murder at the hotel last night?"

"What?" Jimmy and Farrah said in unison.

"Yeah, looks like someone got tossed from his balcony and hit the pool deck face first. Hasn't been identified yet, maybe you should look into it."

"How do you know it wasn't a jumper?" Farrah asked.

"Witness saw some babe make it into the pool from that same balcony just minutes after. The description sounds an awful lot like Jenny Slade. Were you being naughty last night Jimmy?"

Farrah didn't like where this was going and was eager to end the interview. "That's all the time we have now Dirk. Thanks for your time." She terminated the call.

"Was any of that true? Did your childhood drink when I smoke douchebag hero do that to your eye?"

Jimmy gently massaged the new addition to his face and went on to tell her about his men's room invitation to hang with Bernie at a seedy Hollywood hotel bar and their eventual fight over a woman.

"I'm sorry I ever accused you of having a limited sense of adventure."

"Apology accepted."

Farrah was eager to know more about the apparent murder at the hotel last night, but she also wanted to rest up before an afternoon of more interviews. "I don't know about you Doubts, but I'm going to try and get a nap in before we pick up again with the print interviews at noon."

At 12pm, Farrah and Jimmy were to begin the print interview phase of their media tour. Much like the morning radio portion, they were going to be interviewed in rapid-fire increments by journalists and popular bloggers, each asking as many questions as humanly possible in ten minute blocks.

As Farrah was getting up to leave, there was a knock at the door. While Jimmy turned his attention to his phone, Farrah opened the door on her way out to find identical twins with shoulder length blond hair standing in the doorway.

"You're early. Interviews don't begin until noon."

"We're not here to interview you, ma'am," the twins

said in unison while simultaneously flashing their badges.

"I'm detective Murray Nelson and this is my brother, Jeff. We're with the LAPD Homicide Division and have a few questions for Mr. Rella."

Jimmy had buried himself in social media to try and get more information on what had happened at the hotel last night after he left. All accounts he was reading were vague as the decedent's face was so mangled a positive ID had yet to have been made.

"Mr. Rella?" Murray repeated.

Jimmy had become so unaccustomed to hearing his actual last name that he didn't react when it was spoken a second time.

"Doubts, a pair of identical twin detectives are here to see you." Farrah tried her best to get her colleague's attention. He finally looked up.

"Mr. Rella," Murray spoke up, "would you mind answering a few questions for us about last night?"

They were equally ranked detectives, but Murray took the lead in most interactions. Jeff was comfortable being the quiet one.

"Call me 'Jimmy,' and what's this about?

"I think I better stay for this," Farrah said.

"We'd prefer to keep this a private matter with Mr. Rella," Jeff said.

"Well, I'm not just his business partner, I'm also a lawyer. I'd prefer to stay, if it's all the same to you." Farrah turned the 'all-business' switch on and there was no going back.

"Suit yourself, Ms. Graham."

"How is it you know my name?"

"We're big fans, you know, homicide detectives and all,"

Jeff said, earning a disapproving look from his brother.

"How did you know we'd be here?"

"You told the world on Adam Kimmel last night," Murray responded. "Now if you don't mind, I have some questions for you Mr. Rella."

"Call me 'Jimmy,'" he said for the second time.

"How did you get that bruise on your face?"

Jimmy outlined his altercation at The Pulled Plug and it matched what the detectives had seen on YouTube.

"And what brought you to The Pulled Plug last night?" Jeff asked.

"Bernie Deville. I met him at the Kimmel taping yesterday and he invited me to attend an appearance he was making in Hollywood."

"Was anyone else with you last night?"

"Just a girl I met at the bar." Jimmy blushed when he said this now knowing that this girl was an adult actress. "She and I were hitting it off until Bernie butted in."

"We know. The woman you spoke with is Jenny Slade. Makes her living doing skin films in the valley."

"She told me she was in the entertainment business, but I didn't know what kind of business she was in." Jimmy protested.

"Is this the woman you saw?" Jeff showed Jimmy his phone. On the screen was a picture of Jenny dressed in bondage gear wearing a Santa Claus hat and carrying a whip. It was the cover of a recent film entitled How the Gimp Stole Christmas.

By now, Farrah was beginning to think that Dirk Danger was right and that the woman who'd jumped into the pool was the same girl Jimmy lost to Bernie. "Why all the interest in this woman from the bar?" Farrah asked, growing impatient with the detectives' pace.

"You really don't know?" Jeff asked.

"Know what?" Farrah and Jimmy asked at the same time.

"I guess our plan worked," Murray said to his brother, referring to their attempt to keep Bernie Deville's identity out of the news. "Last night, someone tossed Bernie Deville off his third-floor balcony. He's dead."

Jimmy was stunned that Dirk Danger wasn't pranking him during their interview. While he had nothing but contempt for Bernie Deville before going to bed last night, the singer was still one of Jimmy's childhood idols and he was now at a loss for words.

"Why is it you don't seem surprised Mr. Rella?"

Jimmy explained what happened during their last interview.

"We'll have to confirm that," Murray said.

"We'd be happy to share a recording with you," Farrah said. "Now you've asked a lot of questions about the girl, what does she have to do with this?"

"We believe the girl was in the room when Bernie was hurled off his balcony and that she jumped into the pool to avoid the same fate," Jeff clarified. "If we find her, we may be able to find Bernie's killer."

"Unless we already have," Murray looked at Jimmy suspiciously.

"You think I had something to do with Bernie's death?" Jimmy said sounding more surprised than inquisitive.

"Come on, Doubts. That's why they're here," Farrah said stating what was obvious to her. "Isn't it, detectives?"

They responded with stares and silence, a tactic designed to intimidate suspects into talking.

"After I left The Pulled Plug, I took a car back to the hotel. You can verify that with the app company. They are sure to have a record of when they picked me up and when they dropped me off back here."

"We'll do that, Mr. Rella," Murray responded.

"Do you have any more questions?" Farrah asked.

"Nothing at the moment," Murray said. He and his brother got up and left their business cards on the table. "It goes without saying that you will call us if anything comes to mind?" Murray broke his rule about clichés, but couldn't help himself as Farrah was that beautiful and it was his way of making sure she had his number. Out of the two, Murray was more delusional.

"No doubt," Farrah said.

Jeff left his card as well and the detectives exited the room. When Farrah knew they were out of earshot, she turned to Jimmy. "I assume you used your cousin's service last night to come back to the hotel."

"Yes," Jimmy said nervously, he was clearly shaken about the conversation with the detectives.

"The first thing you need to do is call your cousin and get him to pull whatever data he can to prove you were on your way back to our hotel last night when Bernie was killed."

"Absolutely. I'll try him right now but are you thinking what I am thinking?"

"If we find this girl, Jenny Slade, that's another ticket to your innocence."

"Yes," Jimmy replied. "As well as a ticket to our fourth season. You up for some adventure?" Jimmy was confident that his cousin could easily show the cops that he couldn't possibly have been at the Hotel Palomino when Bernie died as he left immediately after the altercation with the singer. As such, he wasn't the least bit worried about being fingered for Bernie's death.

Farrah frowned at Jimmy.

"What's that look for?"

"After we finish up here at 2, I have to head to Glendale and do Tercel's podcast."

"Wait, what? I could really use your help."

"I know, but this is important for the future of the podcast. I'm going on to discuss the patent troll issue with his audience and announce the crowdfunding campaign for our defense fund."

"But this could be our next season!" Jimmy had mixed emotions about Bernie's death; on the one hand, he was a long-time fan but on the other his childhood hero proved to be a major jerk. To make lemons out of lemonade, Doubts thought they could get a season of Uncorking a Murder out of the experience.

"I'm sorry, Doubts, but I'm really doing this for both of us for our long-term future. But I have a thought for you to consider."

"What's that?" Jimmy asked.

"Remember last night during the commercial break, right after our segment on Kimmel?"

"Yeah, why?"

"The producer came out and mentioned something about an argument between Bernie and his manager. Maybe the manager knows something."

"I'm wondering if he's still at the hotel," Jimmy said. "How would you feel if I skipped out on the print interviews to chase him down?"

Farrah smiled. "Go get em tiger. I'll handle the print

vultures, you find Martini."

CHAPTER TWELVE

Promises, Promises

Jenny Slade was awoken up by a boom so loud she expected it to be followed by sirens rushing in from every direction. While she was sprawled out on Terry Tomasulo's bed, the mob enforcer and aspiring writer stirred on his couch. His apartment in El Segundo was a small, L-shaped studio; that it was located on the approach path to LAX explained its affordability and the sound that woke Jenny from a deep sleep. Since opening her eyes, Jenny was contemplating how she could get out of the sex business and out from under Fast Eddie's grasp once and for all.

"You look like you're in deep thought," Terry said from the couch. He offered Jenny his bed when they got to his place earlier that morning, and she was surprised that he didn't make a move on her; perhaps, she'd thought, there's one gentleman left in this town.

"I was just thinking about last night. I'm not sure what to do." Not wanting to pour her entire story onto a stranger, Jenny decided to give Terry a Cliffs Notes version of what she'd been through since coming to LA years ago up until the events of last night.

"The way I see it, you've got a few people who will be eager to find you. The police are looking for you, we already know that, and your over reactive bodyguard who tossed Bernie off the balcony will want to get to you before the cops do."

"As long as you're making a list, add my sleaze ball manager Fast Eddie Costello to it. He's gonna lose his shit when he finds out I'm leaving the industry...again."

"While I don't ever voluntarily interact with law enforcement," Terry said, "I think it's your safest play, especially if you want out of the business."

"I just want to go home."

"LA's finest are likely watching your place and if your manager is as much of a scumbag as you say, that's one of the first places he'll go looking for you so that's out."

"No," Jenny said. "Indiana. My real home."

"I can understand that, but the cops will eventually find you there. It's better you see them on your terms."

"Can I hide out here for a bit, I don't want to risk being seen by anyone until I'm ready to go to the cops?"

"All right, but only for a day. Tomorrow you go to the cops. The longer you wait, the worse it will be. Deal?"

"I promise."

CHAPTER THIRTEEN

Aces High

Detectives Murray and Jeff Nelson had stopped for lunch at their favorite roadside stand, Patrick's Taqueria. How an Irish kid from the northeast was serving the best tacos in LA was anyone's guess, but LA was full of surprises and contradictions.

"Sometimes when I look at you, I feel I'm peering into the eyes of a stranger," Murray said to his brother. They were in the thick of an age-old argument, who was the better Black Sabbath front man. Murray, the traditionalist, was for Ozzy Osbourne. Jeff was in favor of Ronnie James Dio.

"Dio had better range," Jeff argued while taking his first bite. "This pork taste different to you?"

"Different good or different bad?"

"Different different," Jeff replied.

Murray took a bite. "I think Paddy went a little heavy on the seasoning. Here's my take on Dio: his stuff with Sabbath was inferior to Ozzy's, but his solo stuff was awesome."

"The Iron Eagle soundtrack is classic. I'll give you that."

Iron Eagle is an 80s movie about a kid who, with the help of a mechanic, steals a couple of air force jets to go rescue his father in the Middle East. To say the film has plot holes is an understatement.

"The only thing more preposterous than your defense of Ozzy is the plot of that movie."

"Agree to disagree," Jeff used his trademark argument closer.

The brothers threw away the wrappers and waved goodbye to Patrick. Back in their car, they resumed discussing the case.

"What do you think of the kid?" Murray said, referring to Jimmy Doubts.

"Wet behind the ears. Maybe he's our guy, maybe not. If we can prove he was at the hotel when Bernie was killed, I'd put the squeeze on him, until then, all we got is a kid who happened to get into a fight with a guy who was known to be an asshole."

"Yeah, but if anyone knows how to get away with murder, it would be that kid," Murray offered.

"I'm thinking about the girl," Jeff said. "She jumps into the pool and then high tails it out of the hotel without looking for help. She clearly didn't go home last night or to the police station so we can assume she's hiding from us for some reason. Maybe we should reach out to her employer."

"See what you can find on her management, if she has any. I assume someone helps pornstars book gags."

Jeff laughed at his brother's Freudian slip.

"'Gigs,' I mean," Murray corrected.

"It's on my list of things to do."

"Did you ever run the tags from that Cadillac last night?"

Jeff looked at his phone to see if anything came back from his plate inquiry and smiled. "Car is registered to a Terry Tomasulo in El Segundo."

"All right, then," Murray said. "Let's go to the beach."

"It'll take at least an hour. Iron Maiden, Live after Death?"

"Best live album ever."

Jeff reached under the seat and fished around until his fingers found a cassette tape. He looked at it, smiled, and popped it into the tape player. While most people streamed music from their phones, Murray and Jeff Nelson were traditionalists. Their lieutenant had offered them an updated car, but they kept their old Crown Victoria for two reasons: It ran just fine, and it still had a tape player. After waiting a minute for the tape to rewind, Jeff hit play and Murray peeled out to the sounds of Aces High blaring from the speakers.

CHAPTER FOURTEEN

Something to Believe In

Jimmy left Farrah to finish their media tour solo and rented a bike from a kiosk outside the hotel. Given LA traffic, the four-mile ride between their hotel in Beverly Hills and the Hotel Palomino in West Hollywood would be much quicker on two wheels than four.

After going back to his room when the cops left, Jimmy called his cousin and left a message to call him back ASAP. He then called the Hotel Palomino and asked for George Martini's room. Jimmy was relieved when Bernie's manager picked up and was willing to meet in the bar before checking out of the hotel and heading back to the airport.

It took him twenty minutes to get there and he was pleased to see a bike-return kiosk out front. After returning his wheels, Jimmy went in and looked around The Pulled Plug surprised at how many people were day drinking before noon.

"Talk dirty to me kid, what are ya havin'?" The question came from the bartender whose long blond hair and bandana adorned forehead suggested he wasn't just a bartender, but also president of the Brett Michaels fan club.

"I'm actually looking for someone, heavy guy in his 50s, red bulbous nose, likely your first customer of the day."

"Tiffany," the bartender called out to a waitress working the tables, "where did unskinny bop go?"

"I think he hit the can," Tiffany said. "His check's still open." Jimmy looked her over and guessed she was probably an aspiring actress. Her straight brown hair was cut at her shoulders and she had a body to die for — definitely destined for the silver screen.

"He's sitting over there," Tiffany motioned to a table in the corner. "His bags are still by his chair. Have a seat and I'll take care of you."

The waitress walked away towards the kitchen and Jimmy started walking towards where she said Martini had been sitting.

"You want action tonight kid?" The bartender asked as Jimmy started walking away. "Stay away from her. Beautiful but every rose has its thorn if you catch my drift."

"I'll keep it in mind."

Jimmy took a seat at Martini's table and waited for him to come back from the men's room and looked at his phone to pass the time. An exploration of his social media feed was interrupted by a return call from his cousin.

"Joe!" Jimmy said excitedly.

"Your message sounded urgent cuz, I'd have called earlier but it was a late night."

Jimmy knew that, as a developer, his cousin kept odd hours and was understanding of his delayed response.

"Joe I could really use your help with something..."

"Hey," Joe interrupted, "that shit about Bernie was wild. Were you at the hotel when he died?"

Jimmy had seen that his spat with Bernie had gone viral, but so far none of the major news outlets had released the fact that he was killed at the Hotel Palomino the night before. His cousin's reference of Bernie's death caught him off guard.

"I didn't realize that was news yet," Jimmy said. "Look, the cops came by my hotel this morning asking me questions about last night. They saw my fight with Bernie..."

Joe cut Jimmy off, "Yeah, what was that all about?"

"Not important. Listen, I took one of your Fast Lane cars back last night. Is there a way you could have someone from your company call one of these detectives to let them know I wasn't at the hotel when Bernie was killed?"

Joe smiled feeling as if it were Christmas Day, "Of course cuz. Just shoot me their info."

Jimmy caught sight of Martini weaving towards him, the manager was clearly blitzed.

"I'll send you an email. Look, I gotta go. I'll follow-up with you later."

"You bet," Joe replied and hung up the phone.

"If you're looking to settle a score with Bernie," Martini slurred, "I got bad news for you, kid."

"LAPD broke the news to me this morning. They think I had something to do with it."

"You? That's a good one." Martini took a sip of whatever was in his glass.

"They showed me a YouTube video of Bernie kicking

my ass and they think I have a motive."

"There's a long line of people behind you, kid."

"That's why I'm here. I'm curious, at the Kimmel taping yesterday, one of the producers overheard an argument between you and Bernie. What was it about?"

"A private matter." Martini finished his drink and waved Tiffany over. "Can I get another one of these?" He held his glass over his head and shook it so the ice cubes clacked.

"Same?" Tiffany asked and Martini nodded.

"That one's on me," Jimmy piped up.

"You're not a bad kid," Martini said.

"You want anything?" Tiffany asked Jimmy.

"Ginger ale."

"Living on the edge I see," Tiffany said and turned to the bar.

"I did you a favor, now do me one. What was the argument about?"

Martini couldn't argue with his reasoning, anyone who'd buy him a drink was worthy of a return favor. "Back in the day, Bernie was in a very popular band with a few other guys."

"Oh, I know," Jimmy said. He almost professed his love but held back.

"Well, it was a fact he'd rather forget. Anyway, the band's been done for almost two decades and I received an offer a few weeks ago to reunite them for a reunion tour. Big money, too."

"By whom?" Jimmy's inner-detective was kicking in.

"Some former fan who came into some serious cash, but that's not important right now. I talked it over with the other guys who were all jumping at the chance to make some money, but Bernie gave a hard no."

"And that's what the argument was about?"

"Yes. Blew his stack that I would even bring it up. Refused to even let the other guys tour without him."

"Why?"

"In case you don't remember, and kid that shiner on your eye is a good reminder, Bernie was a class-A asshole. Said the only way they could tour without him is if he was in the ground."

"So now that Bernie is out of the way, the other guys can tour," Jimmy observed.

"Probably, after they hire a new lead guitar player, but that problem's solved too."

"How?"

"Guy who wants to fund the tour plays a mean guitar. Seen some video of him shred myself. He's damn good."

Tiffany came back with Martini's drink and Jimmy's ginger ale. She left the check and a pen on the table.

Jimmy removed the lime from the side of his glass and took a sip. "So if they tour on the nostalgia circuit, it stands to reason that you'll make some money."

"What are ya saying, kid?"

"I just think that the two detectives who paid me a visit this morning might find that really interesting."

"Look at me," Martini extended his arms and spilled his drink as he did so. "You think I could throw Bernie off a balcony? While my alibi ain't skintight, it's airtight!"

"Maybe you hired someone to do it."

"I don't exactly have a lot of extra scratch lying around, kid." Martini looked at Jimmy and a lightbulb went off in his head. "You and that girl have a manager?"

Jimmy's jaw went slack. Was the fat manager really

doing business development while discussing the circumstances surrounding his client's death?

"We are self-represented."

"Let me give you my card. I can take you guys to the next level." Martini fished around his pockets for a card but didn't find one. He then opened his wallet and the card Terry gave him last night fell onto the table. He grabbed a pen and wrote his name and number on the back of it.

Jimmy got up to leave, figuring there was no more progress to be made.

"Think about it?" Martini said and then finished his drink.

Jimmy walked past the bar on his way out, and the bartender shouted, "Come back for happy hour, it's nothing but a good time."

"You have a trashcan?" Jimmy asked.

The bartender pointed toward the corner, and Jimmy was about to toss the fat manager's number when he noticed the other side of the card. "BreakaLeg.com?"

"Change of heart?" The bartender asked.

"I may have just been given something to believe in." Jimmy looked around for the waitress and saw her at another table. "Hey, Tiffany," he called out.

"Yes?"

"I won't forget you."

The waitress looked confused. Apparently, she wasn't a big Poison fan and missed the song references Jimmy and the bartender had been throwing back and forth.

He left the Hotel Palomino and used his phone to arrange a Fast Lane car. While he waited, he typed in the web address on the business card and found the address for BreakaLeg.com's Terry Tomasulo written on a screenplay in the writing samples section.

"El Segundo," Jimmy said, "here I come."

CHAPTER FIFTEEN

Door Number Three

Joe Feld was sitting at his desk feeling as if it were Christmas morning and three stars were aligning to brighten his world; his dream of reforming a band he idolized in childhood was coming to fruition, he was about to become twenty-five million dollars richer after the sale of his company went through, and now he had the opportunity to make his cousin's life extremely difficult. He felt as if he were the baby Jesus and the Magi had just showered him with gifts but instead of gold, frankincense, and myrrh he got a dead rockstar, a term sheet, and his cousin's head on a platter.

Everything Jimmy did made Joe feel like a failure. His cousin's academic and athletic achievements came so naturally, whereas Joe had to study and practice twice as hard, and even then, his performance was never up to his father's standards. Jimmy had natural talent and luck, Joe had nothing but wind in his face and pressure from a man whose demands he could never satisfy and whose love he could never earn.

After working his ass off at MIT, Joe earned the top spot in his class. On graduation day, Joe dredged up enough courage to ask his father if he was proud of him. His dad, who'd shown up with a woman half his age, look bewildered. "Proud of you?" he said. "Why should I be proud of you? You did exactly what was expected of you. I'll be proud of you when you do something with my investment in your degree. Ask me then."

Joe loved a challenge and didn't want to settle for working for someone else; he wanted to prove to his father that he could start a business from scratch and make it a success and was convinced beyond the shadow of a doubt that this was the key to earning his father's affection. Armed with technical skills and an active imagination, Joe set out to capitalize on an opportunity he saw in the growing tech-fueled sharing economy.

When app based ride sharing services took off, Joe had an epiphany — none of the services had a built-in rewards system. He drafted a requirements document outlining how a reward based ride sharing system could work, but he had a problem — he had the vision but no way to bring it to life. He needed a financial partner as he didn't want to run to his parents for capital; his father would consider that cheating.

He drafted a prospectus for his business and started down the long road of pitching it to angel investors and venture capitalists, all of whom turned him down reasoning that the ride sharing market was too crowded. When he was about to give up and call his father for a loan, he got a call from Bram Wallachia, an entrepreneur in South Florida who was looking to invest in mobile technologies. Joe pitched Fast Lane over the phone, and

Bram agreed to an investment of a million dollars to help Joe hire the developers who would bring the app to market. In return, he had two demands: one half of the company and that he remain a silent partner. So secretive was this investor that Joe never met him in person; all communication was done over the telephone. There were to be no written records.

Joe was even convinced that Wallachia was using a modulator to mask his real voice; apparently the axiom that only the paranoid survive didn't die in the 80s with stonewashed jeans and glam rock.

Fast Lane was launched less than a year after that conversation and, in short time, took over the markets where it was allowed to operate — Joe finally felt like a success, but it was overshadowed in the family when his cousin's podcast took off.

That was too much for Joe. He wanted to do something about it, but what? Needing inspiration, he confided in Bram, who was all too eager to help him. At the time, Bram said that his reasoning for helping Joe in this matter was driven purely by business — Joe could help him earn more money if he wasn't so distracted by his preoccupation with his cousin.

They invested some of their personal finances in a new venture with the long-term goal of ending his cousin's career and this investment, while a gamble, was about to pay dividends. After the call Joe took from his cousin earlier, he had another opportunity to ruin Jimmy's life, this one with far greater implications than ending his career.

Realizing he never received an email from Jimmy with the names of the detectives investigating Bernie's death, he tapped out a text to his cousin reminding him to pass that information along.

While he waited for a response, Joe decided to watch some of the various viral videos of his cousin's fight with Bernie. He watched a few different ones because they captured the fight at different angles and Joe wanted to soak it all in. If he had more time on his hands, Joe thought he'd like to do a video compilation of Jimmy taking Bernie's punches—he'd use this highlight reel as a motivational tool; some guys watched TED Talks, Joe was the kind of guy who was only motivated by someone else's misfortune.

As Joe watched the clips, something became apparent to him—the attractive girl in the red dress was in all of them. It was almost as if Jimmy was fighting Bernie over her. He also noticed a brute of a man dressed like a cowboy who came in between his cousin and the singer. Instinct told him Jenny and the cowboy were linked, but how?

In another clip, he saw the girl get into the elevator with the soon to be deceased singer. This gave Joe an idea, assuming he could find the girl, maybe he could bribe her to point the finger at his cousin for Bernie's murder.

He started reading the comments section of the videos and saw that one user identified her as pornographic actress Jenny Slade and the cowboy looking guy as her bodyguard; thankfully the blogosphere wasn't lacking for guys who were really into porn – some comments threaded into discussions about what her finest films were (the general consensus was that Forrest Hump, Shaving Private Ryan, and How the Gimp Stole Christmas were numbers 1, 2, and 3 respectively).

After some searching, Joe found the contact information for her manager, Eddie Costello, and decided to play let's make a deal.

Eddie Costello's world had been spiraling around him for a long time and the letter he was holding in his hand was the latest in a long list of personal complications. Given the nature of how he made a living, off the backs of young women, it was ironic that he was the one about to get fucked.

As far back as he could remember, Eddie was infatuated with sex, and a lot of that had to do with his scumbag of a father who, for his thirteenth birthday, gave Eddie a porn tape. To this day, Eddie keeps I Know Who You Did Last Summer in his underwear drawer. If there is one thing Eddie learned from dear old dad, it's that women are nothing more than vehicles for male enjoyment – it was a belief that led to his nickname. Not caring about a woman's pleasure in the act of intercourse, Eddie would climax shortly after the act began — Fast Eddie. The nickname didn't bother him in the slightest. In fact, he embraced the moniker, thinking it made him sound dangerous.

Armed with nothing more than a high school education, Eddie left his hometown of Latrobe, PA and headed to California to pursue his dream of becoming an adult film actor; though he was awoken from said dream abruptly when he found out how little male performers were paid — unless they were willing to do male-on-male scenes, in which case their income potential was unlimited. A macho man like Eddie Costello would have none of that, though.

Not willing to give up on his dream of being in the industry, Eddie needed a plan-b. He thought he'd make a good agent as the prospect of earning a cut of a girl's scenes was a good way to make a living, but he quickly found that most of the girls auditioning were already represented by an agency and unwilling to switch to an unknown — even if he took a reduced commission. He needed a plan-b for his plan-b.

Costello started going back to auditions as a way of conducting market research — he wanted to know how girls found their way into the industry, and, more specifically, how they found their agents. He learned that many had dreams of becoming mainstream actresses and ended up in adult films as a last resort. Most responded to too-good-to-be-true advertisements in magazines, websites, and newspapers and found themselves doing photoshoots, where, over the course of an hour, their clothes were gradually removed.

Eddie didn't have any money to advertise, but he did have an old-world sensibility about him. He decided to meet his potential clients the old-fashioned way and intercept them in person. Most of the girls he met on auditions said they came to LA via bus, so he decided to start prowling the downtown station, where he honed his craft.

Over time, he learned what worked and what didn't. He dressed nice, but not flashy, and won girls over by offering a temporary place to stay, a photo shoot, and a few guaranteed auditions without being pushy. Once he got them interested, he took them to an apartment he rented, where his other clients helped sell the story of his being a savior to aspiring actresses.

His turn from new friend in LA to ruthless agent was gradual, but effective. He'd start off by getting them to sign a contract that gave him exclusive rights to their representation. It was legally binding but could be broken for fifty-thousand dollars; in other words, girls would have to buy their way out of indentured service to Eddie. While they were working to earn that money, Eddie would have his other girls introduce them to alcohol and drugs, with the goal of making them dependent and increasingly vulnerable. He'd then get them started doing webcam shows and would take a portion of their earnings.

Eventually, they'd wind up in the billion-dollar adult film industry, and he'd continue taking a percentage of growing incomes. By the time most saved enough money to buy their contract, no mainstream producer would touch them. With the dream of mainstream success dashed, and their beholden to various chemical addictions, most stayed in the employ of Eddie Costello – it became their only option.

Even though he had dozens of women earning money for him on any given day, Fast Eddie Costello had a big problem that amounted to three letters – I.R.S. As a self-employed individual, Eddie was supposed to pay quarterly taxes on his earnings as well as a self-employment tax; according to the government, he only earned twenty-eight thousand dollars a year and therefore paid next to nothing in income tax to either the federal government or the state of California. But, of course, he was masking his true income.

His scam was pretty common among agents in the industry; he would bill a production company a set fee for each scene his girls performed in and, in turn, he would cut a check for the same amount to the performer. She would then take that check to the bank, deposit a portion of it, and give Eddie his cut in cash. At the end of the year, he only declared a small portion of what the girls paid him —in this way, he was more like a pimp than an agent. He further offset his tax liabilities with questionable business expenses, hair plugs being one.

His lifestyle, though, suggested he earned far north of the reported twenty-eight thousand a year. A home in Palm Springs, sports cars, a sailboat — Eddie surrounded himself with elements of the good life, and because of that, he was always looking over his shoulder for trouble from the government, which had just found him—the letter he was holding from the I.R.S. was proof of that. He had to come up with some big bucks quickly or else go on the run from the law. That, and the problem he had with the missing Jenny Slade, were making his anxiety reach its boiling point.

"Please, walk me through what happened last night one more time," Eddie said to The Cowboy.

"Jenny took the guy to her room and he got physical with her. Started throwing things and then saw the camera. I had to go in and take care of him."

"By body slamming him off the balcony? Jesus H. Christ Cowboy that's extreme even for you." Costello was borderline manic.

"No one saw me, got away clean."

"No one except SLADE, who's conveniently gone missing! What if she goes to the police and fingers you? You are tied to me and I got enough problems on my hands with the feds at the moment."

The issues with the IRS, The Cowboy, Bernie, and

Jenny were just the proverbial icing on the cake. The tech industry had put his main business, pornography, in free fall. Online porn aggregators made adult films practically free, which meant less revenue for all the players involved. On top of that, his role as a "talent scout" was becoming less and less valuable to filmmakers because young women were practically raising their hands and freely joining the sex industry. It seemed that the greater acceptance of porn by the overall population was an occupational hazard to bastards like Eddie Costello who preyed on the dreams of young women in search of fame. How's that for karma?

"What do you want me to do?"

"FIND THE FUCKING GIRL," Eddie shouted. His verbal assault would have continued if not for the ringing phone on his desk.

"Eddie Costello," he said into the phone, trying to sound as calm, cool, and collected as possible.

"Eddie, you don't know me but I think we may have a mutual interest in Jenny Slade."

Costello sat down in his chair, the caller had his undivided attention. "What do you know about Jenny Slade?"

Joe Feld wasn't an actor, but he was about to put on an Oscar winning performance.

"I know where she was last night and I know who she was with," Feld said.

"Yeah, so do millions of other people thanks to Twitter jackass."

"I also know that she was the last person to see Bernie Deville alive. Do millions of other people know that yet?"

Feld was thankful that the police had yet to reveal the

identity of the man killed at the Hotel Palomino the night before, it made his admission to Costello much more threatening.

Costello was silent for a moment.

"Are you still there Fast Eddie? Why do they call you that anyway? It certainly isn't referring to your wit." Feld was superior to this cretin in every way and wasn't bashful letting him know it.

"You smug son of a bitch. Let me tell you something..."

"No let me tell you something, right now I'm the only friend you have. There's a girl out there who I'm guessing you want back in your life before she spills the beans on what her bodyguard did to Bernie last night and, believe it or not, I'm about to try and help you."

"How could you possibly help me?"

"I want to make a deal with you Costello. The police are going to catch up with Jenny Slade sooner or later, the question is what name will she offer them when they do?"

"If I find her first, which I intend to do, I can promise you she won't be going to the police."

"Let's say you do. I'll offer you ten thousand dollars to encourage Jenny to give a false name to the cops."

Five figures for offering a fake name to the cops wasn't a bad deal. The caller had his interest before, but now Eddie Costello was getting excited.

"Whose name?"

"The name of the preppy guy in the video who Bernie punched in the face."

"Jimmy Doubts? The guy from Uncorking a Murder? Why?"

"I'll offer you another ten if I don't have to answer that question."

Fast Eddie thought it over, twenty large wouldn't solve all of his problems, but it would certainly help.

"How do I know you're good for it?"

"You are just going to have to trust me."

"Buddy, I'm not exactly the trusting type. You gotta give me something more to go on than the word of some guy I've never met."

"How about this, I'll give you half when I deliver the girl to you and the rest after she fingers Jimmy for Bernie's death."

Costello couldn't believe what he was hearing. "Did you just say you were going to deliver her to me? How in the fuck are you going to do that?"

"Do you know her mobile phone number?"

"Of course," Costello said and offered the number. "Why?"

"Let's just say I got technology on my side. Do we have a deal?"

"Yes," Costello said and then realized he had no idea with whom he was speaking. "What's your name anyway."

"You can call me Monty Hall," Joe said and then hung up.

"What was that about?" The Cowboy asked.

"Guy who says he can deliver us Slade."

"Problem solved?"

"I don't know this guy from a glory hole in the wall and it sounds way too good to be true. No way I'm putting all my eggs in one basket. Still, if he can find her, who gives a fuck?"

Joe Feld truly believed he was the master of his own universe and fully intended to make good on his promise to deliver Jenny Slade back to her agent.

He knew she lived in LA and, given her age, it was highly likely she had a Fast Lane account. All accounts were tied to a mobile phone number so Joe did a quick search on the number that Fast Eddie had just given him and got a hit for a Michelle Davies in Culver City. The picture in her profile matched the girl from the video. He wrote a business rule into Fast Lane's code to send him a notification should anyone attempt to hail a Fast Lane car using that account. All he had to do was wait.

CHAPTER SIXTEEN

The Humpty Dance

Glenn and Donnie had been in good moods all day since hearing from Martini that Bernie was dead, but couldn't understand why it wasn't bigger news. At two o'clock that afternoon, however, the cat was out of the bag. LA Homicide had identified forty-nine-year-old Bernie Deville as the victim of a murder at West Hollywood's notorious Hotel Palomino. Since then, the news was all over social media — apparently his death gave birth to an unprecedented amount of nostalgia from their old fans who were in the driver's seat when it comes to viral worthy news.

With their band's name all over the place, the lead singer and drummer were eager to capitalize and announce their reunion tour. Hey, Pete Townshend and Roger Daltry of The Who didn't stop their tour when their bass player died of a cocaine overdose. The show must go on — especially for aging musicians desperate to make a few bucks.

"I think we should open the reunion shows with

Humpty Dumpty," Donnie said after taking a toke off the joint Glenn just sparked.

Glenn started laughing so hard he was almost crying.

"I'm going to try Martini again," he said. "I just have to know how he did it."

Glenn picked up his phone while Donnie pretended to fall of the couch and break his neck. This imitation of Bernie's final moment caused Glenn to start giggling again. Well, that and good weed.

"Martini," a voice slurred into the phone.

"He's hammered," Glenn mouthed to Donnie.

"Shocking," the curly haired drummer replied.

"George," Glenn said. "Looks like you took that Hans Gruber suggestion to heart. I didn't know you had those kinds of balls."

"After Humpty Dumpty, let's play Big Balls by AC/DC," the drummer suggested, causing Glenn to lose it again.

"Who's dis?" Martini asked.

"Glenn! Glenn Fr...Beagle. Glenn Beagle." The singer figured he should use his stage name — he assumed Martini was too drunk to recognize his real one.

"Whey're you?" Martini slurred.

"I'm in New York with Donnie," Glenn said.

The manager said, "I finda new geetar player for you," and then made a retching sound.

Glenn put the phone down and looked at Donnie. "I think he just blew chunks."

"After Big Balls, let's play Tossing Cookies." The drummer referenced an original song Bernie had written two decades ago.

Glenn was almost crying again but turned his attention

back to Martini. "Martini old boy, just tell me one thing, how did you do it?"

"Waitress, can you bring me some napkins?"

"Martini?"

"No you worry about dat Glenn. But call dis guy, Max Ruby is his name. His phone number is...oh fug it, I'll email you da numba. But don't fuget he's the guy fronting da money."

Martini's line went dead and Glenn tossed his phone aside.

"What did he say?" Donnie asked.

"We got to call this Max Ruby cat."

"I don't like that," Donnie reminded his former bandmate. "We are the musicians, he's the manager."

"Let's at least give this guy a chance, Martini brought us this opportunity, let's at least give his guy a chemistry check. What's the worst that could happen?"

"Fine," Donnie agreed. "Speaking of chemistry, you got any more herb?"

Glenn rolled another joint and they blazed the rest of the day away.

CHAPTER SEVENTEEN

Running to Stand Still

Without traffic, the drive from Beverly Hills to Glendale should take just under thirty minutes, but at 2pm in LA traffic, it took Farrah closer to ninety. While Jimmy was chatting with Martini, and Bernie's former bandmates were discussing their good fortune on the back of his tragedy, Farrah was listening to Tommy Tercel rant about service animals on commercial flights and praying he would somehow bring the conversation around to their crowdfunding campaign.

"I am just saying we as a society are losing our fucking minds by letting this happen," Tercel was saying about letting service animals on airplanes. "How is a fucking toy dog going to stop you from hyperventilating at thirty-six thousand feet when you hit turbulence? If anything, you are going to squish little Toto when you get scared! And don't get me started on the people who have seizure dogs. If you are going to have a seizure, it's great that Fido can give you a heads up, but how the fuck is that going to help you when you're a few miles over Kentucky?"

Gina, Tommy's "news girl," got up from her desk during this rant, sensing there was no end in sight; in fact, it went on for a solid twenty-five minutes before Tommy put it to bed and got around to introducing his guest, Farrah Graham.

"I should mention we are joined in the studio by everybody's favorite podcasting detective, Farrah Graham. Hello, Farrah."

"Nice to be here with you, Tommy."

"Let me get down to the point of why you're with us. Wait, let me tease that for a minute. First, let me tell you in the audience about the Vibratoe. Oh yeah, Ladies, ever have an embarrassing situation where someone finds a vibrator in your purse? You know what I'm talking about, I know you've been there. Well, kiss those days goodbye. With the Vibratoe, anyone rifling through your purse, be it one of your kids looking for a stick of gum or that nosey TSA agent with the blue gloves, won't come across your battery-operated boyfriend because it is disguised as a fake toe. With 5 different skin shades and three different speed settings, you can't go wrong with the Vibratoe. Just go to www.vibratoe.com/Tommy and order yours today."

Farrah would have wondered why the hell Tommy did a live read for a product so preposterous, but she knew full well that live reads for ridiculous products paid the bills in the podcasting world.

"First of all, congratulations to you on the success of Uncorking a Murder. Fifty million people can't be wrong right?"

"Thank you so much for saying that, we are very..."

"I mean you unseated good old Tommy Tercel for the number one downloaded podcast spot, that's no small feat." Tommy had a habit of cutting his guests off before they could fully answer a question and making an interview that was supposed to be about them entirely about him.

"Are you and that Jimmy Doubts guy of yours working on a fourth season? You know, some of us have to do this every day."

"As a matter of fact, the reason I'm here is because there may not be a fourth..."

"Which brings me to the issue with this patent troll situation. Your show is in jeopardy, my daily show is certainly in jeopardy so Farrah, how about you tell us in your own words what is going on with this patent troll."

"A few weeks ago, I, along with other popular podcasters including yourself and Drew Baron, was served legal papers from a company called Interpersonal Audio. They claim they invented the technology that makes podcasting possible, and they're demanding a significant percentage of past and future revenues. They had nothing to do with our success but want a significant piece of our earnings." Farrah was amazed that Tercel had let her get away with so long a statement, when she looked over at where he was sitting she realized why, he was giving one of his interns a lunch order.

"What do we know about the people behind this, and what is the technology they claim to have invented?" Tercel had read the question from a piece of paper in front of him.

"To answer your first question, absolutely nothing. We can't track down an actual human being at Interpersonal Audio. It's almost like it was setup as a shell company just to bring a suit against podcasters. My guess is they're part of a patent holding company and they troll successful people linked to their patents."

"Sound like quality people. I don't know about you, Farrah, but I'm wired to work hard for my money, not to make it off the backs others."

"I've often wondered how you were wired, Tommy."

"Riddle me this then, what is this mysterious technology they claim to have invented?"

"They claim to own the technology that updates websites to provide access to new podcasts as they become available."

"You're telling me this group of nerds is claiming to have invented a solution for updating audio content? Like no one else on the planet would have eventually come up with that?"

"That's what they claim."

"So what do you propose we do?"

"Here's the thing, we can fight this in court, but it will cost a lot of money. We can reasonably assume they've got deep pockets and, as you know, our syndicators want us to help fund the defense. As a former lawyer, I can also tell you that our legal system is not the fastest in the world meaning we could be stalled for a while unless we act now."

"Should we just throw up our hands and go home? Was it over when the Germans bombed Pearl Harbor?" Tommy joked, dropping one of John Belushi's most famous lines from Animal House.

"No. And I'll tell you why. You, me, and Drew Baron are in the minority when it comes to podcasters in that we make a good living doing it. Our sizeable audience translates into sizable advertising dollars. But most podcasters don't make that much money, and if we gave into this patent troll, they'll have to pay the same vig to this company."

"That will virtually wipe out ninety-nine percent of podcasts."

"It will do nothing but harm the industry, particularly if we have to start charging listeners for the content that they currently get for free."

"Though I'm pretty sure my fans will pay. Hey, fans, that's your cue to call in and let me know how you feel." Tercel started his podcast after years of morning radio and sometimes forgot that his show was taped. This lead to confusion amongst his listeners who tried to call into his show when not listening live.

"This brings me to why I'm really here today. I'm here to protect podcasting as we know it. We've created a crowdfunding campaign to raise money for a legal defense fund to fight the patent troll on our terms. Because if we play on his terms, we'll be running to stand still."

"If it is a he," Tommy interrupted. "We don't know. It could be a she, though it could be a she who identifies as a he. There's no way of knowing, right?"

Farrah stayed on track. If she acknowledged his comment, the conversation would veer off topic and into another one of his rants on gender identity.

"If you want our shows to stay available for free downloads, we need your help. We have different levels of support that your listeners can participate in and you have been kind enough to provide some incentives to your audience to say thanks for helping out."

"Ahh yes, incentives, baby, to help fund operation troll roll. Here goes. A ten-dollar contribution gets you a signed headshot of yours truly. Twenty-five will get you a ticket to one of our live events. With fifty bucks, you get a year's subscription to our premium app, and with the donation of a Benny Franklin, you get a ticket to see me race one of my Paul Newman cars at Laguna Seca on Thanksgiving weekend. Go to www.TommyTercel.com/troll to learn more and make your donation."

"Thanks for having me on your show, Tommy."

"We're going to do some news. Do you have a few more minutes to crack wise while Gina over here tells the audience what's going on in the world?"

"I'd love to, Tommy."

While Tommy's sound guy played an intro for the news segment, Farrah looked at her phone and saw a text from Jimmy.

"Heading to El Segundo to track down a lead on the Bernie thing."

She typed a quick reply, "Be careful."

CHAPTER EIGHTEEN

The Last Mile

Jimmy was in a Fast Lane car heading southwest toward El Segundo. The car's AC didn't work so the driver had all the windows down, giving Jimmy an intimate experience with the sounds and smells of LA. Jimmy rolled up his window choosing perspiration over the offensive sounds and odors coming from outside.

His phone buzzed to announce he received a text message. After seeing it was from his cousin Joe, Jimmy remembered he'd forgotten to send him the detectives' contact information so Joe could prove to them that Jimmy wasn't at the Hotel Palomino at the time of Bernie's death.

Joe: Remember to send me the 411 on the detectives

Jimmy: Sorry, got sidetracked

Jimmy then snapped a picture of Jeff Nelson's business card and sent it via picture message.

Joe: Got it. What you been doing today?

Jimmy: Went back to the Hotel Palomino to meet with Bernie's manager. Who knows, maybe we can get our fourth season out of this!

The thought of Jimmy's star rising over this series of events made Joe's stomach turn. That he may have had a hand in his cousin's success made him furious. If he had any reservations about what he was planning to do, they were gone now.

Joe: Good for you. What's the rest of your day like?

Jimmy: Currently in a Fast Lane car on the way to El Segundo to chase another lead.

This got Joe's attention. El Segundo wasn't too far from Joe's luxury apartment in Manhattan Beach.

Joe: Hey, gotta run. I'll let you know when I talk to the detective.

Jimmy: Thanks cuz, means a lot.

Joe was eager to see what his cousin was up to in El Segundo so he decided to hop in his Tesla and try to find out. He loaded an app that could track any Fast Lane user in transit; it not only told him where they were, it told him where they were going. It only took a minute after plugging in his cousin's phone number to see that Jimmy was on the 405 in Inglewood, heading toward 841 West Grand Avenue in El Segundo. Joe plugged the address into his GPS, which told him he'd get there 3 minutes faster than Jimmy. He peeled out of his driveway and decided to call the detective on the way.

"Do you think Maiden would have made it if Bruce Dickinson didn't come on board?" Jeff asked his brother while stuck in traffic just two miles from the address they had for Terry Tomasulo in El Segundo.

"I liked the Paul DiAnno records, but..."

"All two of them?"

"Why do you always have to cut me off? What I was going to say was — I liked the Paul DiAnno records but will admit that Dickinson was better for the band."

"So a replacement singer can be better than the original. Is that what you're saying?"

"Hagar still sucks, and don't you dare mutter the name Gary Cherone."

Jeff was about to offer support for Van Halen's third lead singer when his phone rang.

"Detective Jeff Nelson."

"Detective Nelson, my name is Joe Feld from Fast Lane. A celebrity customer of ours called our support line and, due to his stature and my relationship with him, the ticket got bumped up to me. I'm supposed to speak with you about it. Does this sound remotely familiar to you?"

"It's a guy from the app Doubts claimed to have used last night," Jeff said to his brother. "Mr. Feld, I am working on a murder investigation and a suspect wants to use the fact he was in one of your cars as an alibi."

"Detective, my uncle was a cop and I'll do anything I can to help. What do you need?"

It wasn't a lie, Joe's uncle — Jimmy's father — was a police officer who was killed in the line of duty.

"Can you tell me if a Jimmy Rella was in one of your cars last night?"

"I'd be happy to look into that but like I said before, this got bumped up to me not only because he's a celebrity, but because of my relationship with this customer."

"What do you mean by that?" Jeff asked.

"Jimmy Rella is my cousin. Our mothers are sisters—I just wanted to be upfront with you about that."

Murray saw the look on Jeff's face change. "What?" he

mouthed.

Jeff covered the receiver of his phone with his palm, "The Fast Lane guy is Doubts' cousin."

"We just need to know where your cousin was last night between 8:30 and 9:30." Based on a statement given by Chrissy Snow, the smoker who heard the crunch of Bernie's body as it slammed into the pavement, the detectives estimated that the time of Bernie's fall was approximately 9:15.

"I'm going to need a few minutes to query the database. Can I call you back in a few?"

Joe knew exactly what he was going to tell the detective. The request for time was a dramatic effect.

"Thank you, Mr. Feld."

"What's up?" Murray asked after his brother hung up.

"He's gonna call us back."

"You know, we can't trust what he's about to tell us. He may be trying to protect his cousin."

"Agreed, we'll need to subpoena the actual records themselves if it gets to the point where Doubts goes on trial for this."

At this point, they were parked in front of Terry Tomasulo's and were staring at the sky-blue Cadillac parked out front.

"Same one as last night," Jeff said.

"Yep," his brother replied. "Should we knock on the door?"

"Let's wait to hear back from the Fast Lane guy."

"Fine," Murray said. "If you were on a desert island and could only bring three albums with you, what would they be?"

The brothers debated this intensely until the door to

Tomasulo's apartment opened and he and Jenny Slade exited.

At the moment, Jenny Slade had six people trying to find her — Jimmy Doubts, Joe Feld, the Cowboy, Eddie Costello, and the detectives. Unfortunately, this was the most interest she'd garnered since coming to California eight years ago, outside of the sex industry of course.

Being holed up in Terry's house all day was starting to get to her, and the mob enforcer turned writer started to notice her jitters.

"Everything okay?"

"Can't we get out of here just for a little bit? I'm starting to suffocate, and if I have to hear one more god damn plane, I'm gonna lose it."

Jenny had been a steady user of cocaine since becoming an adult film actress. She turned to the drug to feel better before shooting scenes – and because she shot scenes no fewer than five days per week, she got intense cravings when it wasn't in her system. She needed to score.

"We can't go anywhere in my car. The cops who were at your place have likely run the plates. I'm guessing it's on an APB or something."

"Shit, grandma's Caddy does stand out."

Jenny wondered how his grandmother would feel about him harboring a pornstar with a coke habit.

"You don't have any blow, do you?"

"Never touch the stuff."

He was being truthful. Terry watched too many of his friends ruin their lives on the Columbian marching powder highway. He knew what happened when withdrawal kicked in and saw the signs presenting themselves; if she didn't get a fix or go under the supervision of a medical professional, things were going to get ugly.

"I need a little to get right."

"You got a connection?" Terry didn't want to condone her use, but he didn't want a hot mess on his hands either.

The look Jenny gave him suggested there actually is such thing as a stupid question.

"Look, I have to get out of here. If we can't take yours, why don't we take a Fast Lane car?"

Terry looked puzzled.

"It's like Uber or Lyft."

Jenny's comparisons didn't help.

"It's like a cab, but cheaper."

"Why didn't you just say so? What's the number?"

Jenny shook her head. "You don't call. You use their app. Give me your phone. I'll download it and sign in with my account."

Terry handed his phone over, and within a minute, she'd hailed a ride and was ogling the car that would be picking them up.

"What's that look on your face?"

She held up the phone for him to see.

"Only in LA could we get picked up in a Tesla," she said. "Let's go wait outside."

Joe Feld was only two blocks away from Terry Tomasulo's when his phone came to life. Jenny Slade's Fast Lane account just arranged a pickup from the same location where his cousin was heading. He accepted the job and made note of their intended destination in Van Nuys. Joe then called the detectives back with a report on his cousin's ride history.

"Someone's coming out of the building," Murray said, thus ending their debate about albums and desert islands. At the same time, his brother's phone began to vibrate.

"The Fast Lane guy's calling," Jeff said. "Keep an eye on them while I take this." He put the phone to his ear. "Detective Jeff Nelson."

"Detective Nelson, this is Joe Feld from Fast Lane. I just finished the data pull you asked for."

"What did you learn?"

"The system shows that Jimmy Rella did hail a Fast Lane car last night. He went to the Hotel Palomino from a TV studio in downtown LA."

"What time was that?"

"The ride initiated at 5:29 pm and dropped him off in Hollywood at 7:14."

"What about after that? Any activity?"

"He called for one of our cars at 8:41 but then cancelled it."

"Is that all?"

"Well, our app uses GPS to guide our drivers directly to their customers. If the app is running in the background on someone's phone, we actually can look at where our customers are at any point during the day. I was able to see that he remained in the vicinity of the Hotel Palomino until 9:45 and then went to a hotel in Beverly Hills."

Joe Feld was a man who took calculated risks, every successful entrepreneur did. In his master of the universe mind, the lie he just told the detectives wouldn't come back to haunt him for two reasons; he had data, (albeit fudged) on his side and Jimmy's very public fight with

Bernie showed motive. Jimmy would, of course, vehemently challenge the lie that Joe told the detectives, but with the one-two punch of evidence and motive, they'd have to side with Feld vs. Doubts.

"This is helpful. Thank you for your time, Mr. Feld."

"My pleasure."

Jeff turned his attention back to his brother. "The kid was lying. We got him at the hotel at the time of the murder."

"That's odd."

"What?"

"This guy just threw his cousin under the bus. I mean, that's good for us, but why not lie about it to help out his cousin?"

"Maybe they ain't that close," Jeff said. "And what about these two?" Jeff asked, referring to Terry and Jenny, who were waiting on the corner.

"I don't know, but if they were leaving, wouldn't they get in his beast of a car?"

Just then, a Tesla pulled up and the pair jumped in. A second later, it tore off.

"Shit!" Jeff said. "Should we follow them?"

Murray didn't reply — his attention was on another car that just parked in front of Terry's building.

"What's today's date?"

"March 21st, why?"

"Christmas is coming early this year. Our guy Jimmy Doubts just showed up."

The two detectives got out of their car and approached Jimmy, who was hunting for Terry's name on the call box outside the door.

* * *

Jimmy felt a tap on his shoulder and turned around to see the two detectives from earlier in the morning.

"Mr. Rella, what a coincidence meeting you here."

Jimmy was dumbfounded.

"What are you guys doing here?"

"Interesting question," Jeff said. "We have a few of our own. Let's take a drive."

The thought of making a run for it didn't even cross Jimmy's mind. He knew the best thing to do was come clean and tell the detectives what he knew. He just didn't want to do that without Farrah present.

"Am I under arrest?"

"Not yet, but it's not looking good."

Jimmy followed the detectives to their car and remained silent during the ride to the station. The detectives, on the other hand, had an intense debate on whether Ozzy's music was better with Randy Rhodes or Zakk Wylde on lead guitar. Murray argued for the former while his brother argued for the latter.

CHAPTER NINETEEN

Dr. Feelgood

Before Jenny and Terry got into his Tesla, Joe shot a text to Eddie Costello asking to meet him at the address Jenny had plugged into Fast Lane when she called for a car. He also told Eddie to bring backup—Jenny's friend looked as if he could handle himself.

"Looks like you guys want to head up to the valley, what you got going on up there?" Joe asked.

"I gotta see someone about something," Jenny responded curtly. She was clearly agitated, a sign of the growing withdrawal from the drug she needed to feel normal.

Something was bugging the mob enforcer turned writer and he couldn't help but scratch that itch.

"What's a guy with a Tesla doing working for an online taxi service?"

It was a logical question, and because he thought of everything, Joe was prepared with an answer, though he resented Terry's characterizing Fast Lane as a taxi service —it was a ride sharing platform based on the sharing economy!

"I sell Teslas. This is a great way to give more people the Tesla experience, up close and personal. Sold three just last week from Fast Lane users."

"Smart," Terry admitted.

"Looks like it's going to take about an hour and twenty minutes to get up there on the 405. The 5 isn't much better. Anything in particular you want to listen to?"

Jenny just let out a sigh, showing her aggravation.

While Joe was driving north on the 405, his phone began buzzing, and when he answered, the car put it on speaker instead of his Bluetooth headset.

"Max Ruby?" everyone heard a drowsy voice ask before Joe transferred it to his earpiece.

"Yes," Joe said. While he didn't recognize the number, there was only one person who knew him as Max Ruby, George Martini.

"It's Glenn Beagle, I believe you know my manager George Martini?

"Yes, he and I have been in discussions about getting you guys to tour."

"Well I'm not sure if you heard the news, but our guitar player had a bit of a fall and will be unable to tour with us."

"Is he okay?" Joe said, digging deep to find a scrap of emotion hiding at the bottom of his soulless body.

"Let's just say all the king's horses and all the king's men couldn't put Bernie together again."

Joe heard laughing in the background; Donnie couldn't contain himself.

"Look, I don't know how much Martini has told you about me, but I really want to see you guys back on tour.

The fans would love it. I'd love the chance to play with you guys, of course that wouldn't impact my decision to finance you, that comes with no strings attached."

"That's why I'm calling. Me and my bandmate Donnie would like you to come to New York for a chemistry check. If you've got the chops and we can all get along, the gig is yours."

"So you want me to come to New York?"

There was a pause, then Glenn hurriedly added, "You gotta come on your dime though!"

They couldn't afford to drive themselves out of New York, let alone fly someone they didn't know there.

"Not a problem. When do you want me?"

"Let's see, today is Friday, how about Saturday?"

"Next Saturday?"

"No, tomorrow." In Glenn's mind, there was no time to waste. They had to capitalize on the newfound buzz after Bernie's plunge.

"Well sure, I can fly to New York tomorrow," Joe said excitedly. "Where do I go once I get there?"

"I tell you what, I got a friend who owes me a favor at a limo company called Greenfield Livery. Someone will be waiting for you in baggage and he'll take you to a place we can meet. Just call me later with your flight number."

"Greenfield Livery?"

"Yes," the singer confirmed.

Terry made a mental note of this as Carbona had an ownership interest in Greenfield. Hell, he had an ownership interest in every livery service operating in New York, New Jersey, and Connecticut.

"I'll get the flight number to you later. Thanks, Glenn."

There was no reply. The singer had already hung up.

"Planning a trip?" Terry asked from the backseat. "Isn't Saturday a pretty busy day for a car dealer?"

The nosey thug in the back was starting to get annoying. "It's an opportunity I can't refuse," Joe said and then turned up the music, signaling the conversation was over.

While Terry could only hear Joe's side of the conversation, his wheels were turning—the street smarts he'd acquired over the years told him something was amiss; of course, Joe Feld had no way of knowing that in the back seat of his Tesla was Terry Tomasulo, surrogate son of Anthony Carbona's, who had been hired by Feld himself to break Bernie's legs if need be. This one little piece of knowledge would have saved Feld a lot of heartache.

"Fast" Eddie Costello was waiting in room 803 of the Airtel Hotel across the street from the Van Nuys airport. While Van Nuys didn't have the same cache as West Hollywood, it attracted its fair share of hard living souls looking to self-medicate, and the Airtel was the biggest pharmacy in town.

Eddie Costello not only introduced Jenny Slade to coke, he introduced her to a dealer called The Fencer, due to the fact that he wore a fencing mask whenever doing business. No one, not even Eddie, knew what he really looked like.

Not wanting to rely solely on the mystery man Monty Hall to track down Jenny Slade, and knowing his starlet's dependence on cocaine, Eddie called The Fencer and asked that he let him know about any contact from Jenny. Considering how many customers the sleaze-ball sent his way, The Fencer called immediately after hearing from the on-the-run actress. When the guy who called himself Monty Hall sent him a text earlier with the address of The Fencer's hotel-based operation, Fast Eddie marveled at how things were turning around for him. Considering the unique circumstances of where Jenny was being dropped off, Costello agreed to accept the promised first payment later in the day as he certainly didn't want to keep ten-thousand bucks with him at the Airtel.

The Fencer was never in the same room at the hotel between sales. Once a deal went down, he packed up and went to another room. This was done to prevent anyone from pointing law enforcement, or rival dealers, to his specific whereabouts in the joint. It also meant that his customers had to get a room assignment prior to scoring dope.

It was a simple two-call system for past customers; one call to say when they'd like an appointment and another, once on the premises, for a room number. For new customers, there was an intense screening process that preceded a first meeting — The Fencer was nothing if not safe.

"When she calls, point her to room 803," Eddie told the dealer.

"Roger that," The Fencer said.

Joe pulled into the parking lot of the Hotel Airtel. "I would really appreciate a 5-star review," he said, fully committing to his role as a Fast Lane driver.

Jenny tapped a note on her phone and received a response seconds later.

"Room 803," she said to Terry.

They got out, and Joe rolled down his window. "Do you want me to wait for you?"

Terry waved him off and caught up with Jenny, who was practically speed-walking toward the hotel.

"This place looks pretty seedy," he said. "Are you sure you want to be here?"

Her eyes suggested it was the last place she wanted to be, but that major jones for blow kept her going.

They passed the front desk where, in the middle of the afternoon, there was a line three-people deep. The guy in front was complaining that he had no hot water.

"I am sorry, sir, but we've never had this problem before," the receptionist said, unconvincingly.

"Bullshit," said the second person in line. "I've got no hot water either."

"Me either," said the third.

"Quality place," Terry said as he hit the button for the elevator. "What's the plan after we get you feeling right? Talk to the cops?"

"Score coke and then hit the precinct?"

"This is LA. Stranger things have happened." Terry then realized something. "You don't have any money, do you?"

"Nope."

"This just keeps getting better and better." Terry checked his wallet and saw that he had a hundred and twenty bucks on him. "A buck twenty enough?"

"For now," Jenny replied.

The ride to the eighth floor was insufferably long, particularly for Jenny, whose anticipation for a fix made every second feel like an eternity.

"I picture a hamster on top of this thing in one of those

little hamster wheels running his little hamster legs as fast as he can to move this elevator up and down."

"Terry?"

"Yes?"

"Shut the fuck up."

They exited the elevator and stood in front of door 803. Terry stepped in front of the door and Jenny put a hand on his shoulder.

"This guy doesn't like surprises. He's not going to like that I brought you here."

"I can handle myself," Terry replied and knocked on the door.

"When she gets here, please avoid the temptation to throw her off the balcony."

"She should be here by now, Eddie. What if that masked freak is fucking with us?"

"He wouldn't do that," Eddie said. "I'm one of his best customers."

They heard the elevator bing in the hallway. Eddie cut the lights, and The Cowboy moved to the door.

"Remember the plan?" Eddie asked.

"You open the door and I clobber the first person to walk in."

"That's right."

"Even if it's Jenny?"

"Especially if it's Jenny." The Cowboy's crush on her had waned. He clenched his hand into a fist after hearing the knock on the door.

CHAPTER TWENTY

Under Pressure

Jimmy Rella was an unabashed mama's boy. His mom, Diane, worked her butt off to raise him, and because he knew how much she'd sacrificed, he always did his best and stayed out of trouble, which is why he caught her off guard with the news that he was being questioned for murder. Most guys in his shoes would call a lawyer first, but Jimmy Doubts needed to hear his mother's voice.

"James Angelo Rella, if you are playing a joke on me, so help you God I will take the next flight to California and hunt you down with my shoe."

While Jimmy was a good kid, he was known for playing practical jokes on his mother. When one of his ruses was up, she'd chase him around their home with a shoe.

"Mom, this isn't a joke. I'm at the police station now. They haven't charged me yet, but it's not looking good."

"Tell me everything."

So he did. Jimmy told her about his pitching Reasonable Doubts to an "entertainment executive," the subsequent altercation with Bernie Deville, and then being approached by the cops.

"Did you tell them you couldn't have had anything to do with it?" Diane sometimes forgot that her son was a twenty-seven-year-old man, in her mind, he was still a six-year-old boy who needed his mother's help.

"Of course! I told the cops I couldn't have been involved with Bernie's death since I was in a car back to my hotel at the time. I took one of Joe's Fast Lane cars and asked him to call them with proof."

"Do you think he forgot? He's probably preoccupied with the sale of his company."

"No, he didn't forget. He even reminded me to give him the detectives' information which I did, yet here I am."

"You never know, that kid was always an asshole."

Jimmy's mother had the cleanest mouth of anyone he knew, so hearing her swear caught him off guard.

"You're right about that."

"Of course, I'm right, I'm your mother. Where's Farrah?"

Jimmy gave her an overview of what they are dealing with regarding the patent troll and how she has been preoccupied dealing with that.

"Listen, mom, my phone's about to die. Can you reach out to Farrah and tell her where I am?"

"Of course."

"Thanks, mom. I owe you one."

"You owe me a lot more than one. Stay safe. What have I always told you since you were a baby?"

"Everything is going to be okay."

"That's right. Just have a little faith and remember that your mother loves you."

"I love you, too."

An hour later, detectives Murray and Jeff Nelson walked in with a cup of coffee and a yellow legal pad. They always made suspects wait alone before starting an interrogation in earnest as they found it helped with the confession process.

"How about you save us a whole lot of time and just write down a confession?" Murray asked.

"If you make this easy for us, the DA will go easier on you," Jeff added. "You might be looking at involuntary manslaughter and not second-degree murder."

"I didn't do anything!" Jimmy protested. "Did you check with the Fast Lane people? They can prove I wasn't even at the Hotel Palomino when Bernie died."

"As a matter of fact, we did check with them," Jeff said. "They said the GPS coordinates from your phone put you at the hotel until 9:45 pm, just after Bernie was tossed from his balcony."

"What?" Jimmy asked. "Who did you talk to?"

"Some guy named Feld?"

"Joe Feld?"

"What's he a friend of yours?" Murray asked. He knew the answer, but was curious to see if Feld was yanking his brother's chain when he claimed to be Doubts' cousin.

"He's my cousin." His mother's characterization of Joe as an asshole was in consideration for understatement of the year.

"Did you say cousin?"

"Yes, Joe's mother and mine are sisters."

It was Jeff's turn to poke at Jimmy. They found the one-two punch was helpful at breaking down suspects. "If you're not going to write a confession, why don't you at least tell us how you wound up at Terry Tomasulo's place this afternoon."

Jimmy closed his eyes and took a deep breath. He knew he had to play it straight. "I went back to the Hotel Palomino this afternoon and met with Bernie's manager, George Martini."

"Now why would you do a thing like that?" Murray interrupted.

"Well, I was trying to start the process of clearing my name."

"I know you and your podcasting partner like to play detective, but leave the police work to us."

"I stand by our track record. Anyway, Farrah and I were on Adam Kimmel's show last night and Bernie was the musical guest. He and his manager got into a blowout before he went on and I wanted to find out what they were arguing about."

"Martini didn't tell me about an argument," Murray said to his brother.

"Why would he?" Jimmy replied.

Jeff's glance to Murray suggested they take their conversation about Martini offline.

"And Terry Tomasulo?" Jeff asked.

"Martini wound up pitching me his services as a manger but didn't have a card, so he wrote his number on the back of someone else's — Terry Tomasulo's, of Break a Leg productions." Jimmy handed the card to Jeff. "Ever hear of him? Oh, of course you have. You were waiting outside his apartment when you picked me up."

"Watch your tone," Murray advised. "Tomasulo's not a suspect. You are."

Before Jimmy could reply, there was a knock at the door. Murray answered it and had a whispered exchange with someone. Jimmy prayed it meant Farrah had arrived. The detective closed the door and sat back down.

"Well, this just got really interesting," Murray said.

"How so?" Jeff asked.

"Jenny Slade just showed up and wants to talk about last night. Sit tight, Jimmy Doubts, we'll be back."

Jimmy was relieved and hopeful Jenny would set the record straight, but then he remembered one of his mother's trademark sayings—"keep your hopes high but expectations low."

He was about to be disappointed.

Before Jeff and Murray met with Slade, they had a discussion about Jimmy.

"I don't think he did it," Jeff said. "How many killers call their mother before their lawyer?" The twins had listened in on Jimmy's conversation from the other side of a two-way mirror.

"This is LA, stranger things have happened," Murray argued.

"This thing about the cousin is a jagged little pill to swallow," Jeff said. "When Feld first called, I remember him saying that his uncle was a cop killed in the line of duty. I wonder if he meant Jimmy's dad."

"I think I remember that from season 2 of Uncorking a Murder."

"We are going to need to put a little pressure on Feld."

"Agreed."

"Ready to talk to Slade?"

"No, let her stew for a minute. Coffee?"

"Sure."

The brothers went into the breakroom to grab a dose

of caffeine and got into an argument over who was a better guitar player, Eddie Van Halen or Steve Vai. Murray argued for the former and Jeff for the latter.

"After leaving Van Halen, David Lee Roth found a better guitar player than Eddie," Jeff argued.

"He also had an all dwarf security team," Murray reminded his brother, "so let's not use Diamond Dave as the poster boy for a human resources professional."

"Yeah, I think Dave took his Snow White alter ego a bit too far. Still, Vai is better than Eddie."

"Mountains of cocaine will do that," Murray said referencing Roth's well known love affair with the drug back in the 80's. "Look, Vai's got great technical skills, but put him in Van Halen and they wouldn't be as good," Murray countered. "Plus, they'd need a new name."

"The drummer is still a Van Halen," Jeff argued.

"What great bands are named after drummers?"

"Fair point."

Their argument was interrupted when their administrative assistant came in to let them know a Farrah Graham was there to see them.

"Show her to our suspect and let her know we'll be with them shortly."

Then the brothers went in to hear what Jenny Slade had to say.

The last two hours of Jenny's life had been among the scariest she'd ever spent — and she worked in the adult film industry. Her expectation of a quick transaction with The Fencer was squashed when Terry was attacked as soon as they stepped into room 803.

Terry insisted on going in first, which was a good thing

for Jenny, as he took a big hit from The Cowboy that knocked him out cold. While the writer/mob enforcer was face down on the floor, The Cowboy grabbed Jenny and Eddie made it clear that she needed to identify Jimmy as the person who threw Bernie off the balcony or he'd have to see that harm came to everyone in her family. What choice did she have?

Eddie gave her a little coke to make her feel right and then drove her down to the precinct, leaving The Cowboy to handle Terry Tomasulo. All she heard Eddie say to the man in the vest was, "Take care of him and do it the right fucking way."

Now, sitting alone in the interview room, Jenny started to cry, thinking how far her mama's little angel had fallen since coming to LA.

The door opened and snapped Jenny from her mental pity party; at first, she thought she was seeing double. The men, who identified themselves as detectives Murray and Jeff Nelson, were carbon copies of each other.

"Are you guys twins?" she asked.

"Same father, different mothers." To Jeff, that joke never got old. To his brother, it was as stale as the coffee in the precinct's breakroom.

"Pardon my brother," Murray said. "He thinks that line is actually funny."

"I've heard worse," Jenny replied.

"We've been looking for you for a while, Ms. Slade," Jeff asked. "Where have you been?"

Jenny anticipated that question. She initially planned on telling them she went to the emergency room to get checked out after jumping into the pool, but if they checked her story — which she assumed they would —

they would quickly find that it was a lie.

"I was a little freaked out about what happened so I stayed at a friend's."

"And why did it take so long for you to come in today?" Jeff could have asked why she got into a Tesla out front of Terry Tomasulo's house, but decided not to push her yet. The time would come when they needed to turn up the heat, but that time wasn't now.

"Look, I'm still wigged out about last night. I saw someone get killed."

"Which is why we need to talk to you. Can you walk us through the events of last night?"

Jenny took a sip of water and began telling the detectives about going to the Hotel Palomino the prior evening to participate in a new type of adult entertainment.

"This I gotta hear," Murray said.

Jenny took another sip. "My manager is working with a new production company on something called reality porn."

The brothers put down their pens and listened intently. Living in LA for so long, they had seen and heard it all, but this captured their interest.

"Please continue," they said in unison.

"Sounds more exciting than it is. It's shot hidden-camera style to give it authenticity."

"Who set you up with the gig?" Jeff interrupted.

"My manager, Eddie Costello."

"So you're at the bar," Murray said. "What are you supposed to do?"

"The working title of the show is Fantasy First Dates. The idea is that I come on to an average Joe type of guy in a hotel bar, I mean really come on to him, and then take him to a room where, you know."

"We don't know," the brothers replied, once again in unison.

"Fuck him. Hidden cameras catch it all. Afterwards I tell the guy about the camera bit and get him to sign a release."

"Who would be stupid enough to do that?" Murray said.

"The idea has some holes in it, but my manager wanted me to try it anyway. Last night was supposed to be our pilot." For obvious reasons, Jenny left out the bit about Eddie planning on blackmailing any holdouts.

The detectives raised their eyebrows at the same time giving her the green light to continue.

"Last night I see a guy dressed like he just walked out of a J. Crew catalog like he was from Connecticut or something. He stood out to me as the perfect mark for the pilot, so I approached him."

"Do you remember what his name was?"

"Jimmy something. Anyway, we hit it off and he tells me an idea for a gameshow, things are going great. I got him on the line."

"Is this the guy you were talking to?"

Murray showed Jenny a picture of Jimmy Doubts.

"That's him," Jenny confirmed. "Anyway, another guy comes up to us. Bernie Deville. I recognized him from his old band and thought he'd be better for our pilot, you know cause he's famous, so I pivoted and started talking him up."

"How did Jimmy react?" Murray asked.

"Like he had his whale logoed skivvies in a bunch! He

started picking a fight with Bernie, not smart if you asked me. Bernie had him in height and weight."

"They fight?" Jeff asked, knowing the answer.

"Yeah. He started mouthing off to Bernie and got clocked in the face."

"What happened next?"

"Jimmy learned his lesson, or so I thought. I saw him leave the hotel bar when I went up to my room with Bernie."

"You said you thought Jimmy learned a lesson, what did you mean by that?"

"I take Bernie upstairs, and we start to party."

"Wait, what do you mean by party?" Murray asked.

Jenny looked down, she was afraid of incriminating herself by admitting to drug use. "Bernie did some blow."

"Just Bernie?" Jeff asked.

"He did it all," Jenny admitted.

"Continue."

"There's a knock at the door and it's the guy who pitched the gameshow idea to me." Fast Eddie spoon fed Jenny this entire story, enabling her to set up Bernie's murder as a crime of passion. "He acted like a caged animal just freed."

"So he's in the room, and then?"

"He immediately went for Bernie. Everything happened so fast, before I knew it he was throwing Bernie off the balcony."

"Wait a minute," Jeff interrupted. "Bernie Deville was six feet three inches and a solid two hundred and twenty-five pounds. You mean to tell me that five foot ten Jimmy Rella, weighing a buck seventy-five soaking wet, if he's lucky, managed to not only overpower Bernie, but throw him off the balcony? Sorry, I'm not buying it. What really happened?"

Murray gave his brother a deadly look. "Ms. Slade, we need a minute."

She watched as the two left the room.

Everyone at the precinct was used to the brothers arguing about music, but they were shocked when they heard them getting into it about a case.

"What the hell are you doing in there?" Murray asked. "She's an eye witness — our only eye witness, mind you — and you're pushing back because you don't believe the little preppy bastard in that room over there is capable of doing something like this? Do I understand that correctly?"

"Her story is, what was the term you used earlier? Oh yeah, fishy!" Jeff argued. "Pornstar pitches us the idea of Reality Porn, strike one. That whole idea is so farfetched I don't even know where to begin to poke holes in the premise. Pornstar poses the possibility that a scrawny little guy like Jimmy tosses someone taller, heavier, and stronger — snowblind mind you —off a third story balcony, strike two. Pornstar jumps out of building and into the pool after seeing someone murdered and doesn't go directly to the cops or to seek medical attention, strike three. Want to add a strike four? She winds up with a known mob associate! She's lying through her teeth, Murray."

"Have you considered the possibility that this might be a publicity stunt gone wrong? The kid was on Kimmel's show last night as was Bernie. They both need headlines so maybe some plan they concocted backfired."

"Okay, to your point," Jeff said, "what are the chances

that the kid and Bernie appear on the same late-night talk show followed by the same reality porn pilot? Murray, it makes less sense than a KISS farewell tour."

Another thing the brothers agreed on, Kiss would never retire. Gene Simmons, the band's bass playing demon in charge, would take the stage until he was buried in his own KISS coffin — and even then, he'd likely have his heirs sell tickets to his funeral.

"What do you suggest we do, ignore her?"

"No, but let's buy ourselves some time."

"What are you thinking?"

"Follow my lead."

While the Nelson twins were gone, Jenny started thinking about her life before moving to LA. A-student, plenty of friends, promising future. But that was so far in her rearview now.

"Is it too late to change?" she wondered. "Once this is all behind, I'm moving back home."

She realized it was an empty promise. It was one she'd made — and broken — to herself at least a dozen times. She was stuck and didn't know how she could ever become Michelle Davies again.

Just as she began to sink into hopelessness, the detectives returned.

"We appreciate your patience, Ms. Slade," Jeff said. "As a matter of procedure, we need you to write down everything you just told us and sign it."

Jenny looked puzzled.

"It's a matter of procedure," Murray added.

"Take all the time you need," Jeff said. "We'll be here for a while. Try to remember as many details as possible, and be sure to write down the name and contact information of your manager."

Jenny's mouth went agape. Fast Eddie made it crystal clear that she was not to point the cops towards his direction.

"What do you need that for?"

Jeff and Murray exchanged glances. "You mentioned your manager set you up for that gig last night, right?"

"Yes."

"Well, we just have some standard questions for him. Unless you can think of any reason why we shouldn't call him."

"Umm, no." Jenny didn't sound convincing. "I'll put that in my summary."

"Good," Jeff said. "We'll leave you alone for a bit. And remember, no detail is too small."

"Okay."

The detectives got up and left Jenny alone. Jeff jiggled the door handle behind them to give her the impression that she was locked in.

Her heart sank. She didn't start writing for ten minutes.

"Nice touch on the door," Murray said as they walked to the conference room where Jimmy was.

"How do you want to handle this?" Jeff asked.

"Time for you to follow my lead."

They entered the room and found Farrah sitting next to Jimmy with her hands folded on the table, all business — a stark contrast to the disheveled podcaster they met earlier in the day.

"Is my client being charged with anything?"

"Client?"

"I'll remind you that I'm a lawyer admitted to the bar in California. James Rella has retained my services so I will repeat my question gentlemen: Is my client being charged with anything? A simple yes or no will do." She left out the part where she was a patent attorney, not a trial lawyer, but what they didn't know wouldn't kill them.

The brothers exchanged glances and Jeff nodded to Murray, suggesting he take the lead.

"I'll be blunt Jimmy, Jenny Slade just told us she watched you throw Bernie Deville off the balcony."

"What?" Jimmy said, his voiced pitched as high as a soprano's.

Farrah's response surprised everyone—she began to laugh.

"I'm glad you find this funny," Jimmy said.

"Jimmy Doubts over here could barely lift all one hundred and seventeen pounds of me," Farrah said. "You think he tossed someone the size of Bernie Deville off a balcony. She's lying."

"Thanks for the vote of confidence," Jimmy said under his breath.

"Ms. Graham, we've got GPS data putting Jimmy at the Hotel Palomino at the time of the crime; we've got motive, given the altercation with Bernie, and we've got a witness who just pointed her finger at your client. As improbable as it is that your client tossed a man much taller and heavier off a balcony, this is LA — stranger things have happened."

"What's this about GPS data?" Farrah asked.

"This is the best part," Jimmy said sarcastically.

"Your client told us he took a Fast Lane car back to your hotel last night after the fight with Bernie. We checked with the company who did a data pull and they have Jimmy's GPS coordinates at the Hotel Palomino when Bernie was tossed off the third floor."

"That's your cousin's company," Farrah said to Jimmy.

"My cousin is the one who called them. Christmas is going to be awkward this year," Jimmy resigned himself to humor to combat the terror he was feeling inside.

"Why would he lie to the police?" she asked.

"Who says he's lying?" Murray challenged.

"My cousin and I are not particularly close," Jimmy said, "but I can't imagine why he would say I was still in Hollywood when I was clearly at our hotel in Beverly Hills."

"Jimmy, this may sound like its coming out of left field, but was your father a cop?"

"Yes, he died in the line of duty when I was very young. Why?"

"Your cousin mentioned his uncle was a cop," Jeff said, "I wanted to see if he meant your dad."

Jeff wasn't sure what to believe, but he didn't want to lock up a cop's son if the only evidence against him was based on the testimony of a porn star and a tech guy who may have questionable motives.

"Do you have anyone who can place you at your hotel around 10pm last night?" Murray asked. "Ms. Graham, did you see Jimmy at all?"

"I was at a dinner in Malibu and came back after Jimmy. We had an early morning, so I went straight to bed."

"There must be security camera footage of me coming back around then," Jimmy said.

"Put that on our list of things to follow up on," Murray said to Jeff.

"Detectives, at this time do you feel as if you have enough probable cause to arrest my client and book him for the murder of Bernie Deville?"

The room went silent. Jimmy felt a bead of sweat travel from the middle of his back to his waist. Later, he would recall being able to hear his own heartbeat.

"Yes," Murray replied.

Jimmy's head sank to the desk.

"But we also have reason to believe that something is off with Jenny's story."

Jimmy's head rose from the desk.

"That's why I'm not going to charge your client with anything for twenty-four hours," Murray said. "During that time, we're going to follow a few more avenues. If nothing else pans out, we will arrest Mr Dou...I mean Rella, by this time tomorrow."

"Don't get too comfortable and don't try and run," Jeff said, he clearly didn't have the same issue with clichés as his brother, though his tone suggested he was quite serious.

The detectives got up to leave, but Jeff stopped short of the door. "What kind of car does your cousin drive?"

"He was recently posting pictures on Facebook of his Tesla, though I'm sure he has others. Why?"

"Just curious."

The detectives escorted Farrah and Jimmy from the interview room then went to rejoin Jenny Slade.

"Think it's a coincidence we saw Slade get into a Tesla outside Tomasulo's?" Jeff asked.

"Nope. You should have used your superpowers to get that license plate."

"Mea culpa," Jeff replied.

When they walked in, the Nelson brothers found a woman whose eyes looked bee-stung – she'd clearly been crying. Jeff left the room for a box of tissues and handed it to her when he returned. In turn, Jenny presented her letter, which Jeff slid into the inside pocket of his blazer.

"Aren't you going to read it?" she asked.

"In time," Jeff replied. "That friend you were with last night, they have a pale blue Cadillac Coupe Deville?"

"How did you..."

"How long have you known Terry Tomasulo?" Murray asked.

"Who?"

"Don't play dumb," Murray said, turning on the heat. "We saw you leave his house this afternoon and get into a Tesla. We would have followed you, but we saw Jimmy looking around your place so we picked him up instead."

Jenny wasn't surprised the cops tracked her to Terry's given they were outside her place last night when she and Terry drove by in his boat of a car, but how the hell did Jimmy know about him?

"I just met Terry last night. The Tesla was a Fast Lane car."

The brothers exchanged glances. Jenny calls for a Fast Lane car and is picked up in the same make as Jimmy's cousin?

"The kid didn't kill Bernie, did he?" Jeff asked.

Jenny began to cry and shook her head. Tears ran down her cheeks.

"Tell us who did." Murray pounded his fists on the

table.

Jenny's sobbing became louder and louder until it was uncontrollable. She grabbed a tissue and blew her nose — it turned bright red with blood. She looked at it, felt dizzy, and blacked out. A moment later, she was having a full-blown seizure on the interview room floor.

CHAPTER TWENTY-ONE

Big Yellow Taxi

Farrah and Jimmy grabbed a yellow taxi cab from the police station – they were done with Fast Lane.

"Take a good look at me and what do you see Farrah?"

"A guy who needs to stop wearing khakis?" Farrah quipped.

"Wrong!" Jimmy's John McLaughlin-esque shouting annoyed the cabbie, who was already nervous about making a pickup at the station. "A guy that will get the shit beat out of him in prison."

Jimmy crumpled in the back seat. He was doubled over like he had menstrual cramps.

"Relax, Doubts," Farrah said, rubbing his back in a motherly way. "If they really thought you did it, they wouldn't have let you go. They're good cops. My gut tells me they don't believe Jenny Slade's story."

"I want to believe you," Jimmy replied, "but..."

Farrah couldn't resist cutting her partner off: "You have doubts?"

He would have laughed if he weren't so scared. "How

did it go with Tercel today?" Jimmy thought changing the subject would keep his mind off of prison shower scenes.

"Since announcing Operation Troll Roll, we've already raised $95,000. I expect it to pick up steam as more people download the episode."

"Well, I guess if we beat the troll, we'll have content for our next season," Jimmy said with a snicker.

Farrah didn't want to admit it, but she was thinking the same thing. "It's going to be fine, Doubts, but I think we need to help the Nelson twins out a bit."

"What are you thinking?"

"First, we need to figure out what your cousin's up to."

"For the life of me, I have no clue."

Farrah's phone buzzed and she looked at it. "Interesting."

"What?" Jimmy asked by Farrah kept reading. "WHAT?" Jimmy pleaded.

"I had a connection of mine in the patent office track down some information about Interpersonal Audio. After some digging he said that Interpersonal Audio was only incorporated a few months ago. Also, around the same time, the patent being used to go after podcasters was transferred from a bankrupt tech company to..."

"Let me guess," Jimmy said, "Interpersonal Audio."

"Correct, but that's not all."

"What else?"

Farrah continued to read the note from her contact. "There's a pending transfer of ownership happening with the patent our troll is using to come after podcasters."

"So?"

"Does the name The Universal Products Company ring a bell?"

"UPC? I think that's the name of the company my cousin is selling Fast Lane to."

"Oh my God," Farrah said, "your cousin is trying to fuck you on multiple fronts."

"What do you mean?"

"If your cousin is selling his company to UPC, that means they get all of Fast Lane's assets. I'd bet my life that if we dug deep enough, we'd find that Interpersonal Audio is actually owned by Fast Lane."

"That little prick!"

"What did you do to piss him off?"

"I don't know. He was never nice to me, but I can't for the life of me understand why he'd do this. Can your friend in the Patent office link Interpersonal Audio and Fast Lane?"

"Unfortunately, I've run out of favors with Gordon."

"Who's Gordon?"

"Keep up Doubts," Farrah said while rolling her eyes. "He's my friend in the Patent Office."

"Yeah, but you never mentioned his na..."

"I have an idea," Farrah said cutting Jimmy off. "Let's track down someone at UPC and do what we do best."

"Which is?"

"Finding the truth."

Jimmy shook his head concerned that Farrah was overestimating their odds. "How do you know they'll even give us the time of day?"

"I'm Farrah Graham, everyone wants to talk to me."

"Confident are we?"

"Doubtful are we?" Farrah replied.

"But why Joe would lie to the cops is only one question we need to answer," Jimmy observed. "We also have to find out why someone killed Bernie."

"Pop quiz, Jimmy Doubts, where would you start?"

Jimmy thought for a moment, "His former bandmates."

Farrah rolled her eyes. "Are you secretly still a mega-fan and just want to meet them all?"

"I'm being serious. When I saw Martini earlier today, he told me that someone offered them money for a reunion tour but they had some contract stating they couldn't tour unless all agreed. Bernie was the holdout.

"Sounds like motive to me," Farrah said and then went quiet.

"What's the matter?" Jimmy asked. "You're lost in your head."

"Something's bothering me about Jenny showing up at the police station."

"You don't say?" Jimmy said sarcastically. "It's bothering me too."

"The detectives said she'd just left Tomasulo's place when they approached you at his building, right?"

"Yes."

"And then she shows up at the station a few hours later. Why didn't she come over sooner? What was she doing that entire time?"

"We can't get close to Slade out of fear that we'd be intimidating a witness," Jimmy observed. "Maybe this Tomasulo guy knows."

"I guess we just added another name to our interview list."

"Yes, indeed," Jimmy agreed.

CHAPTER TWENTY-TWO

Dazed and Confused

El Camino's are not the best for transporting bodies. First off, anyone passing in an SUV could easily spot the body-shaped mass in the bed of the vehicle. Second, should The Cowboy hit a pothole, there was a slight possibility that Terry's body would bounce from the bed of the car-truck and create quite a mess on the 101, which he was taking to Agoura Hills where a former Major Leaguer known for his bad temper was waiting to help dispose of Tomasulo's body. Indeed, there are many other vehicles suited to the task The Cowboy was faced with, but nothing came between Greg Page and his El Camino—not even a stiff.

After Fast Eddie left with Jenny, The Cowboy stayed at the hotel and literally beat the life out of Terry Tomasulo. He was smart enough to know he couldn't leave a body in a hotel room that could be traced back to his boss, which left him with a five foot nine-inch problem.

In true cowboy fashion, he had no plan for how he was going to get out of the hotel undetected, so he called an acquaintance, "Nasty Boy," Bob Hagan and asked for advice. The former major leaguer suggested The Cowboy wait until nightfall and then take Terry, Weekend at Bernie's style, down to his car and drive him up to Agoura where they'd dissolve him in chemicals, then bury the bones deep in the nature preserve near Nasty's house. Turns out, Nasty had just spent the last seven days binging Breaking Bad, but the truth was, he didn't have the means (or guts) to dissolve a body. Still, this was LA and he didn't want to lose face.

When nightfall came, The Cowboy realized he needed help getting Terry's body down stairs — someone to play Jonathan Silverman to his Andrew McCarthy. That wasn't going to happen, though, so he came up with a plan B— pull the fire alarm, throw Terry over his shoulder, and rush him out. It was a stroke of genius except for the fact that the whole thing was caught on camera.

Huffing and puffing after carrying Terry down multiple flights of stairs, The Cowboy threw him in the bed of his El Camino, covered the body with a tarp, and weighed it down with some rocks and a crowbar. Then, he was off towards Agoura Hills.

After a 30-minute drive on the 101, The Cowboy exited the highway and got caught at a red light. He reached down to grab the bag of chew he kept in the ashtray and put a pinch of the cherry flavored tobacco in his lip, oblivious of anything going on around him. A few minutes later, he turned into the driveway belonging to Bob Hagan, World Series champion from the Cincinnati Reds who earned his nickname for his propensity to bean key opponents.

"Really inconspicuous car, Cowboy," Nasty said as he

met Greg in the driveway.

"She runs just fine, Nasty."

The two became acquainted during a bar fight at The Canyon Club in Agoura Hills. Hammered drunk, Nasty began heckling the headlining band — Night Ranger — when they started playing their 80s power ballad, Sister Christian. Apparently, the guy next to him had chosen Sister Christian as the first dance at his wedding. Next thing anyone knew, fists were flying and Nasty took a few shots to the face; unaware that a Night Ranger fan could be so good with his fists.

The Cowboy, itching for a fight, started throwing punches just to get in on the action. He and Nasty ended up back to back, and the two laid out no fewer than 8 men between them before getting tossed from the club. It was the first and only time in recorded history that Sister Christian led to a fight — it's time had come.

Ever since that night, The Cowboy and Nasty were in a serious bromance.

"Where's Darla?" The Cowboy asked, referring to Nasty's wife.

"Home."

"She's here?"

"No, back in Cincinnati with her mom and dad."

"Oh," The Cowboy said. "Sorry."

There was a little sadness in Nasty's eyes but he fought it off. "Fuck her. Let's see this problem of yours." Nasty had never seen a dead body before, and his stomach was turning about the prospect, but he didn't want to disappoint The Cowboy.

"Probably blue by now," The Cowboy said.

Nasty pulled up the tarp, relieved there was nothing

underneath.

"What the fucking fuck?"

"That's what I call a curveball," Nasty said.

"Fast Eddie is going to kill me."

"Listen, it probably rolled off into a ditch or something. It's no big deal. I'm sure it's fine." As Nasty as Hagan was, his affection for his brother-in-mayhem encouraged him to try and ease his mind. "Beer?"

"Why the fuck not?" The Cowboy said. "I'm probably fucked, may as well get fucked up."

When The Cowboy's sucker punch dropped him in room 803, it had been so long since he'd taken a good punch that Terry Tomasulo almost forgot what it felt like. He was dazed and confused, and just as he started to come to, another beating commenced. Realizing he had the lower hand, Terry decided to take his beating like he did when he was a kid, without defending himself. Instead, he slowed his breathing and started meditating until he was completely numb.

Luckily, Terry had taken advantage of all southern California had to offer and got in with a group of aspiring writers who touted the benefits of transcendental meditation — though he never anticipated it saving his life.

Unable to feel a pulse or see his chest rise, The Cowboy assumed Terry was dead, so he made the arrangements to get rid of him in Agoura Hills. Terry heard it all and knew exactly where he was headed when The Cowboy dropped him in the bed of his El Camino.

Since it was well after rush hour, traffic on the 101 northbound was moving at a brisk pace. His severe pain wasn't being helped by the constant bouncing up and down in the car-truck, but Terry knew he couldn't make a move until the vehicle came to a stop, and due to the free-flowing traffic, that wouldn't be until The Cowboy exited the 101.

After twenty-ish minutes, Terry felt the car decelerate and veer to the right. Once the vintage vehicle came to a stop, Terry peeked from the tarp and saw there were no cars behind them on the exit ramp. He quietly hauled himself from the bed of the El Camino and rolled into the high grass on the side of the road. The Cowboy, busy stuffing a pinch of chew between his lip and gums, was oblivious that his cargo had rolled itself to freedom.

Terry knew the area pretty well – it was near an old Hollywood filming location setup to look like a western town. As a film buff, he'd visited it often since moving to California but had some trouble finding the entrance to the trail at night. Fortunately, thugs like The Cowboy weren't the sharpest knives in the drawer and left Terry's cell phone in his pocket. After using it to navigate a mile to the old town, Terry sought refuge inside a makeshift saloon. Once settled, Terry called his surrogate father, Tony Carbona, and made him aware of his present situation including everything from meeting Jenny Slade to chaperoning her to the Valley to score drugs, and the beating he took at the hands of a guy dressed as a cowboy.

"Did you say Fast Lane?"

"Yes, Don Carbona," Terry said.

"And you heard this guy say he's going to New York?"

"Yes, later this morning. Whoever he's meeting is arranging a limo for him through, get this, Greenfield Livery."

"Listen Terry, I know you are in a lotta pain, but it would be very helpful if you could remember anyding about this driver of yours, particularly his name."

Terry closed his eyes and tried to remember the conversation. He heard a name, but what was it?

"It will come to me in a minute."

"Gianni," Carbona shouted off the phone. "Get me a sweater, would ya? Sorry Terry, it's cold as tits here in Pompano. My cheeks are like rubies."

"Ah, that's it!" Terry blurted. "Max Ruby! That's the driver's name."

"If anyone made a limo reservation under that name with Greenfield, I'll find him. It's about three in the morning here in Florider so I'll make a few calls in New York first thing in da morning. We got time on our side anyways. Even if your guy gets the first flight out, he's not getting to New York until 3:30 or 4. Now, tell me again exactly where you are, and I'll send someone over to get ya."

Terry relayed his whereabouts to Tony Carbona, ended the call, and drifted into a deep sleep which he didn't wake from until he heard the sound of a car with a damaged muffler pull up outside from the makeshift saloon. Though it was still dark out, Terry was able to make out the outline of his 1979 Cadillac Coupe De Ville. He heard the driver's door open and close and saw his friend Nicky Casperello approach the makeshift western bar.

"Things slow at Vertigo tonight?" Terry asked after his friend entered through the swinging doors. Nicky was an associate of the Carbona family who ran a popular nightclub in Hollywood.

"Hell no, but when Don Carbona calls I put people in front of profits."

"Why did you bring Maria?" Terry named his car after the grandmother who had given it to him.

"I thought you might like to nap in the back seat while we drive up to the doctor. It's a long drive to Santa Barbara."

The family had access to a doctor in Santa Barbara with a no questions asked policy for Carbona associates.

"How did you get her started without the keys?"

"Some questions are better left unanswered."

"Well, she's a lot better than this floor." Terry smiled thinking of his oversized back seat, on which he slept on many occasions. He handed Nicky the set of keys he had in his pocket and then terry climbed in the back seat and fell back asleep.

CHAPTER TWENTY-THREE

And the Cradle will Rock

Jimmy struggled to get to sleep that evening as the events from the past two days played on an endless loop in the theatre of his mind, but out of all the of the exciting things he'd experienced, the one thing he couldn't stop obsessing over was the betrayal by his cousin.

As his eyes finally started to feel heavy, he remembered something his Italian grandmother told him to do when faced with a difficult situation: Sleep on it. She said when his mind was at rest, it could do a better job of processing information, and that the answers to difficult questions would come to him in his dreams; he kept this in mind as he drifted off to sleep. After only a few winks, he shot straight up in bed having just fully recalled something that happened to him in his childhood, the memory so vivid in the stillness of Jimmy's room that he could practically see the events of 20 years ago play out before him.

The floor of the Palace Theatre packed with little kids all

dressed in brightly colored long sleeve tee shirts impatiently waiting for their four musical heroes — The Beagles — to take the stage. At the time, the band was at the height of its popularity with the kindergarten set, who loved the easy melodies and silly lyrics that parodied classic rock songs from acts including The Eagles and The Beatles.

For the parents, the band played music that was palatable; The Beagles were innovators in that regard. Something for everyone, or so their business plan said. While parents dreaded taking their kids to see performers such as Barney or Raffi, they found themselves actually enjoying the music of Bernie, Glenn, Donnie, and Randy Beagle.

In the Palace Theatre that afternoon there were many more moms than dads, a dynamic that was entirely by design. In addition to being talented and approachable, the four members of The Beagles were also very, very attractive, and while the band made its living by entertaining children, they were no strangers to entertaining young mothers between sets.

Glenn was the lead singer and rhythm guitar player. He was recognized by his long sleeved yellow tee shirt and mustache which was reminiscent of the rugged macho look of the 1970s. His large nose was fodder for jokes that were made at his expense by his bandmates.

Bernie played lead guitar and was the principal songwriter. He wore his blond hair in typical 90s fashion; shaved at the neck and over the ears but long on top. Kids also recognized him by his trademark red tee.

Randy had pin straight brown hair that covered his eyes and partly obscured his babyface. He played bass for the band and, like his bandmates, had his own color teeshirt (blue). He also was known for the Wayfarer style sunglasses he wore while performing; largely to hide his often bloodshot eyes and dilated pupils.

Every band needs a drummer and The Beagles had Donnie — the only member of the band with curly hair. In addition to his drumming duties, he would trade off singing with Glenn and kids were amazed at how he could sing and drum simultaneously. His assigned shirt color was purple; a fact that he was none too happy about since kids referred to him as Barney Beagle in reference to the popular dinosaur of the same color. That's what you get for pulling the short straw when colors were assigned.

In addition to the colored tees, each band member wore matching socks which could easily be seen given that, no matter the season, each performer wore cargo shorts as part of his uniform. Hey, it was the 90s and cargo shorts were still in.

As six-year-old Jimmy Rella and his mother Diane were looking for their seats, they bumped into Diane's sister, Anne, and her son, Joey.

"What are they doing here mother?" Joey asked angrily. He was dressed in a yellow shirt because that's what the lead singer wore, and Joey had to be front and center in everything he did.

His question was a logical one; six months prior, Jimmy's father, a police officer named Angelo, died in the line of duty while attempting to thwart a robbery. He left his family with no savings and zero life insurance. Diane had a job as a secretary at a Catholic high school but her salary was barely enough to make ends meet. The fact that she was taking her son to a Beagles concert, where tickets sold for sixty bucks a pop, was certainly surprising, given the state of her finances.

"It's good to see you, too," Diane said to her nephew.

"He doesn't even have a real Beagles shirt," Joey said to his mother.

Jimmy clutched his mother's leg. He was always uncomfortable around his cousin, who bullied him every chance he got. But it was true, Jimmy didn't have an authentic Beagles shirt — his Red Bernie Beagle shirt was a knock off. When you have to cut corners to feed and clothe your family, Diane argued it didn't make a whole lot of sense shelling out thirty bucks for a tee shirt her kid would outgrow in a few months. As such, for three dollars, she ordered a long sleeved red tee shirt from the Sears catalog, bought a stenciling kit from a local craft store, and handmade Jimmy's shirt. He didn't mind at all — he was proud to wear it.

"I'm surprised to see you here," Anne said to her sister.

Anne married rich and lived in the upscale town of New Canaan, CT. Her husband had done so well on Wall Street that even her money had money.

"I won the tickets from a radio show," Diane replied. She didn't need to justify her presence at the concert to her uppity sister, but doing so led to fewer questions — and Diane hated her sister's questions.

Just then, the house lights flickered. Anne and Joey took their seats in the front row (center stage, of course) while Jimmy and his mom took their seats in the third – if not for winning them from a radio station, they'd have been in the balcony (if they had gone at all). A moment later, a man in a suit, his hair slicked back, came on the stage — he was George Martini, band manager and one of the many characters they employed to add color to their show.

"Boys and girls," Martini said into an old-fashioned telescopic microphone, "The Beagles!"

Ed Sullivan was likely turning over in his grave, but the crowd of kids went crazy and jumped out of their seats. The band took the stage and launched into crowd pleasers, such as Take It to the Hydrant, New Dog in Town, and I Want to Sniff Your Hind.

Fans knew they always played The Long Walk right before intermission, and it was after this song that Anne approached her sister.

"Would you mind watching Joey for a few minutes?"

Diane was put off by this request. She knew her son always felt uncomfortable around Joey — there was something about him that creeped her out, too.

"Where could you possibly be going?"

Shaking off Diane's question, Anne said, "It's cool, just do me this favor, sis?"

"Whatever."

"I don't want to sit in the third row!" Joey screamed.

"It's only during intermission, baby. Mommy will be right back. Promise."

Anne didn't wait for a reply before going off with a massive human in a shirt with "Security" printed between the shoulder blades.

After taking both boys to the restroom, Diane had to explain to Joey why she couldn't buy him a soda and popcorn—he didn't show any sympathy for his aunt's financial state and threw a hissy fit on the way back to their seats. The house lights started blinking as they navigated their way back, an activity made unnecessarily difficult by Joey's constant attempts to break away from his aunt's grasp.

When they got closer to their section, all three were relieved to see Anne back in the front row. Diane thought she looked a little disheveled, compared to pre-intermission.

"Where did you go, mommy?"

"Mommy went to go arrange a special surprise for you!"

The band took to the stage for Act II and rolled right into Scratch Me Do, which they followed with Let It Pee, We can Walk It Out, and a number of other songs about typical K-9 activities.

After playing Kibble Sunrise, Glenn Beagle, his yellow shirt soaked through with sweat, got on the microphone and addressed the fans.

"Now is that special time where each Beagle picks one lucky boy or girl to join them on stage."

This was the event during a Beagles show; to be called up by Glenn, Bernie, Randy, or Donnie was akin to being picked first in gym class, an experience Jimmy never had. Anne's extracurricular activity during intermission was designed to ensure her son's selection by Glenn Beagle, who always picked the third child to come on stage.

Donnie picked a purple-clad girl in back and Randy called up a pair of twins in matching blue shirts. Glenn looked in Diane's direction, caught her eye, and smiled. Then he picked a different child clad in yellow to bring on stage. Her heart sank and Joey started balling.

Bernie, as usual, picked the last child to come up. "Well I guess it's up to me now," he said. "Let's see, who's it gonna be?" He looked left and right, even up toward the mezzanine, giving false hope to those in the cheap seats.

Then his eyes rested on a boy in the third row who appeared to be wearing a homemade Bernie Beagle tee shirt.

"You in the third row there," Bernie pointed toward Jimmy, who pointed an index finger at his chest, as if to ask, "Me?"

"Yes, you with the homemade tee. Would you like to join us on stage?"

Anne turned around and shot her sister a look of death. Little Joey became inconsolable.

A moment later, a security guard escorted Jimmy and Diane on stage to join the other children and their parents. Together, they all sang a final song, Bones Will Keep us Alive.

After the last note rang out, Glenn, Bernie, Randy, and Donnie all walked to the center of the stage and shocked their fans with the following statement.

"Tonight was an extra special show for us…" Glenn said.

"After ten years of making children laugh and dance…" Bernie continued.

"We've decided to make a change," Randy said.

They let that sink in a moment before Donnie took the mic. "This is not only the last Beagles concert on this tour, it will be our last concert ever."

In unison, the band proclaimed, "Thank you for being the best fans ever."

And with that, the band left the stage, the house lights went up, and the sound of weeping filled The Palace theatre in Stamford, Connecticut.

Jimmy looked at his phone — 4:30 in the morning. He

considered calling Farrah, but decided not to wake her. She could be a bit volatile when she didn't have enough sleep. Instead, he got out of bed and called his mother to see if she remembered the events of that day similarly. It was 7:30 her time and he knew she'd be up.

"That's exactly how I remember it," Jimmy's mother said, "but I also remember why I had to take care of your little brat of a cousin during intermission."

Jimmy remembered his aunt disappearing during intermission, but didn't know where she actually went. "What do you mean by that?"

"Well, you're old enough, I guess. During intermission, your Aunt Anne went backstage and spent some intimate moments with the lead singer."

"Aunt Anne was a groupie?"

"Let's just say your Aunt Anne wanted to guarantee that your cousin was chosen to join him on stage at the end of the show, so she hunted down good old Glenn and..."

"I don't need the details, mom, but this reminds me, there's something I left out about my meeting with the detectives." Jimmy clued his mother in on what happened in the interrogation room, how Joe lied to the cops about Jimmy's whereabouts.

"That little monster," Diane said. "If I can ever get my sister to return my calls I'm going to...."

"This isn't Aunt Anne's fault," Jimmy interrupted.

"No, but she raised that little spoiled brat and she wasn't actually the poster child for sisterhood."

"Well, let me know if you hear from her. I'm curious as to how she would defend him. You know, there's another thing that's bothering me."

"What's that?" Diane asked.

"When Joe returned my call, he knew about Bernie's death yet it hadn't been reported on the news at that time that Bernie was the one who died at The Palomino…oh my God!" Jimmy said.

"What?"

"What if Joe had something to do with Bernie's death?"

"That's a little far fetched even for your asshole of a cousin."

"This is LA, I'm learning that nothing is far fetched out here." These words were spoken by a guy who almost wound up on a reality porn pilot and was fingered for murder.

"When are you back?" Diane was eager to see her son and didn't like him being so far away. "I can't wait to see you."

"Wish I could tell you."

"Okay, well, it's 4:40 in the morning your time and you need to try and sleep. I'll call you when I get back from school."

"School on a Saturday?"

"Open house for prospective parents and the principal wants his best cheerleader there to greet them."

Jimmy hoped the school's administration knew the gem it had in his mother. He ended the call but knew he was done with sleep for the night and prayed to Our Lady of Google and got to work on some Beagles research.

One of the first returns to his search was the website for Glenn's autobiography entitled Mommies and Me: My Time in The Beagles. Jimmy laughed but caught himself when he remembered what his aunt did backstage. The website provided a phone number for press inquiries, which Jimmy wrote down, figuring he'd call it at a more reasonable hour.

After additional searches came up without viable leads, Jimmy turned on the TV, deciding to unwind with a little mindless entertainment. He debated watching a movie, and pay per view seemed to be luring him toward the adult genre. His interest was piqued by the picture of a sultry brunette with a pixie cut, but then he realized who it was – Jenny Slade.

"No thank you," he said, and flipped to the news.

CHAPTER TWENTY-FOUR

Free Bird

Joe was making his way to Los Angeles International Airport to catch a 6:45am flight to New York. Traffic on Sepulveda was light and the Fast Lane car he was in got him to LAX in record time. After his ride, he was pleased that the app's algorithm told him that trip was on the house – even though he technically was the house. "This," he thought, "is going to be my day."

He had only two pieces of luggage, an overnight duffle bag for his clothes and a hardshell guitar case housing his 1957 black Fender Stratocaster. Joe idolized Eric Clapton and recently bought this look-a-like of Slowhand's trademark guitar for somewhere in the five figures. When an airline representative suggested he check it, Joe scoffed. The thought of some baggage handler making minimum wage throwing it carelessly into the belly of the plane sent shivers down his spine. His cousin potentially wasting away in a California prison didn't bother him one bit—his prized guitar getting damaged in transit, however, was too much for Feld to handle.

As far as assholes went, Joe Feld broke the mold.

Joe loved to fly – the longer the flight the better. He loved the freedom of being able to detach. No email. No texts or calls, a policy he adhered to even though most flights offered WiFi. On this flight, he planned on doing nothing but enjoying free cocktails – a first class perk – and listening to Beagles tunes so they'd be fresh in his ear when he met with Donnie and Glenn.

Joe was the kind of guy who had a hard time letting go of slights. While it had been over twenty years since his mother took him to see The Beagles perform, the fact that his cousin — wearing his ridiculous homemade Bernie Beagle shirt — got called on stage at the end of the concert burned him to this day. To add insult to injury, he'd recently read Glenn Beagle's autobiography— a tell-all about what life is really like in a touring children's band —wherein he recounts a sexual encounter with the mother of a fan during intermission of their final performance. When he read, *"I pulled back on her ponytail while she bent over in front of me and saw an amazing sight, a little butterfly tattoo on the small of her back. Man I loved 90s girls, and they always liked it Beagle style,"* Joe knew right away that Glenn was describing his mother. She had gotten that tattoo as a birthday gift from his father and he remembered her leaving him with his aunt during intermission. Knowing that his mother gave it her all to get him picked to go on stage but that his cousin got the nod only amplified the anger and jealousy he felt toward his cousin.

He had every Beagles CD and every DVD. As a kid, he wrote each of them thoughtful, handwritten letters at least once a week. He had his mother send them each a personalized gift on their birthdays and had every piece of Beagle merchandise that was ever made. He supported them with his time, attention, and parent's money – they returned his loyalty by leaving him in a lurch and calling it quits the day he gets to see them in concert without calling him up on stage. This was a wrong that had to be made right; Joe Feld himself was about to see that his loyalty and fandom were going to be thanked.

The moment he signed the term sheet to sell his company, he started his talks with George Martini. He had done enough research on each of the four Beagles to know that three out of four were in dire straits and would be amenable to a tour. He didn't want to fund a reunion tour just to make money, hell there was no real indication that he'd make any at all as nostalgic kids acts are not exactly in demand. No, all of this effort was because Joe wanted to live out his childhood dream of becoming part of the band. That one of the founding members had to die for him to have that opportunity didn't bother Joe in the slightest. He was Joe Feld, and he was a master of the universe.

CHAPTER TWENTY-FIVE

Pacing the Cage

Jimmy paced nervously in his hotel room, expecting the Tom Petty twins to come knocking on his door any minute.

There were three things on the agenda today: speak with at least one member of The Beagles, get a meeting with someone at UPC, and track down Terry Tomasulo, presumably the last person who saw Jenny Slade before she showed up at the police department.

Jimmy picked up his phone and dialed the number he wrote down in the middle of the night. After multiple rings, her heard a voice on the other end.

"Hello?" a groggy voice said, more question than statement.

"I'm looking to get a hold of Glenn Beagle," Jimmy said, trying to sound as polite as possible.

"What the fuck time is it?"

Jimmy looked at his watch. It was 7:30am LA time. "10:30."

"Why the fuck are you calling me so early, man?"

"Is this Glenn?"

"Who the fuck do you think it is? What do you want?"

Jimmy was surprised that the number for press inquiries on the book's website was actually the singer's personal number.

"My name is Jimmy Rel....Doubts from the Uncorking a Murder podcast." Jimmy thought he might get more mileage if he gave his stage name. "I'm doing a story on Bernie Beagle's death. Do you have a minute?"

Glen really didn't want to talk, but any publicity was good publicity. Given that he was going on tour with a new incarnation of The Beagles soon, he sucked it up and agreed to an interview.

"Yeah, hold on a second."

The singer grabbed his bong from the nightstand, packed its bowl, blazed it up and took a big hit. If he was going to do an interview, he may as well wake and bake.

"Shoot," Glenn said, exhaling a big cloud of smoke.

"Do you know anyone who might want Bernie dead?"

Jimmy was surprised when his question was met with a fit of laughter.

"What's so funny?"

"That's a long list, my friend. Let's see, all his bandmates, a countless number of men whose wives slept with him in our prime, his manager. I can go on. Do you need more than that?" A rational person might hold back the dirty secrets of a kids-oriented band, particularly one trying to stage a comeback, but Glenn wasn't rational (as evidenced by his tell-all autobiography).

"Was he that bad a guy?" That punch to the face the other night told him Bernie was a jerk; he just didn't know the extent of Bernie's jerkiness.

"That mother fucker held all the publishing rights to our songs and made millions of dollars off our music every year while me and the other guys went broke. We wanted to tour in order to keep the lights on, you know what I mean, but Bernie didn't give a shit. He's like the fucking honey badger when it comes to the shits he couldn't give. Talk to our manager, George Martini. He'll give you an earful."

Glenn took another hit. "If you ask me, though, it all happened for the best. We are hiring another guitarist and hitting the road to make a little bank. Martini's problems are also solved."

"How so?"

"The guy's got more debt than Greece. He'll be able to pay that back and still have some jingle in his pocket after this tour is done."

"How did you guys get a tour planned so quickly?"

"Quickly? Who said anything about quickly?"

"Bernie just died a couple days ago."

"Buddy, this tour has been in the works for months. Some promoter approached our manager a while back offering us each a quarter of a million bucks if we would get back together for twenty dates."

A million dollars was a hell of a lot of money for a washed-up kids group to net on a reunion tour. At an average cost of forty bucks a ticket, cheaper than the sixty they could get in their heyday, the band would have to sell over twenty-five thousand tickets to make that kind of money before expenses. That's a lot of tickets for a kids' band that hadn't toured in over twenty years. Jimmy thought that this promoter was either stupid or had some irrational fascination with The Beagles.

"So when does the tour begin?"

"Obviously, we have to get a new guitarist on board, but we are auditioning someone tonight."

"That's fast," Jimmy said. Bernie's body wasn't even cold yet, and they were already auditioning his replacement. Something was off there.

"Care to share his name for our story?"

Glenn took a third hit off his bong. "Why the fuck not? Some guy named Max Ruby, our manager found him."

Max Ruby? When Jimmy was little, he used to watch a cartoon called Max and Ruby on one of those cable networks devoted to kids; if his memory was correct, it was the same network that televised The Beagles TV show. His mother hated that cartoon—she couldn't stand the whiney characters as they reminded her too much of her nephew Joe.

"Let's say it works out with this Ruby guy. When's the first gig?"

"I want to start it off where we ended it twenty years ago, at the Palace Theatre in Stamford, CT. How wild would it be if some of the kids we played to that night came back with kids of their own?"

"Pretty wild," Jimmy said. "Got a date in mind yet?" reiterating his original question.

"Martini is shooting for April 1st."

April Fool's Day, Jimmy thought. "That's only a few weeks away!" Jimmy said. "You must be pretty sure about this new prospect."

"Our manager liked him and sent us a recording. I think he's going to work out just fine. Awe, shit!"

Jimmy heard glass breaking in the background. "Shit man, I gotta...fuck!" Another scream. Something had taken Glenn's attention away from the call.

"Sounds like you have your hands full. I think I have all I need for this interview."

"Right, whatever. Listen, if you have any kids or nephews, or some shit, come out and see us. We put on a great show."

Some memories are better left in the past, Jimmy thought. "Sure thing."

Jimmy ended the call after another childhood memory was obliterated.

On his way to the shower, he was interrupted by a knock and feared it was the Nelson Twins coming to haul him off to LA County Lockup. He was relieved to see Farrah's smiling face through the peephole.

"Doubts, I haven't got all day," Farrah said through the door. "Put some pants on, we don't need a repeat of what happened at my house in Chatham."

Farrah would never let him forget the time little Jimmy slipped out of his boxer shorts one morning last summer.

Jimmy opened the door and Farrah immediately looked him up and down.

"I'm glad you have clothes on, but you need to change."

"Why?" Jimmy was wearing khaki pants and a button-down shirt, his standard uniform.

"You look like a square. We're going to UPC to meet with Allison Hart. Dress like an entertainment type."

"And how does an entertainment type dress?"

"I don't know, ratty pair of jeans and a hoodie?"

"I own none of the above."

"Fine, but at least untuck your shirt."

"Wait, who's Allison Hart anyway?" Jimmy said while following Farrah's wardrobe instruction. With his shirt now untucked he looked like a rebel at a prep school.

"Big wig at UPC. Turns out she played a key role in the decision to purchase your cousin's company."

"And you know this how?"

"Being famous has its privileges."

Jimmy wondered if he would ever enjoy the special treatment that fame brings. "How about you meet with her and I try to find Tomasulo?"

"No dice. Her assistant said the only way she would meet with me is if you came along. Apparently, she's a fan of the doubting one."

This made Jimmy perk up. "You don't say," Jimmy said excitedly. "But I have to brush my teeth."

"You haven't brushed them yet?"

"Of course I did, but I want them to be minty fresh for our meeting."

"You are a piece of work, Doubts. I'm going downstairs to rent a car at the Hertz counter in the lobby. I can't take riding in cabs any longer."

"Can I drive?" Jimmy asked. The kid loved to drive but was terrible at it. The old Jeep he kept at his mom's place had so many dings and dents his mother said it was as pockmarked as Jan Michael Vincent.

"Maybe later," Farrah said, knowing full well it was the last thing she'd let him do.

CHAPTER TWENTY-SIX

My Generation

Detectives Murray and Jeff Nelson were in their car drinking coffee and taking a break from discussing the Deville case. Their night ended with an argument about Jimmy's innocence and, while the two enjoyed arguing, they didn't want to revisit that one just yet.

"I got a note from Nikolay this morning," Murray said. Nikolay was the former lead singer of the Russian glam metal band Gorky Park, which gained popularity in the late 80s after the era of Soviet censorship started to subside with the rise of Mikhail Gorbachev and his glasnost policy reforms. The Nelson brothers met Nikolay Noskov and his bandmates when they shared a bill at The Troubadour in West Hollywood. They quickly hit it off, and Gorky Park liked the Nelson brothers so much that they hired them as roadies for a trip back to Russia to play the Moscow Peace Festival in 1989; it was a trip the twins would never forget.

The festival was a who's who of 80s glam bands. Headlined by Bon Jovi, it also featured Motley Crue, Ozzy

Osborne, The Scorpions, Cinderella, and Skid Row. It was the brainchild of infamous band manager Doc McGhee, who handled the affairs of both Bon Jovi and Motley Crue. As a condition of his parole for drug smuggling, McGhee agreed to use his influence in the music world to start an anti-drug foundation known as Make a Difference. While the festival was designed to raise money for McGhee's foundation, most of the event's performers were known to abuse every substance they could get their hands, or noses, on.

"He back in the band?" Jeff asked

"Said he's retired. He's a judge on a Russian version of X-Factor and says he's happy spending time with his grandchildren."

"Good for him. He came out a survivor. That said, Big Sasha was a better singer." Jeff couldn't resist sharing his view that the band's bass player, and sometime vocalist, was technically a better singer than their original front man.

"Speaking of survivors, any word on Jenny Slade?"

After Jenny's seizure at the precinct the night before, paramedics took her to the nearby UCLA medical center; since she had no family or real friends in California, Jeff went with her to the hospital, completely forgetting to read the confession he stuffed in his suit jacket pocket.

"I called Dr. Pansky and got her into his rehab center. She'll be transferred there when UCLA feels she's stable enough to travel."

Dr. Andrew Pansky is an addiction specialist known best for his work on a popular radio show called Sexline. The Nelson brothers befriended him a few years back when they did a side security gig for him and his Sexline partner, podcaster extraordinaire Tommy Tercel.

"How is good old Dr. Andrew doing?"

"Unfortunately better than ever, with the use of opiates on the rise."

Dr. Andrew couldn't keep up with the demand for help at his Pasadena rehab center and was now referring addicts to competing centers in the greater LA area, but due to his friendship with the Nelson's, he agreed to help Jenny Slade.

"I hope she gets the help she needs. Hard to do without family support."

"I called the girl's parents last night. They're flying out today to be with her. That reminds me," Jeff reached into the pocket of his suit coat remembering he put it there just before her seizure, "I never actually read her confession."

Murray looked at his brother and rolled his eyes. "Come on, it probably just reiterates what she told us in the interview room last night, that Jimmy Doubts did it."

Jeff opened the envelope and read the letter. "Holy shit!"

"What?"

"I love it when you're wrong," Jeff said excitedly.

"Don't leave me in suspense."

"On Wednesday, March 2nd, I was partying with Bernie Deville at the Hotel Palomino. About ten minutes after arriving into my room with Bernie, Greg Page, a bodyguard assigned to me by my manager Eddie Costello, stormed into the room after Bernie became abusive. Greg lost his temper and eventually threw Bernie off the balcony. I'm desperate to get away from Eddie and decided to take my chances and jumped off the balcony and into the pool. Eddie Costello lives in Van Nuys and if you find him, he can lead you to Greg, who goes by the nickname The Cowboy. Once you find him, you'll know why. I'm sorry I lied to you about Jimmy, he's a sweet kid and had nothing to do with it."

"Mother of pearl," Murray said sounding like their father.

"The plot thickens," Jeff observed. "I guess we're off to Van Nuys to find this Eddie Costello guy."

"Don't get all soft on me and tell the kid he's off the hook," Murray warned. "Like I said last night, it's better if he thinks he's facing time. It can only benefit us."

"At last we agree on something."

"How about a little music for the ride to Silicone Valley?"

"Good idea."

Jeff reached into the backseat for a sleeve of cassette tapes and found Stairway to Heaven/Highway to Hell, a compilation featuring all the bands from the Moscow Music Peace Festival. Each track was a cover originally performed by a band who lost a member to drug or alcohol abuse; the proceeds of each sale went to the Make a Difference Foundation.

Jeff pushed the cassette in the tape player and hit rewind.

"How suspenseful," Murray muttered. When the tape stopped rewinding and Gorky Park's cover of The Who's My Generation began, he said, "Nice."

CHAPTER TWENTY-SEVEN

Union of the Snakes

While it was a Saturday morning, Allison agreed to meet Farrah and Jimmy at the UPC offices in downtown LA. Like Farrah, Allison was a workaholic and no stranger to weekend hours – she'd have been there anyway even if she didn't get a request to meet with Farrah. The request came from her boss, Brandon Master, the president of the Universal Products Company. Farrah knew that UPC played in the entertainment space and had used her name to track down Master. When she spoke with him, he pointed her to Allison Hart, though he didn't fully brief Allison Hart on what Farrah wanted, details were for the little people.

Farrah and Jimmy showed their IDs to a security guard who checked their names against a guest list. Apparently it was as hard getting into the UPC building as it was an LA Nightclub with the Kardashians inside.

"Ms. Graham, you are all set but Mr. Rella, I don't see your name." This news was broken by a sassy Latina named Martina. Her bleach blond hair was pulled into a tight ponytail and Farrah noted to herself that it was time to get her roots done.

"That's odd," Farrah said, "I spoke with Allison Hart's assistant Marios and he confirmed that both Jimmy and I would be meeting with her at 10:30."

"I am sorry, ma'am, but I have no James Rella in our system. If he's not in our system, I can't let him up."

Ever since a recent on-set stabbing during a UPC live event, the receptionist had been taking her job as first line of defense very seriously. Had Jimmy been there by himself, he probably would not have been able to convince her that the Jimmy Rella on his license was the same as the Jimmy Doubts on the list. But the calm competence Farrah projected was as good as any government-issued ID and Martina eventually relented.

"Ms. Hart's office is on the 39th floor. Take the second elevator bank on your right. Her assistant will meet you in the lobby."

"Thank you," Farrah and Jimmy said simultaneously.

"Be sure to bring that badge back when you're done, Papi," Martina said and winked at Jimmy. "If I'm not here, let me give you my number so you can call me to let me know you dropped your badge off."

She wrote her number on a business card and handed it to Jimmy, who smiled awkwardly and slid the card into his pocket.

"At a loss for words, Doubts? Sounds like she wants a taste of the doubting one." Farrah asked as they walked toward the elevators. She knew Jimmy clammed up in front of beautiful women. She'd witnessed it countless times.

"I'm fine," he said.

"Listen, this Allison Hart woman is quite pretty. Try to stay focused up there."

"Hey, it's me," he said, doing his best Harrison Ford as Han Solo impersonation.

The ride to the 39th floor took only fifteen seconds, and the rapid ascent made Jimmy's ears fill with fluid. He pinched his nose and blew to release the pressure.

"Ouch!" he proclaimed.

"What in God's name are you doing?"

"Had to pop my ears."

"You're going to make some woman very miserable someday," Farrah said as she strode off the elevator.

"Farrah and Jimmy?" asked a high-pitched voice belonging to a rail thin man with perfectly manicured facial hair and a Bluetooth headset protruding from his ear.

"Yes," Farrah said.

"I'm Ms. Hart's assistant, Marios. Follow me to her office, m'kay."

Marios walked at what Jimmy considered six-pack speed, an accelerated pace typically undertaken by his friends who were at least a six pack into a night of drinking. For some reason Jimmy didn't understand, his friends always walked faster while intoxicated.

They made numerous turns as they navigated their way to a corner suite of offices. Allison's suite had a desk for Marios, a few couches for her guests' comfort, and a closed door with ALLISON HART on the nameplate. UPC didn't have an open floorplan, it was as traditional as they come.

While Allison was in her early thirties, she was old school

when it came to meetings. She always had guests wait a few minutes to remind them who was in charge. She didn't do this to be a bitch; rather, she did it because, even in 2017, women weren't treated with the same seriousness as men. It was her subtle way of maintaining the upper hand with people who may be looking to take advantage of her.

Allison's Job at UPC was to create reality TV shows that were used as vehicles for product placement. While in business school at Harvard, she realized that traditional advertising was on the decline — consumers had started time shifting their TV viewing and fast forwarding through commercials. On top of that, streaming services such as Netflix and Hulu were eating traditional broadcast networks for breakfast, lunch, and dinner. She also saw another trend — traditional networks kept recycling the same ideas; how many medical dramas, police procedurals, or situation comedies could viewers swallow?

While earning her degree, Allison was given the opportunity to pitch Brandon Master, the president of UPC and a Harvard graduate, on her idea to create reality TV shows that essentially served as commercials for UPC products. She argued this would kill two birds with one stone; compelling reality shows would fill the void that unoriginal programming left in its wake and consumers, who normally zapped advertisements, would be fed a steady stream of UPC product placement. He loved the idea and guaranteed her a job upon graduation.

The first show she created for UPC was called Bling it On with T-Bang, a celebreality show based on the wild life of Thaddeus "T-Bang" Stevens, the son of an A-List actress and a powerful entertainment attorney. The show wound up quadrupling the sales of UPC's Lust brand of body sprays targeted to tween boys who idolized T-Bang.

Given the success of Bling it On, Allison was asked to make lightning strike twice, this time for UPC's Believe brand of skincare products. The marketing team was launching a new line targeted to women in their 50s and Allison thought she struck gold when 80s heartthrob Blaze Hazelwood, the star of primetime soap opera Casa Grande, unknowingly appeared on Bling it On. She put together a show called Return to Casa Grande featuring Blaze and his former castmates, but the production process provided more twists and turns than any soap opera could. The project crashed and burned during a live morning news segment when the show itself was being announced to the world; though the debacle that was Return to Casa Grande is a story for another time.

Since then, Allison had risen through the management ranks at UPC where Brandon kept pushing her to find new path's for growth and Allison had her eyes set on the mobile app market as a hunting ground for increased revenues. For this reason, she was part of the due diligence team when UPC threw its hat in the ring to purchase Joe Feld's company. While working Saturdays didn't bother her, it did get to her assistant Marios who negotiated a 30% bump in salary when working every other Saturday became the norm.

Feeling as if she kept her guests waiting long enough, Allison opened the door and found a stunningly beautiful woman of about forty and a younger man in his late twenties — Farrah Graham and Jimmy Doubts. Allison thought neither had a "face for radio." It was a shame they weren't in front of a camera. Maybe she could change that.

"Farrah, Jimmy, I'm Allison Hart. Nice to meet you."

Farrah smiled back and extended her hand. Jimmy looked like a deer in headlights. Farrah nudged Doubts and brought him back to reality.

"Sorry, nice to meet you."

Allison smiled at Jimmy. "Follow me. Can I get you anything, coffee, tea, water?"

"Cold shower?" Farrah whispered into Jimmy's ear.

"What was that?"

"Cold water for me please," Farrah replied.

"Hot tea for me," said Jimmy.

"Marios," Allison called to her assistant, "can you get a water for Farrah and a hot tea for Jimmy?"

"Right away," her assistant replied with a sigh.

Farrah and Jimmy sat on Allison's couch while she took a chair facing them; had this been a meeting with another UPC executive, she would have opted to remain behind her desk, but she wanted Jimmy and Farrah to feel at ease.

"I was excited to get Brandon's call last night, Farrah, though Brandon didn't tell anything about what you're looking for. I'm a big fan of Uncorking a Murder, perhaps you want to make it a TV series?"

"Interesting thought, but that's not why we're here," Farrah said and looked at her partner. "Jimmy, why don't you take us through the events of the other night?"

Fearing he'd gone into another trance, Farrah was about to snap her fingers in front of his face when Marios came in with their drinks. This seemed to bring him back to the present moment.

"Have you heard of Bernie Deville?" he asked.

"Of course," Allison replied. "He was just murdered."

“Right,” Jimmy said. “We were on Kimmel with him the night he was killed and, after the taping, I met him at the Hotel Palomino.”

“Why in the world would you go there?” Allison asked. “Nothing but aging rock stars and sluts.”

“Tell her about the porn star you pitched a gameshow to.”

“You are never going to let that go, are you?”

“Game show?” Allison’s ears perked up. She was, after all, an opportunist at heart.

“That’s not important right now,” Jimmy replied. “Can I continue?”

“Please.”

He then told her about the altercation he had with Bernie in the bar and his subsequent meetings with the cops as he is a suspect in Bernie’s death.

“While I find this fascinating, I’m having a hard time figuring out why we’re talking.” Allison was charming, but she was also a Type-A executive working on a Saturday and this conversation didn’t seem to be relevant to anything of business interest to her.

Jimmy then divulged that Joe Feld is his cousin and the role he played in misleading the cops about his whereabouts.

“So Joe Feld is your cousin? Interesting,” Allison replied.

“Why interesting?” Farrah and Jimmy asked at the same time; they were always echoing each other.

“I was part of the management team at UPC that looked into your cousin’s company. I met with him a handful of times and found him to be quite cold. Nothing like you, Jimmy.”

This made Doubts blush. Farrah thought she was going to lose him to fantasy again. Fortunately, she was mistaken.

"That's kind of you to say. Joe and I were never particularly close."

"Guys, I'm sorry while all of this is intriguing, why are you telling me?"

"Your company is buying all of the assets of his company right?"

"Yes, and?" Allison was becoming impatient.

"Can you look into your due diligence files and see if there's any link between Fast Lane and a company called Interpersonal Audio?"

"If you give me a good reason to."

Farrah then explained the issue she and other podcasters were facing with a patent troll.

"That's unbelievable but again, I have to ask, why should I care."

Jimmy spoke up, "We believe that Fast Lane somehow owns Interpersonal Audio and that Joe Feld is systematically trying to ruin my life."

Allison was now intrigued; if what Jimmy and Farrah proposed was true, it would make for a very interesting story—perhaps something she could sell within UPC.

Allison picked up the phone on her desk. "Marios, bring me all the due diligence files on Fast Lane."

Moments later, Marios dropped a stack of folders on Allison's desk then turned on his heels to leave.

"We had to do a forensic audit of your cousin's company," Allison said to Jimmy while reacquainting herself with the file. "The results came back pretty standard except for one oddity. We found that he had a silent partner by the name of Bram Wallachia whom Joe didn't tell us about."

"That name sounds familiar," Farrah said, but couldn't put her finger on it.

"He's the ultra-secretive type," Allison said. "But as part of our deal, we had to know more about him since he technically owned part of your cousin's company."

"Joe never said anything about business partners," Jimmy said. "He always talked about building that company himself."

"He didn't," Allison said. "Wallachia gave your cousin the seed money to start his company. In addition to that, he also held a patent filed under an LLC."

"Interpersonal Audio," Farrah and Jimmy said at the same time.

"We did some more digging and it turns out the original holder of that patent sold it to Wallachia six months ago."

"Union of the snakes," Jimmy said.

"You look too young for a Duran Duran reference," Allison remarked.

"He could also quote the band Poison chapter and verse. Doubts here was born two decades after his time. Plus, I could say the same thing about you." Farrah offered a wink and a smile.

"It can't be a coincidence that my cousin is in cahoots with the patent troll looking to end our careers," Jimmy said.

"There's definitely something bigger at play here," Farrah observed. "We have to find out more about this Wallachia character."

"Good luck with that," Allison said. "To say he's

secretive is an understatement. It took weeks just to uncover what little we could about him. No personal information or background, all we know is really based on what your cousin told us and some legal filings."

"Or maybe it's an alias," Jimmy muttered. Something about the name was familiar to him too, but like Farah, he couldn't put his finger on it.

"In light of what you're telling me, I'm going back to the board and recommend we re-evaluate the pending deal for Fast Lane."

"Can you do that?"

"There's a character clause in our term sheet, which gives us the right to terminate a pending contract if our reputation might be in jeopardy. Between a dead musician, potentially lying to the police, and this patent business, Joe Feld likely isn't someone we should be getting into business with." This was all true, but Allison also thought she could earn her company more money if she could ink a deal with Farrah and Jimmy for an Uncorking a Murder TV show—a deal that was unlikely if UPC was in business with Feld.

Farrah looked at a picture on the wall of Allison next to a guy with multiple gold chains around his neck and laughed.

"What's so funny?" Allison asked.

"Character clause? Isn't that you with T-Bang?"

Years ago, T-Bang wreaked havoc in Hollywood with his merry band of misfits. He was the poster child for bad behavior.

"Say what you will about Thaddeus Stevens, but he helped us double the sale of our Lust brand. And, I'll have you know, he's a successful pediatrician now, we apparently scared him away from the entertainment industry. Hey, when things calm down, I'd love to talk about bringing Uncorking a Murder to the small screen. I think it would be a smash hit."

"Let's cross that bridge when we come to it," Farrah said and offered her hand to Allison. Jimmy did the same and Allison walked them back to the elevator, giving her assistant a break from at least one menial task.

"So, Doubts, that gameshow idea?"

Farrah anticipated Jimmy stumbling over his words, but he managed to hit Allison with a high-level overview of Reasonable Doubts.

"I kind of like it," she said.

"Really?" Jimmy asked.

"Call my office sometime." Allison handed him her card. "My direct line is on there."

The elevator doors opened and Farrah got in; Jimmy remained in the lobby, unable to move.

"Uh-hem," Farrah coughed, pulling Jimmy from his daydream.

"Right then, gotta go."

"Call me," Allison said.

"I will," Jimmy said eagerly as the doors closed.

"Two numbers in one day, smooth operator," Farrah said.

Jimmy smirked but quickly went back to business. "I know Terry is on our list, but what do you say we let the police tackle that one? We have some new stuff to look into with this business partner of my cousin's."

"I was thinking the same thing. We need to find out more about this business partner," Farrah said, throwing emphatic air quotes around "business partner."

CHAPTER TWENTY-EIGHT

Eyes Without a Face

Anthony Carbona was relieved to find the mercury in the thermometer on his balcony north of 70. "How do you like that, Gianni," he said to his son, "it may be a beach day after all."

"Love it or List it is about to come on, pop," Gianni said from the family room. Anthony Carbona ran a large and sophisticated organized crime operation, but devoted every Saturday morning to his one guilty pleasure, HGTV. He considered it Saturday morning cartoons for adults.

"I'm coming. We hear anyting about da matter in California?" Carbona's New York accent was thicker than usual, likely because he was hungover. He attended a homemade wine tasting at the Knights of Columbus hall in Ft. Lauderdale the night before and a stinger always brought out the Bronx in Anthony, who always spoke vaguely in his home as he assumed it was bugged.

"The doc in Santa Barbara said he's surprised our friend can walk, but he should be okay. Broken nose, a few ribs, a few missing teeth. Says he put him on some pain killers to take care of the pain."

"Are we all set with da udder matter?"

"Yes. Greenfield said he'd take care of it personally."

In the early 1980s, The Carbona family ran every limo service in the greater tristate area. An upstart livery service run by a young entrepreneur named Sandy Greenfield started eating into Carbona's business, so Anthony had a sit down with the guy challenging his profits.

Greenfield was wet behind the ears and fresh out of business school when he started his limo service in New York. Carbona, feeling generous, was willing to give the kid a pass because he clearly didn't know how things worked in The Big Apple. He explained the way of the world and gave the upstart two options: have his livery service join the "family business" and kickback a fee for every ride, or take his chances.

Greenfield, green in every sense of the word, chose the latter. A week later, all the cars in his fleet were vandalized. When he called the police to file a report, the officers who showed up shrugged and said there was nothing they could do.

The young entrepreneur fixed the cars, but the same thing happened a week later. After that, he gave in and agreed to partner with Anthony Carbona. In the thirty-five years since, no cars in his fleet have been vandalized, and while the relationship cut into his profits, Greenfield made a very good living.

"What time the kid get in?"

"3:30. JFK."

"Any idear where he's supposed to go from dere?"

"Some studio somewhere downtown."

"Cuttin Room?"

"Yeah."

Looking to diversify his money laundering operations outside of the restaurant industry in the 90s, Carbona started buying recording studios. It was a great scheme; Carbona charged local bands next to nothing for studio time, but his ledgers showed extensive billings that were paid for by profits from his illegal operations. The Cutting Room in downtown Manhattan was a Carbona family operation.

"Even betta." Carbona looked at his watch. "About tree hours before this Ruby guy lands. Tell Greenfield to bring one of dem iPads with him so we can have a facey book chat on his way."

"Facetime," Gianni corrected his father.

"Whatever da fuck it's called. I wanna see this Max Ruby face to face, and I ain't leaving Florider for New York when it's still below freezing up dere."

"Your iPad charged?" Gianni asked his father. He knew his dad would fly off the handle if his tablet was dead when he wanted to chat with Feld.

"Whaddya think I'm a moron? Of course it's charged. Show me how to facechat."

Gianni decided not to correct his father again and tapped the FaceTime icon on the iPad's home screen.

"Give me dat!" Carbona snatched the tablet from his son's hands and held it close to his face, as if he were reading a newspaper.

"All I see is my eyes, no face."

"You are holding it too close, pop."

Carbona extended his hands until his face showed up on the screen.

"I look like a slice of week-old Gabagool!" the older

Carbona exclaimed. "Now I know why your mudda left me."

Gianni laughed at this observation, but his father's looks weren't what pushed his mother from the marriage; it had a lot more to do with the infidelity and heavy drinking.

"I'm gonna shower. DVR this show and Property Brothers for me, will ya? I may be a while."

Gianni, good son that he was, grabbed the remote control and did as his father requested.

CHAPTER TWENTY-NINE

Shout at the Devil

Detectives Murray and Jeff Nelson were driving through the San Fernando Valley as the last notes of Motley Crue's cover of Rock and Roll were playing over the car's speakers. "Think they'll get back together?" Murray asked.

"Crue or Zeppelin?"

Murray exhaled loudly.

"The one whose drummer didn't die," he said.

Zeppelin's drummer, John Bonham, was considered one of rock and roll's greatest. He died in 1980 after choking on his own vomit, an occupational hazard for rockstars.

"Zeppelin could tour with Bonham's son," Jeff argued. While Jason Bonham didn't have the same success as his father, he was an accomplished drummer in his own right.

"True," Murray admitted, "but Robert Plant can't hit those high notes anymore."

"But Zeppelin could tour with..."

"Don't you dare say David Coverdale!" Jeff had once argued that Coverdale was as good as Plant and Murray didn't want to resurrect that argument.

"Then to answer your original question— Motley Crue will get together for a reunion tour no later than next year. Mark my words."

"You sound pretty sure of yourself on that," Murray observed.

"The music business is in the tank. Most bands spend more on producing an album than they take in from sales after everyone takes their cut. Kids don't buy albums anymore, which means the only reason to put out new music is to get people interested in a new tour."

"So, each of those guys is popular enough to tour on their own," Murray countered.

"Yeah, but who the hell wants to see them solo? They'd basically be playing in a Motley Crue tribute band. Once they realize they won't make any money touring, Nikki and Vince will get together and convince Tommy and Mick that the world wants Motley Crue back. And you know what, it'll work because together they play some pretty great music."

Feeling bested in the argument, Murray changed the subject. "How far away are we?"

Jeff looked at his phone. "GPS says one mile. Oh, and make a right here."

Murray hastily made a right-hand turn from the left-hand lane, cutting off a car as he did so. The driver honked his displeasure.

"Can you give me a little fair warning next time?"

"Nice Van Halen reference." While the band's fourth studio album didn't include a popular single, Jeff had always considered Fair Warning his favorite of the David Lee Roth era records (but would argue that Van Halen III with Gary Cherone on lead vocals was a better album).

"What did you learn about this Costello guy?" Murray asked.

On the drive to Van Nuys, Jeff reached out to a friend of theirs in Vice and read his assessment of Costello word for word. "Real scumbag. Preys on young girls coming off busses in LA. Promises them fame and fortune and everything that goes with it."

"Sounds like every other Hollywood dirtbag."

"Yeah," Jeff said, "but this one leads them into a life of porn. He's the worst of the worst."

"Don't these girls have a choice?"

"Think about it, you get off a bus that you were on for God knows how many days with not much more than a suitcase and a dream. Someone tells you a story you're desperate to hear and agrees to represent you, even offers you a place to stay. Then you wind up in a house or apartment full of women in the same situation, some who no doubt continue to help him sell the story he told you. Next thing you know, your auditions all have one thing in common – you're asked to remove your clothes in each of them."

"Aren't most people smart enough to sniff out this bullshit?"

"This is LA, the place where dreams are bought and sold, the land of make believe. All rational thought is suspended when one feels as if they can accomplish their dreams."

"Class-A dirtbag, no doubt, but it doesn't sound like he's doing anything that's technically illegal. Immoral, yeah, but not illegal."

"We aren't here to investigate the legality of his

operation," Jeff reminded his brother. "We're here to push him on Page."

"Let's say he gives up Page," Murray said, "how do we get him to stop ruining the lives of young women?"

"Let's table that," Jeff replied. "His house is three down on the right."

"The one with the serial killer van out front?"

"Yep."

Murray brought their car to a stop just shy of Costello's house. A moment later, Costello's door opened and the brothers saw their man walk across his lawn and get into the van — he was holding a brown paper bag and screaming at someone on the phone, so preoccupied with his rage he didn't notice the Nelsons' Crown Vic.

"Speak of the devil, and the devil appears," Murray muttered.

"Want me to flip on the lights?" Jeff had his finger on the switch. He was eager to take down Costello.

"Hold up a second," Murray said. "I got an idea. Let's follow him a bit. Maybe he'll take us to this cowboy character."

"And if he doesn't?"

"Then we'll pull him over for a busted taillight." Murray pointed toward the back of the van where, sure enough, the driver's side taillight was out. "How about some tunes for the ride?"

Jeff reached into his box of cassettes and put one in the tape player — Motley Crue's Shout at the Devil.

"Another home run," Murray said, pulling away from the curb to follow Costello's white van.

CHAPTER THIRTY

Prowler

Eddie Costello woke up on his couch at approximately one o'clock in the afternoon. After dropping Jenny off at the police station the night before, he waited out front to take her home. He got nervous when he saw the ambulance pull up and even more nervous when he saw his little starlet rolled from the precinct on a gurney and placed in the back of it. Had he known what Farrah and Jimmy looked like, he would have lost his shit when they left the police station prior to the ambulance's arrival.

Costello considered following the ambulance to wherever it was taking Jenny, but thought better of it when he saw one of the detectives jump in the back.

He was reasonably certain Jenny followed the plan to finger Jimmy for the murder—threatening to kill a girl's family can go a long way; that said, a small bit of uncertainty gave him anxiety and there was only one way Eddie dealt with anxiety, by going on the prowl.

Last night, while Jenny was being rushed to UCLA Medical Center, Eddie took a drive downtown and hung out by the Greyhound station to await the fresh meat coming in from Middle America. Some guys go fishing to clear their thoughts and become one with nature, but Eddie Costello found that dreadfully boring; he'd rather spend his time fishing for women to feed his little corner of the sex industry.

Without any success at the bus station that evening, he dipped into his Skittle bag of prescription pills and took three at random. This cocktail of unknown medications knocked him so hard on his ass he hallucinated that Tiger Woods was sitting in his passenger seat and told him not to drive home from the club, which was good advice from Tiger considering Fast Eddie wasn't actually at a club. Costello went with the apparition's guidance and called a Fast Lane car to take him home.

When he woke up, all memories of the night before were gone from his mind. He panicked when he didn't see his car in the garage, but then the pieces of the puzzle slowly came together and he called The Cowboy for a ride.

"You sound like shit," The Cowboy said.

"And you sound like fucking Rick Dees," Eddie retorted, invoking the name of the veteran radio DJ known best, to his embarrassment, for the 1978 hit Disco Duck.

"Who?" The Cowboy asked.

"Never mind," Eddie said. "I need a ride. How soon can you get to my house?"

"This time a day, forty-five minutes?"

"Forty-five minutes? You live in fucking Reseda."

"Ain't in Reseda now," The Cowboy replied. "I'm with Nasty Boy up in Agoura."

"Please tell me you two took care of our little friend from last night."

This was the moment The Cowboy was dreading. To numb his fears, he took a long swig from the bottle of Canadian Club he'd opened earlier in the morning.

"Beat him senseless."

"I hope his own mother won't recognize him. What you do with the body?"

The line was silent.

"Page, what the fuck did you do with the body? Please tell me it's coyote food in one of those nature preserves near Nasty's house."

"It rolled out of the El Camino's bed between Van Nuys and Agoura."

When Eddie Costello heard those words, he almost threw up.

"I'm sorry, I thought you just said it rolled out of the bed of your El-fucking-Camino. My hearing isn't so good, could you tell me what you just said again?"

"You heard me right the first time."

"You moron! Dead bodies just don't roll out of the bed of trucks!"

"I'm telling you that's what happened Eddie."

"Riddle me this, how did you kill him?"

"Beat him to death."

"Newsflash, cowboy, he wasn't FUCKING DEAD!" Fast Eddie was so angry, veins were popping from his skull and his pulse had doubled since starting this conversation.

"Stay at Nasty Boy's place. I'll call a car to take me there."

Eddie hung up on The Cowboy and then hailed a Fast Lane car to take him to Agoura Hills. The car closest to him wasn't a car at all, but a van. Putting his vanity aside, Eddie decided to take it even though he normally wouldn't be caught dead in such a vehicle.

Eddie's phone vibrated a few minutes later to tell him his Fast Lane driver was arriving and, while walking to the van, he called the guy he knew only as Monty Hall. It was not, what you might call, a civil conversation.

Detectives Murray and Jeff Nelson followed the van through Reseda until it merged onto the parking lot that was 101 north; the brothers crawled along a few cars behind to avoid being spotted, and as they hit Woodland Hills, Jeff's phone began to ring. He recognized Farrah's number and answered immediately.

"Detective Jeff Nelson."

"Jimmy, watch out for the curb!" Farrah shouted. She'd decided to let him drive — she couldn't take LA traffic any longer — and regretted her choice the moment they left UPC's offices.

"Everything okay over there?" Jeff asked.

"Sorry, I made the mistake of letting Doubts drive. "We just had a very interesting meeting."

"Meeting?" Jeff asked and rolled his eyes. The thought of Farrah and Jimmy playing detective didn't sit well with him. "Why don't you start by telling me who you met with."

Farrah reasoned there was no reason to hold back the fact they were meeting with Allison Hart from UPC and told the detective.

"What's she got to do with any of this?"

"Joe Feld is selling his company to her's and she was involved with the deal."

"What does that have to do with anything?"

Farrah explained how a patent troll had recently surfaced and brought a lawsuit that could effectively end their show.

"I remember you mentioning that during your interview with Kimmel." As part of their research, the detectives had rewatched the entire interview Farrah and Jimmy did on the late night show. "But what's that got to do with Bernie?"

"As part of the process to buy Joe's company, UPC had to look into his business in more detail. Turns out he has a business partner."

"I'll broaden my question, what does it have to do with anything?"

"Joe Feld's business partner holds the patent that's being used to ruin our show."

The pieces of the puzzle were starting to come together in Jeff Nelson's mind. He started thinking out loud. "Feld allegedly lies to us about his cousin being at the scene of the crime. A pornstar then fingers your boy Doubts for Bernie's murder but then recants it..."

"What do you mean recants it?"

"Stop killing my train of thought," Jeff said. "You get sued by this patent troll who turns out to be in business with Doubts' cousin. It doesn't explain a motive for Bernie's death, but it definitely casts a shadow on Feld, especially if we can make a connection between him and Jenny Slade. Any idea where he is now?"

"Doubts, any idea where your cousin is?"

Jimmy shook his head.

"No," Farrah said into the phone.

Murray interrupted, "The van's getting off in Agoura

Hills."

"We gotta go," Jeff said.

"Wait, is Doubts off the hook?"

Murray heard Farrah's question from his brother's handset and nodded his approval to let his brother tell Farrah that Jimmy was clear.

"He's off the hook," Jeff replied. "But listen, don't do anything stupid. Leave the police work to us."

"Of course," Farrah said, fully intending to break that promise.

CHAPTER THIRTY-ONE

High and Dry

Joe's flight from LA landed forty-five minutes early at JFK, though the excitement of an early arrival was offset by having to wait thirty minutes for the plane's assigned gate to open up. The travel gods are funny like that — they giveth and taketh away.

Since he was in first class, Joe Feld was one of the first passengers off and walked down the jet bridge with his guitar case and overnight bag. He followed the signs for baggage claim and ground transportation, which led him down an escalator where a number of men in dark suits held placards with names on them; Joe thought they looked like undertakers. If he only knew.

Halfway down the line, he spotted a bald man holding a sign that said "Ruby." Joe approached, introduced himself, and handed the driver his overnight bag. When the driver offered to take his guitar, Joe shook him off.

As they walked to the parking garage from the terminal, Joe quickly realized he wasn't prepared for the weather; March was still more lion than lamb in the greater New

York area. The driver opened the rear passenger door for Joe, who slid in and switched on his phone.

"Going to the Cutting Room?" the driver asked.

"Yep," Joe said curtly, not bothering to look up.

"Car should be nice and warm in a minute."

"Whatever," Joe said dismissively. His phone began ringing before they left the airport. It was Eddie Costello.

"This better be good," Joe said.

"It's pretty fucking far from good," Eddie barked. "We got a problem."

"What kind of problem?"

"You know that guy who was with Jenny at the hotel yesterday?"

"What about him?"

"He's gone."

"Gone?"

"Yeah, like nowhere to be found. If he gets to the cops, he could poke holes all over the story my girl told them yesterday."

"I thought you said your guy was going to take care of him. What the fuck happened?"

"That's what I'm about to find out," Eddie said. "You know, I regret ever meeting you, no amount of money is worth this shit."

"Are you sure your girl went to the police?"

"Drove her myself, but she left in the back of an ambulance!"

"Ambulance? Did she tell them about Jimmy?"

"I don't fucking know Monty fucking Hall, she's not taking my FUCKING CALLS!"

"Shit, shit, shit," Joe accentuated the profanity by beating his fist into the limo's back seat. "How hard could it be to get a whore to lie to the cops?" Joe asked.

"You know what, fuck you!" Eddie said. "I called to give you a heads up. If the cops come calling on me, I'm pointing the finger at you. Why the fuck was it so important to set that guy up?"

"Does it matter?" Joe asked.

"You know what matters?"

"What?"

"FUCK YOU!" Eddie screamed.

Then the line went dead, just like Bernie.

Joe looked out the window and saw that the Van Wyck expressway was practically a parking lot.

"They call it an expressway, but there ain't nothing express about the Van Wyck today," the driver piped up from the front seat.

Joe rolled his eyes at the attempt at small talk.

"Hey, you ever wondered why you park in a driveway and drive on a parkway?" The driver was trying to push Joe's buttons. It was working.

"I'm sorry, can we play a game called shut the fuck up?" Between the hangover that was setting in from the drinks he had on the plane, the bomb Costello just dropped in his lap, and the traffic they were in, Joe Feld wanted to be alone with his thoughts.

"Sounds like you're having a bad day," the driver muttered.

"How about you keep your thoughts to yourself Morgan fucking Freeman?" Joe said referencing the movie Driving Miss Daisy.

"Call me Sandy and it's about to get worse," the driver replied and threw a tablet computer into Joe's lap.

* * *

Anthony Carbona had just gotten out of the shower and was in the nude when Gianni knocked on the door.

"Waddya want?" Carbona asked through the door.

"Greenfield just texted me pop. He's in traffic on the Van Wyck and Ruby's got the tablet in his lap."

Carbona opened the door, and Gianni was aghast at the sight of his dad in his birthday suit.

"Set me up with da Instaface thingy."

"FaceTime, pop. Don't you want to get dressed?" Gianni handed him a bathrobe.

"For dat bum? My bathrobe will do! I'll get dressed before I go to Matarano tonight." Carbona put on the bathrobe and sat on his bed.

The elder Carbona had plans to go to a swanky Italian restaurant in Ft. Lauderdale that evening. He was bringing a new lady friend who was younger than his son. She was a little peeved that they were eating so early, 5pm, but after 8, Cafe Matarano turned into a nightclub and the loud music bothered the mobster.

Gianni opened the app on his iPad and handed it to his father. "It's ringing. Remember, hold it a little bit away from that fachia brute of yours."

The term was one Gianni's grandmother always used. While it translates to ugly face, it was often used in their family as a term of endearment.

"Get outta here," Carbona barked and Gianni left the room.

"What the fuck is this?" Joe said to the driver, whose name he already forgot.

"When it starts ringing," Sandy said, "answer it."

Joe looked down as the tablet started ringing. He hit

"accept call" but saw only a pair of eyes staring at him.

"Who the fuck is this?" he said. He regretted those words a moment later when the caller's face came into frame.

"No, who da fuck is..." When Joe's face came across Carbona's screen he said, "well what do ya fucking know?"

"Anthony?"

"Cut it with the Anthony, Feld, you and I are no longer on a first named basis. Why are you in one of my cars going by the name Max Ruby?"

"How did you...why are you?"

Joe was bewildered that he was talking face to face with the guy he hired to take care of Bernie. What the hell was this about?

"Wassamadda, cat got your tongue?" The mobster was impatient.

Joe's mind raced, trying to figure out what Carbona could want.

"Last night I got a call from one of my associates, said he was beat to a pulp in some roach motel in the valley."

Joe thought of the guy with Jenny Slade yesterday. *Oh shit*, he thought to himself.

"I can see it in your eyes that there's some recognition there. That's bad for you Feld."

"Mr. Carbona I..."

"Shudup!" the mobster said. "Now tell me why one of my guys is suffering from broken bones and don't give me any bullshit about getting some band back together, which actually reminds me of something."

"What's that?"

"My guy, who you drove to his beating, was da guy who

was supposed to have a sit down with Bernie on Thursday. I don't know about you, but I call that irony."

"Mr. Carbona, I had no idea the guy with Jenny was your guy. I swear to God."

"Let's say I believe youse, dat don't change the fact that you drove my guy to a beating he's lucky to be recovering from."

"It wasn't supposed to go this way..." Joe went on to tell Carbona his real motivations to get The Beagles back together and why it was so important to have Jenny lie to the police about who she saw kill Bernie.

"All to live out a dream of being in a fucking kid's band? Youse got some serious issues Feld. If you make it back to California in one piece, I highly suggest some therapy."

In addition to HGTV, Anthony Carbona was also a big believer in the talking cure.

"Are we good then?"

"Good?" the mobster said with a laugh. "You got some sense of humor, kid. We are pretty fucking far from good."

"How far?"

"First off you have to go back to California and personally apologize to Terry Tomasulo."

"Who?" Joe asked.

"For such a smart kid, you really lack some critical thinking skills. He's my guy whose nose is on the wrong side of his face at the moment."

Humbling himself and apologizing was not a skill in Joe's wheelhouse, but he figured he could make an exception.

"Fine. Anything else?"

"Dis business with your cousin, it upsets me. You gotta

make things right by him." Carbona may have broken many a man's bones in the course of his business, but he was a strong believer in the sacredness of the family.

"I'll make sure his name is cleared. Anything else?"

"Yeah, I think I told you before that I control the livery business on the east coast. Just so happens I'm in da market for some new technology."

"You want me to build something for you?"

"Nah, you've already built it."

"I don't understand."

"How in the name of Jesus, Mary, and St. Joseph did you beat out my kid at MIT? You are going to sell your company to me."

Joe's stomach dropped. "I'm sorry, it's too late for that. I already have a twenty-five-million-dollar deal with UPC. Are you counter-offering?"

The question made his driver laugh out loud.

"Kid, you just did something no one has been able to do in a few decades, make Sandy up there laugh."

"I don't get it..."

"I'm not offering you money kid, I'm offering you your life." Carbona stared at Feld silently.

"There's no way my business partner will...did you say my life?"

"Don't make your problem with your business partner my problem. If youse needs a little business advice, I'm sure your driver Mr. Greenfield will be happy to share his experience with you while he chaperones you back to California. Isn't that right, Sandy?"

"Any time, boss."

Joe was beyond speechless.

"But I have an audition..."

"Let me guess, you are meeting with Bernie's bandmates."

"They are expecting me..."

Carbona interrupted, "Audition is cancelled, kid. No time like the present to start making amends."

"But I'll be left high and dry!"

"No buts! Now Mr. Greenfield is going to make a big ol' U-turn and take you back to JFK. Can I count on you to live up to your word, kid? I would be shocked if you didn't, and I strongly advise you not to shock me."

"Yes, fine, whatever."

"Good! Now a word of advice— Mr. Greenfield isn't a tall guy, but he really likes first class. Treat him right, kid."

Anthony Carbona looked away from the screen for the first time since he started talking to Joe. "Gianni," he screamed. "How do you turn this mudda fucking thing off?"

The connection died at the same moment Joe's phone started ringing. He saw an LA number and picked it up, thinking his day couldn't get any worse. He was wrong.

"This is Joe," he said somberly.

"Joe, this is Allison Hart at UPC. I'm sorry to call you on a Saturday, but it's important that we speak."

CHAPTER THIRTY-TWO

Foolin

Donnie and Glenn were in the smallest of The Cutting Room's studios waiting for Max Ruby to show up. Donnie was behind his drum kit while Glenn was warming up at the mic and reflecting on how they got to this point in their lives. The two had been friends for four decades and were as close as brothers; it was a friendship that predated the Beagles and lasted through the band's highs and lows.

They met in the fourth grade when Glenn moved to Connecticut and entered St. Cecilia school in Stamford. While Donnie was a Stamford native, it was also his first year at the school. His parents had pulled him from public school due to concerns for his welfare – little Donnie was beaten up nearly every day, either for his lunch money or for looking weird, or both. The two bonded immediately over their shared love for music, which was fitting because their new school was named after the patron saint of music.

Glenn begged his parents for a guitar and received one for his 12th birthday, the same year Donnie bought a second-hand drum kit with the money he earned from his paper route. The two would tool around in Donnie's garage for hours at a time and did little else — sports didn't interest them and girls were not on their minds, yet. The monotony of hearing the same notes and beats over and over was too much for Donnie's wealthy parents to handle so they registered both their son and his friend Glenn in music lessons and, over time, they got pretty good.

In high school, they met a bass player named Randy and formed a trio that played local dances, battle of the bands contests, and the occasional sweet sixteen party. After high school Randy went to train as a carpenter while Glenn and Donnie enrolled at the University of Connecticut, where they met Bernie, a lightning fast guitarist who grew up on a strict diet of Joe Walsh, Jeff Beck, and Jimmy Page. It was Bernie who would push them from being a cover band to writing original music.

While playing fraternity parties on the UCONN campus, The Ladykillers — as they were then known — would throw an original song between covers and found, to their delight, that the crowds reacted favorably.

While Bernie studied business, Glenn and Donnie studied early childhood development, not because they had a strong desire to work with kids, but because the ratio of men to women in that major worked entirely in their favor.

Their major required graduating seniors to work in the on-campus daycare facility; to pass the time, Glenn and Donnie would play music for the kids — the former on acoustic guitar and the latter banging drumsticks on an overturned pickle bucket. The kids took to them immediately, and parents eventually began asking Glenn and Donnie to perform at birthday parties. They got regular feedback from parents that their music was not only entertaining the kids, but was palatable to the adults, as well.

As part of his major, Bernie took a class in entrepreneurship that required he write a business plan for a new idea. When he asked his advisor for guidance, he was told to focus on an unmet need and to craft a plan around that. He knew he wanted to do something around his one true love—music—but each time he started drafting an idea, he realized it had already been done. While listening to Glenn and Donnie talk about all the hot moms they were meeting at kids' birthday parties, an idea hit him like a lightning bolt — what about building a business around a music act that appealed to both children and parents?

Bernie began conducting market research by going to Glenn and Donnie's weekend gigs and asking parents what was missing when it came to children's music. Most of the parents he spoke with loathed the high-pitched singing and crappy melodies of the popular kids' musicians of the time—this knowledge got Bernie's creative juices flowing. He started writing kid friendly parodies of classic rock songs from bands like The Beatles and The Eagles and found that both kids and their parents went crazy when Glenn and Donnie played them. He needed to come up with a name for the band and scribbled down The Beagles one night before going to bed.

The next morning, he met with his advisor who urged him to flesh out more details about how the band could be turned into a brand. For that, Bernie sought counsel from a marketing professor who reminded him that big brands employed signs and symbols to help their product stand apart from competition. He discussed this with Glenn and Donnie who made the observation that kids are drawn to bright colors. It was Donnie who had the idea for the shirts and Glenn who had the idea for pairing wacky socks and cargo shorts — Bernie built both into his plan.

Another meeting with his advisor led Bernie to start building out the revenue model. In addition to royalties and ticket sales, he dreamt of merchandise and filming videos that would intersperse sketches and live recordings. He included all of this in his plan and submitted a final draft to his entrepreneurship professor — he earned an A on the project.

Upon graduation, he decided to put his money where his mouth was and convinced Glenn and Donnie to form The Beagles. Their old friend Randy, who was making a steady living as a carpenter, joined the band to earn extra money on the weekends. As their popularity on the kids' birthday party circuit grew, so did Bernie's ambition. He convinced the guys to join him in putting up money to record an album then found a manager, George Martini. With Martini, they quickly moved beyond the party circuit and began opening for popular acts like Barney and Raffi.

Martini's involvement, combined with their talent, took the band to the next level. Soon they were headlining gigs and pulling in serious cash. Another album followed and then, per his business plan, Bernie started producing videos, which took off and propelled The Beagles to national exposure and their own show on a cable network targeting kids.

Over time, a combination of vast disposable income, growing egos, and creative differences gnawed away at the friendships that surrounded the band. The monotony of playing the same songs over and over also took a toll and the guys began doing what other touring musicians did to entertain themselves – they turned to drugs, alcohol, and women.

After ten solid years of touring and cranking out music, tensions approached a boiling point. The pot boiled over when Martini got drunk and let it slip that Bernie, who held publishing rights for the music, was making way more money than everyone else. Since they all had more money than they ever dreamed of the guys acrimoniously called it quits in 1995, right before the show that Jimmy Doubts and Joe Feld attended with their mothers.

Glenn's walk down memory lane was interrupted by his old friend Donnie.

"I thought he was going to be here around 4. It's 5:15 and no sign of him yet. Where the fuck is he?"

"He'll be here," Glenn assured his bandmate.

"Why the fuck did we have to do it here anyway?" Donnie was upset he had to drive his drums in from Connecticut, where he was living with his octogenarian parents.

"What, you'd rather we audition this guy at your parents' house? Besides, we got the studio for a hundred bucks."

"Yeah, well, I gotta be home by eight. My father was very clear on that. He needs the van back."

The conversation was interrupted by the studio's receptionist, Nikki Anne, who told them they had a phone call that they could take in the control room. She did a quick in an out of the studio because Glenn and Donnie gave her the creeps.

"You know who she reminds me of?" Glenn asked.

"Oh yeah, fire crotch herself, Ella Jackson. Marlboro, MA 1992. Right?"

"Bingo."

Twenty-five years ago, The Beagles played an old ice rink outside Boston. After the show, a young red-headed mother came backstage with her twin boys who were eager to meet the band—but not as eager as she was. Bernie and Randy kept the boys entertained during an extended meet and greet while Glenn and Donnie partied with their mother.

"You think Nikki's about twenty-five?" Donnie asked.

"I'm twenty-two, asshole," she shouted from down the hall. "Now pick up the goddamn phone. Mr. Carbona is an impatient man."

"Hi, you're on with Glenn and Donnie," Glenn said, mimicking a radio DJ.

"How are youse boys enjoying the studio today?" There was a lot of background noise, as if Carbona was calling from a restaurant, which, of course, he was. Cafe Matarano was always bustling with activity and noise—even at 5 o'clock.

"Fine, I guess. Receptionist could be a little more friendly."

"Why don't youse boys put that in the comments box on your way out. I'm calling because I got some unfortunate news for youse."

There was a pause on the line.

"Excuse me," Carbona called out to the waitstaff. "Can I have another Chardonnay?"

"Well, don't keep us waiting," Donnie said impatiently.

"I suggest you watch your tone. It's hard to play music without fingas."

Glenn placed his hand over Donnie's mouth; he sensed Donnie was an offhand comment away from actually losing his fingers.

"What the news?" Glenn asked.

"The guitar player you guys are waiting for ain't gonna make it. Let's say he's had a change in his priorities."

"How did you..." Glenn began but was cut off.

"Never mind dat," Carbona said. "But today is your lucky day because I have a business proposition for youse. Call it a silver lining."

"We're listening," Glenn said.

"My granddaughter is turning five in a few weeks and I want to do something special for her. She's my first grandkid and it would mean the world to me if you Beagle guys could reunite to play her birthday party."

"We need a fourth member."

"Come on, fellas. Do it as a trio. She ain't gonna know the difference. I remember youse guys from when my sons were young. I'll make it worth your while."

"Really?" Donnie said with an opportunistic smile.

"Sure. One-hundred each."

"Thousand? That's a very generous offer..." Donnie began but was distracted by a fit of laughter coming from the other end of the phone.

"That's a good one, buddy. No, not thousand. Hundred. As in, you each will get a hundred bucks to play the gig."

"Are you foolin us? Is this some kind of joke?" The drummer's temper was starting up.

"I'm not fa fa fa foolin, gentleman." Carbona was in a playful mood and thought he'd drop a Def Leppard reference on the boys; Adam Kimmell wasn't the only one who had a fine appreciation for the boys from Sheffield.

Donnie and Glenn were silent.

"Do I take your silence as a no? How about this, I'll throw in free limo transportation to my daughter's house up in Connecticut. Give yas the real star treatment."

Glenn grabbed Donnie's arm in anticipation of him saying something impulsive, something that could cost him a lot more than his fingers.

"Mr. Carbona," Glenn said, "thanks for the offer, but we're supposed to go on tour in a month."

"Well, I hate to continue being bearer of bad news, but the tour's been cancelled, guys. Stop by and see Nikki on the way out. She'll have the contract ready for you. See yas in a month."

Carbona hung up and Glenn did the same. The bandmates stared at each other in disbelief.

"Mother fucking fuck," the drummer said. "I'm never going to get out of my parent's basement."

CHAPTER THIRTY-THREE

Shock Me

Nasty Boy was skimming leaves from his pool while The Cowboy sat at his table downing another 7&7. "Your face looks about as green as the water in my pool." Nasty Boy's filtration system was on the fritz and every few days he had to shock his pool to kill the algae.

"Eddie's almost here and I'm in some deep shit."

"Why are you scared of that guy anyway? We can take him."

Bob Hagan earned his nickname by drilling batters, but players weren't his only victims — he fought umpires and managers, including his own, and once threw a ball into the stands out of frustration and struck a woman in the head. After retiring from baseball, he took various jobs in broadcast media but lost all of them for making incendiary comments over the airwaves.

"I work for him," The Cowboy said. "Who else is going to pay me to do what I do?"

Nasty Boy stopped skimming his pool for a minute. "What do you do anyway?"

"I make sure no one fucks with my boss or any of his girls."

"Hey, I know a smalltime mob enforcer in LA. Maybe he could get you some work."

"What's his name?"

"Tomasulo."

"Never heard of him."

"Works for the Carbona family, based in New York. Last of the great families. They don't get involved in drugs or whoring — stick to the classic Italian stuff; rackets, protection, gambling, that kind of shit."

"No whoring, huh?"

"Yah, rumor has it old man Carbona made a promise to his mother that he'd never get involved in anything disrespectful to women. If he ever caught his guys freelancing in the sex business, he made sure they understood his position on the matter."

"Maybe I'll look him up."

"Worth a shot, given your situation with Eddie."

Nasty Boy's dog started to bark loudly. "Sounds like he's here."

"So this is how the other half lives," Murray observed as he followed the van onto Trail River Drive, one of Agoura Hills' swankier streets.

"Looks like he's stopping," Jeff said. "Do a quick fly by and park across the street so we get a good look at the door."

Murray drove down the road a couple blocks, then turned around and parked across from the house. Eddie was waiting at the door, still holding the brown paper bag he brought from his house. A dog started barking just as the door swung open.

"Oh my god!" Murray said. "Look who it is."

Jeff strained his neck to see.

"Is that?"

"E.R.A, 2.98. Strikeouts, 645. Saves, 89. The one and only Bobby Hagan."

While the Nelson detectives were rockers at heart, they were also baseball fanatics.

"Now what's a guy like Nasty Boy doing with the likes of Eddie Costello?" Jeff asked.

"Let's go in and find out." Murray reached for the door.

"Let's hold back for a few," Jeff replied.

"We can't just wait here; the Crown Vic stands out like a sore thumb with all these imports parked on the street." Murray had a point, every other car on the street was a luxury import.

They continued to watch the door as Eddie Costello removed his shoes and entered the house.

"I have an idea," Jeff said, staring at the El Camino parked at the house. "What year you think that El Camino is?"

"84."

"Me too. Think they can see me from in there?"

Murray glanced toward the house. "No. Looks like Nasty Boy likes his privacy. I think those are blackout curtains."

Jeff got out and walked to The Cowboy's ride; the driver's side window was open and he reached in and pulled a lever to pop the hood. He took a quick look under and smiled at his brother. He closed the hood gently then reached back into the car to turn on the headlights.

"Wiring's all fucked up," Jeff said as he slid back into

the Crown Vic. "Common problem with 84's. Battery will die in a few minutes."

"If they wanted to leave, can't they leave in Hagan's car?"

"Not if you're blocking the driveway."

Murray drove to the top of the street, then turned around and blocked Nasty's driveway.

"You worried about being outnumbered by one?" Jeff asked.

"Nope."

"Me neither."

"While we wait," Murray said, "who was better in The Misfits, Danzig or Graves?"

"Danzig put them on the map, but Graves had a cleaner tone. I'm going with Graves."

"Danzig, every day of the week, and twice on Sunday."

Nasty Boy opened the door and saw scrawny little Eddie Costello standing on his doorstep.

"Alex, right?" Nasty Boy always called Fast Eddie by the wrong name to humiliate him; it always worked.

"Eddie," he replied. "And you know that. I'm here for The Cowboy."

"Cowboy's out back. Come on in, but take off your shoes. Nobody drags mud into my house."

Eddie looked down at Nasty Boy's feet. "You have your shoes on."

"And this is my fucking house. Take off your fucking shoes or I'll cut off your fucking feet."

Nasty Boy was in no mood to take any shit.

"You remember what I did to Teufel Shuffle in 89?" The pitcher thought everyone remembered that beanball and the ensuing brawl.

"Who?"

Hagan stepped closer to Costello, "Just take off your goddamn shoes."

Fast Eddie removed his shoes, not out of respect for the former pitcher but to get on with it. He followed the former major leaguer into his house.

"Where's Cowboy?"

"Out back," Nasty said, clearly upset at having to repeat himself. The former ballplayer flared his nostrils to intimidate Costello — that one didn't work. "What's in the bag?"

"It's as great big bag of fuck you!" Fast Eddie said.

Nasty turned around, "Your mouth is writing checks that your body can't cash."

Costello rolled his eyes at the Top Gun reference that Nasty just laid on him.

They walked through the foyer, into the kitchen, and out to the patio where The Cowboy was finishing a cigarette.

"Do you mind if we have a moment alone?" Eddie asked.

"Yep," Nasty said and remained on the patio. He took off his shirt, revealing his once muscular body and numerous tattoos. Since his playing days, Hagan had put on an extra sixty pounds and none of it was muscle.

The Cowboy stood up and faced his employer. "I don't think I want to work for you anymore."

"Is that so?" Eddie said. "Jenny Slade said that to me once."

"What about it?" Nasty Boy replied.

"I missed the part where this was any of your goddam

business," Eddie retorted then reached into his brown bag and pulled out a Taser, which he pointed directly at Nasty Boy's chest. He squeezed the trigger and two dart-like electrodes hit Hagan squarely in the right nipple. The former pitcher dropped to the ground and started convulsing.

"The fuck?" was all The Cowboy could muster.

"We're leaving now," Eddie said.

The Cowboy got up. While he had size on Eddie, his boss had two things on him—a dash of crazy and a weapon. As such, he thought it best to comply.

Costello knew he only had a few minutes before Nasty Boy recovered from the blast, so he decided to bypass walking through the house and led The Cowboy through the gate on the pool deck which led to the driveway. That's when he saw a Crown Vic with two blond cops sitting inside.

"Fuck!" he said and started walking hastily to the El Camino. Eddie wondered why the cops weren't getting out. He got his answer when The Cowboy's El Camino didn't start.

"Shit, shit, shit!" Costello said, banging on the steering wheel like a chimpanzee.

"Mr. Costello, I do not believe you are authorized to have such a weapon," Detective Nelson said while tapping on his window and pointing at the Taser Costello hastily put on the dash.

"All right, Cowboy," Murray said to Page. "Put your hands where I can see them. We're going on a little trip."

The Nelson brothers handcuffed both Fast Eddie and The Cowboy and led them to their Crown Victoria. Eddie started mouthing off to Jeff who "accidentally" bumped

Costello's head on the doorframe while pushing him into the backseat. A moment later, Bob "Nasty Boy" Hagan came out from behind his fence looking like something the cat dragged in.

"That fucker tazed me!"

Jeff turned around and saw the former pitcher approaching the car.

"Nasty Boy," Jeff said, "I was in the stands in San Diego back in 89 and saw your immaculate inning."

This admission stopped Nasty Boy in his tracks. "Really? You a fan?"

"Of baseball, yes. Of former pitchers who harbor criminals such as The Cowboy over here, not so much."

"About that," Murray said. "How about you give us a written statement about whatever you and The Cowboy over here were talking about before that piece of shit showed up?"

"Or?" Hagan asked.

"Or we make room for three in the Crown Vic," Jeff piped up.

"And I gotta warn ya, the AC isn't working and me and my brother have what you might call unique taste in music."

Murray reached into the car for a pad and paper, then walked them over to the former pitcher, who began writing as if his life depended on it. When put to the test, the brothers-in-arms loyalty Nasty had with The Cowboy disintegrated under duress. Hagan may have been nasty on the pitcher's mound, but the prospect of carnal knowledge in a California prison was enough to throw Page under the bus.

Nasty handed the pad back to Murray who read what

was written on it immediately and smiled. "All this is true?"

"On my daughter's life," Nasty replied. "What happens next?"

"We arrest this son of a bitch. You may be called to testify against him. That going to be a problem?"

Nasty looked over at The Cowboy sitting next to Fast Eddie in the Crown Vic, "Not at all. The guy is a maniac."

"We'll be in touch," Murray said and then walked to the car.

Bob "Nasty Boy" Hagan then waved goodbye to two of his biggest fans. When he caught Eddie's eye, he offered a one-finger salute.

While pulling out from in front of Nasty's house, Murray handed the statement to his brother. "It's always best to read these things right when you get them." Murray ribbed his brother for not doing the same with Jenny Slade's confession the night before.

"You can't make this shit up," Jeff replied. "The truth is stranger than fiction."

"What's it say?" The Cowboy asked.

"It says you need to pick better friends," Murray quipped.

Jeff had a cassette loaded in the Crown Vic's tape player, a little something special for The Cowboy. When his brother turned off of Hagan's street heading back towards the 101 highway, Jeff hit play, and the sound of David Lee Roth and Van Halen singing Happy Trails came blasting through the speakers.

"Last song on Diver Down," Murray said. "Nice."

"Fuck you," The Cowboy said, to which the Nelson

twins sang, “Bum-ba-dee-da, bum-ba-dee-da, bum-ba-dee-da-dee-da-dee-da.”

CHAPTER THIRTY-FOUR

Unchained

Dr. Robert Fauci was not a native of Santa Barbara but a transplant from Larchmont, NY where he ran a medical practice after being discharged from the Army after the Korean War. His wife of 40 years, Marie, was diagnosed with Multiple Sclerosis and her neurologist suggested that she'd be more comfortable in a drier climate. They explored many areas out west before settling on Santa Barbara, largely because it was one of President Ronald Reagan's favorite places. Dr. Fauci considered himself a Reagan Republican and if the town was good enough for Ronnie and Nancy, it was good enough for them. Marie passed away five years ago and Robert retired from practicing medicine, but he spent a few days a month tending to patients who couldn't afford healthcare. Contrary to what some people think, not all Republicans are heartless.

In 1953, during the last year of the Korean War, Robert took care of a soldier who was suffering from an infected bullet wound in the thigh. Supplies of antibiotics were low and there wasn't much Dr. Fauci could do for the patient except manage his pain. On his death bed, the patient, an Italian immigrant eager to serve his adopted country, asked Robert to track down his wife and son stateside should the doctor make it back alive and tell them that their husband and father died bravely. The patient's name was Fabio Carbona, his son's name was Anthony.

Dr. Fauci honored the request.

He found Anthony and his mother living in a Bronx tenement and saw that they were always taken care of. At 83, Dr. Fauci remains a father figure to Anthony Carbona and, while the good doctor kept his nose clean of Anthony's professional life, he never refused doing a favor for Anthony when that favor meant saving a life. Since moving out west five years ago, those favors were rare, so he was surprised to get a call to help an injured Carbona associate.

The house he purchased with his wife was the rectory to a closed Spanish mission, and with the house came the condemned church. As a practicing Catholic, the thought of tearing down a house of God didn't sit well with Robert, so the old structure remained on his property. When he got the call from Carbona that two of his associates wanted a word with the man he'd been treating, Dr. Fauci opened the old church for the meeting; some lines he wouldn't cross for his adopted son — his personal living area was one of them.

The mob boss assured the doctor that the meeting would be peaceful, a confession of sorts, and what better place to do that than in a church? Sandy Greenfield called to let the doctor know that they were on their way from LA and had just passed Calabasas. Dr. Fauci took care of his patient by changing his dressings and treating him with some morphine to help with the pain. Terry had never been a drug guy, but the pain radiating from his broken ribs, nose, and jaw motivated him to take a very small amount; enough to treat the pain but not enough to go all Kurt Cobain.

Greenfield called again, letting him know they were ten minutes away from the address of the church, so Dr. Fauci walked Terry to the confessional where he'd placed two chairs divided by a privacy screen. With Terry settled, Robert went outside to wait for Greenfield and the penitent, Joe Feld. When they arrived, the doctor walked them halfway down the aisle to the confessional.

"I've never seen one of these before," Greenfield said.

"Judging by your last name, I can't imagine that you have," Robert replied.

"We Jews have one day a year where we ask forgiveness of our sins. You Catholics are supposed to do it what, every week?"

"We are not allowed to receive the Eucharist unless we are in a state of Grace, and the only way to achieve such a state is through the sacrament of reconciliation."

"Well this young man is certainly in need of some reconciliation. I assured Mr. Carbona I wouldn't leave him alone with Terry after what happened. Is there room for three in there?"

Joe Feld fidgeted, nervous enough about what he had to do with Tomasulo. To him, three was definitely a crowd.

"Typically, confession is a private matter between the confessor and the vehicle of absolution. You and I will wait out here, if anything happens to Terry, we'll hear it.'

"Listen to me," Greenfield said to Joe, "if anything

happens to Tomasulo, your own mother won't recognize you. Do you understand me?"

Robert was uncomfortable hearing this kind of talk in general, let alone in a church, but he understood that the Carbona family had its ways. Arguing with them was swimming against the tide.

"I understand," Joe said, nervously.

"Good."

Joe entered the confessional and noticed how quiet it was inside—so quiet he could hear Terry's labored breathing.

"Open the screen door," the voice on the other side of the privacy screen said. Penitents could choose to keep the screen door closed if they felt more comfortable not looking the priest eye to eye; Terry, though, wanted to look into the eyes of the person whose actions put him in this state.

Joe Feld slid the door open and took a deep breath.

"Look, I never intended for..." He was cut off.

"Save your apology. I want to know why this happened."

"I don't even know who did this to you!"

"Maybe that's true, but you drove me to them and if you hadn't done that, I wouldn't be laboring to talk right now, would I?"

Joe closed his eyes and considered his surroundings. While he was raised Catholic and Confirmed in the church, he hadn't stepped foot inside one in at least fifteen years.

He remembered going to confession as a kid, but he never told a priest his real sins, largely out of fear that he'd be in there a long time saying his penance. Nevertheless, he took a deep breath and began talking.

When Feld was done, Terry said, "Anyone ever tell you that you got a problem, Joe?"

Feld just nodded.

"What do you know about this Cowboy guy who beat the shit out of me?"

"Nothing, but I have the contact information for his boss. Fast Eddie Costello will know how to get in touch with him." Joe looked at his phone wrote down Costello's mobile number and passed it through the screen.

"You are absolved from your sins, my child," Terry said to Joe's relief.

"I kind of feel better," Joe admitted as he reached for the door.

"Not so fast," Terry said. "You have to do a penance."

Joe looked confused.

"Everything you just told me, you're now going to tell the police. And I'm going to make sure you keep the story straight."

CHAPTER THIRTY-FIVE

Warrant

Jimmy and Farrah drove down to the precinct where detectives Murray and Jeff Nelson were about to interrogate Greg "The Cowboy" Page and "Fast" Eddie Costello. The Nelson's thought Farrah and Jimmy would like to see an interrogation from the other side of the glass and invited them down to watch.

"I prefer the view from in here," Jimmy said.

"No doubt," Murray replied, satisfied with his pun. Farrah snickered.

"We're going to do a little back and forth with these two," Jeff said. "This observation room was actually designed for that purpose." He pointed to the window on opposite sides of the room. "When we've had enough of one, we'll go to the other room and start on the other; all you have to do is turn around. Any questions?"

"Why are we starting so late?" Jimmy asked, it was close to 11pm.

"We've been holding them here for about five hours; we find a little alone time expedites the interrogation process."

"Who are you going to start with?" Farrah asked.

"Costello," Murray said. "He seems to be the brains. Our goal is to have him roll on The Cowboy.

"No time like the present," Jeff said, and the two exited the observation room but not before dimming the lights and turning up the speakers.

"You okay with a mid-afternoon flight back tomorrow?" Farrah asked as the lights went out. "The 2pm flight gets in around 10:30."

She and Jimmy had plans to record Drew Baron's podcast the next morning at 11 and then head directly to the airport.

"I'd say let's take the 4pm, but I don't want to get in after midnight."

"I know how you get when you don't have enough sleep, Doubts. We can always cancel with Baron."

"No way. I couldn't go with you to Tercel, there's no way I'm missing Baron."

Their conversation halted when the door to the first interview room was opened and Eddie Costello was led inside. They turned around to see The Cowboy trotted into the other room.

Costello was alone for a minute before Murray and Jeff entered the room.

"Can I get you anything?" Jeff asked. "Cup of coffee? Water?"

"Go fuck yourself!" Costello replied.

"Someone's in a bad mood," Murray observed.

"Why am I here? You got nothing on me."

"Tell me," Murray said, "how does a low life like you not have a record? I have to admit I was surprised when we couldn't find even a moving violation on you."

"That's right, clean as a whistle," Jeff added.

The fact is, Costello had no record because of a tendency to roll on anyone who could implicate him; plus, he kept his hands a bit cleaner than his soul—of course that wasn't saying much.

"Why are you guys wasting my time? I had nothing to do with what happened to the singer."

"Jeff, did you say anything about a singer?" Murray asked.

"Nope. I was going to ask him about something else but now that he mentions it...I'd like to hear all about how one of his girls winds up in a room with a guy who got tossed off his own balcony."

Costello rolled his eyes and then described his idea behind Fantasy First Dates.

"It's funny, that concept mentions nothing about throwing the star of the pilot off the balcony. Was this an improv show?"

"I got nothing to say about that."

"You know what Jeff," Murray said, "I did a little digging on our friend here. Did you know he's got some issues with the IRS?"

"You don't say? Fine upstanding citizen like Fast Eddie Costello over here, I'm shocked."

"Why are you guys busting my balls?

"Your friend Jenny Slade doesn't have too many nice things to say about you," Jeff added.

"I gave her a better life than she would have had if she stayed in Wisconsin."

"Indiana," Jeff corrected.

"Whatever."

"You turned her into a drug addict pornstar. You're a real modern-day Mother Theresa."

"Who?"

"Never mind," Murray said. "Tell us about The Cowboy."

"Greg Page came to work for me a few years ago," Costello said.

"In what capacity?"

"Security. There are a lot of creeps in my business. I hired him to protect me and my girls." Costello managed to say this with a straight face.

"Any idea why he was at the Hotel Palomino the other night?"

"You'll have to ask him. What he does on his own time is his business."

"So you didn't send him there last Thursday night?"

"Nope."

"You sure about that? Jenny referred to him as her bodyguard."

Eddie relented, "Alright, she's been giving me some trouble so I had him keep an eye on her. So what?"

"And he didn't mention anything about killing Bernie Deville?"

"Who?"

"How about Terry Tomasulo?"

"What is this, the name game? Never heard of any of these guys."

"Murray, Mr. Costello has a really bad memory. Early Alzheimer's?"

"Nah, it's late, maybe he just needs some time to think. Why don't you and I go talk to The Cowboy. Maybe something he tells us will jog Freddie's memory."

"Eddie, asshole."
"Right."

The detectives left Fast Eddie and joined The Cowboy. Inside the observation room, Farrah and Jimmy turned around to watch the detectives continue their work.

Jeff decided to dig into The Cowboy first. "Greg 'The Cowboy' Page. Anyone tell you that you look like Lemme from Motörhead."

"Who?"

The late Lemme Kilmister was one of the most recognizable figures in hard rock. Anyone who spent time on the Sunset Strip would know him.

"We just had a nice conversation with your boss," Murray said. "Real stand up guy."

"He's all right," The Cowboy said.

"I'd rethink your position on him," Jeff added. "He just pegged you for throwing that singer off a balcony."

It was a simple interrogation trick — convince one suspect that another rolled on him to coerce a confession.

The Cowboy remained silent.

Back in the interview room, Jimmy turned to Farrah. "When do you think he'll lawyer up?"

"When he gets nervous. I don't think he's there yet."

"We had a little time to look into your background, Cowboy," Jeff said. "Looks like you have some anger issues. Aggravated assault, assault and battery, assault with a battery..."

"That wasn't my fault," The Cowboy protested. Two years ago, he was in an automotive store and accidentally dropped a car battery on a shopper's foot. Charges were filed, but later dropped, after the accuser had a change of heart (after Page paid him a visit, of course).

"The truth is," Murray said, "we really don't need your confession since we have this." He handed The Cowboy a copy of the statement Jenny Slade signed the day before. The Cowboy read it, ripped it into little pieces, and shoved them in his mouth.

"Get this, Jeff. He thinks I gave him the original."

"He's much dumber than he looks," Jeff said.

There was a knock on the door and Murray got up to answer.

"Detective Nelson, there's a couple of guys here who say it's very important that they speak with you."

"This really isn't a great time..."

"Their names are Joe Feld and Terry Tomasulo."

Murray smiled and turned to his brother. "You'll never believe who's here."

Jeff raised his eyebrow.

"Tomasulo and Feld."

"No shit?"

"No shit!"

"Well, Cowboy, looks like your day just went from bad to worse."

"I don't think The Cowboy here knows those names. Let's see, Tomasulo was the guy who accompanied Jenny to Van Nuys yesterday. Ring any bells?"

"I want a lawyer."

"You're going to need one."

Terry Tomasulo and Joe Feld were brought to an interview room where they were told to wait for the detectives running the investigation into Bernie Deville's death.

"Are you sure this is a good idea?" Joe said. "What if they arrest us?"

"What if?" Terry replied.

"I don't want to go to fucking jail!"

"Stop being a little bitch," Terry said. The only silver lining Terry saw is that he may very well get a good story out of it and turn that into a screenplay. He was about to dole out a little more Bronx knowledge on Feld when detectives Murray and Jeff Nelson entered the room.

"I'm going to go out on a limb here and assume you're Joe Feld," Murray said.

Feld responded with a nod. He tried to make it look cool; in reality, he looked like someone with a neck spasm.

"What happened to you?" Jeff said, nodding toward Terry.

"I'm still in an incredible amount of pain, Detective, so Mr. Feld over here is going to tell you the story."

The detectives looked at each other, then at Feld, who remained silent for a minute.

"Be sure not to leave out the part where you lied to us about your cousin," Murray said.

Joe looked at the ground and a cold sensation came over his body, as if the temperature in the room suddenly dropped. He began to shiver.

"Suit yourself." Jeff got up and removed a pair of handcuffs from his pocket; this motivated Feld to start talking.

"Last week, I flew down to Florida to meet with a guy named Anthony Carbona." Feld had to be careful here; he didn't want to implicate the mob boss in a crime.

"What's a tech genius like you meeting with a mob guy?"

"Mr. Carbona prefers the term self-made businessman," Terry clarified.

"And I'm Eddie fucking Van Halen," Murray said.

"Vai was better," Jeff whispered in his brother's ear.

Terry decided not to push his case any further.

"I was about to come into a lot of cash," Joe said. "The one gift I wanted to give myself was to tour with a band."

Feld now had the detectives' attention—they too had been bitten by the music bug and knew the sacrifices they had been willing to make in order to play.

The expression on Terry's face suggested this was going to be good.

"I didn't have much of a childhood," Feld began. "My father loved money, my mother loved things, and I was always getting in the way. I had everything a kid could ask for, yet I felt as if I had nothing. The one thing I had was music, and my favorite band was The Beagles. I would fall asleep to their music every night, even after I was too old to be listening to it. The Beagles were my escape."

Joe's legs were fidgeting. Jeff looked under the table and saw that Feld was wearing bright yellow Glenn Beagle socks.

"What does this have to do with Carbona?" Jeff asked.

"When I was a kid, my mother took me to see The Beagles when they came to Connecticut. At the end of their concerts, each member would select a lucky child from the audience to come on stage and join them for the last song."

"Let me guess," Murray said, "little Joey Feld, Connecticut's cookiest Beagles fan, wasn't chosen."

"Bernie had the last pick, and he selected..."

"Your cousin Jimmy," Murray and Jeff said at the same

time. Wonder twin powers activate.

"Yes. I've followed each of their post-Beagles careers and knew Bernie was the only one actively making music and still making money in the business and that the others were down and out. I thought I'd approach the guys with the idea of a tour — they'd make some money and get back on their feet, and I'd live my dream of playing with The Beagles. There was just one problem."

"What was that?"

"Bernie. I counted on him not wanting to tour. From what I'd read, he wanted to put the past behind him. I didn't realize he would block the other guys from making a living."

"Couldn't they tour without him?"

"No. The contract that terminated the band clearly forbade them from touring as The Beagles unless everyone agreed to it. Bernie didn't agree."

"Who did you approach with the offer to tour?"

"Their manager, George Martini. He confided that he could also use the money — he was in deep with gambling debts. So I flew down to Florida to meet with Carbona."

"Not for nothing," Jeff said, "but why would a guy like Carbona meet with you?"

"I went to college with his son Michael and he met with me as a favor to him. That, and I agreed to pay him seventy-five thousand bucks to threaten Bernie."

"That's a lot of dough to spend to be able to play with a washed-up kids group," Jeff observed. "If most of these guys were in such bad shape, I bet you could have paid them a grand each, rented a Knights of Columbus hall, and put on your own show."

"Yes, but not as the Beagles!" Joe protested. Didn't

anyone understand what this band meant to him?

"You are one sorry sack of shit," Jeff said, slamming his palms on the table. Murray eyed his brother disapprovingly at his use of a cop cliché.

"And what about you," Murray said to Terry, "wasn't that your car we saw driving by Slade's place the other night?"

"Yes, it was," Terry said through his teeth. "I had a meeting at the Palomino that night. When I left, I came across a woman trying to get a cab. She was soaking wet and had no money, so I offered to help."

"Chivalry isn't dead," Murray said. "What kind of meeting did you have at the hotel?"

"Joe, why don't you tell them?"

"I'm asking you!" Murray snapped back.

"Mr. Carbona asked me to visit with Mr. Martini and Mr. Deville," Terry said. "To negotiate an agreement."

"So you're the guy that he hired," Murray pointed at Feld, "to take care of Bernie?"

"Yes."

"And that's why you were at the Palomino that night?"

"Yes. I was with Martini in the lobby when we heard about the jumper."

"So Bernie dies before you have a chance to meet with him?" Murray asked.

"Yes. I told my boss what happened and he told me to go home."

"So you got mixed up in this entire thing all because you were trying to help the girl?"

"Pretty much."

"Did you give Martini a business card?" Jeff asked recalling how Jimmy said he tracked down Tomasulo.

"Yes. He offered to make some connections for me."

"Only in Hollywood," Jeff said.

"The only thing left for us to know is why you lied to us about your cousin's whereabouts," Murray said. "We know he didn't kill Bernie and that he wasn't even at the Palomino when Bernie died."

"While you're at it," Jeff added, "tell us why finding Jenny Slade was so important."

Terry winced at the memory.

"When I heard my cousin got into a fight with Bernie the night he died, I thought I could set my cousin up for the singer's murder. Lying to you and my finding Jenny Slade served that purpose. I bribed Eddie Costello to encourage Jenny to say Jimmy threw Bernie off the balcony."

"In a city as big as LA, how the hell did you find her?"

"My app, Fast Lane. On Friday, I got a notification that Jenny Slade had logged into her Fast Lane account and requested a ride up to Van Nuys, so I decided to drive her myself. I arrived at the pickup location..."

"Tomasulo's place in El Segundo?" the detectives asked in unison.

"Yes. I took them up to a hotel in Van Nuys."

"And when we got there," Terry spoke up, "I had the shit beat out of me by a guy dressed like a cowboy."

Terry went on to say that he overheard Eddie threatening Jenny's family, that he'd kill them if she didn't go to the police and blame Jimmy for Bernie's death. He also told them how playing dead saved his life and that he was thankful the Cowboy drove an El Camino and not a truck with a covered bed.

"He pulled the fire alarm to make carrying me out of

the hotel look inconspicuous. I bet the hotel has some camera footage of that."

The detectives looked at each other and Jeff made a note to get that footage.

"You can't make this shit up," Murray said to his brother.

"So can I go now?" Joe asked.

"Oh sure, we'll call you a cab."

"Really?" Joe asked, "I can just use a Fast Lane..."

"No, asshole. You're staying here," Murray interrupted then turned to Terry. "Mr. Tomasulo, we'll need a sworn statement from you. Can you write with that hand?"

"No, but I can dictate with my mouth and sign something."

Just then Murray had an epiphany, "Before that, Mr. Tomasulo, would you mind doing something for me?"

"What?"

"We've got Costello and The Cowboy in separate interview rooms, and both abut an observation room with two-way mirrors. I want you to stand in that room, and I'll turn the lights on..."

"Then they'll see me," Tomasulo said.

"Exactly," Murray said. "Watch Joe for me, will ya?"

"Don't worry about Joey boy," Jeff replied. "He isn't going anywhere."

Farrah and Jimmy were waiting for the Nelson twins to come back to the observation room. To pass the time, they studied Eddie Costello and The Cowboy; while the later was acting cool as a cucumber, the former was coming unglued. It was now well after midnight and he was losing more than his patience—he was losing his cool.

Eventually the twins returned with Tomasulo in tow; Jimmy thought the guy looked as if he'd gone twelve rounds with Mike Tyson in his heyday.

"Farrah and Jimmy," Murray said, "Meet Terry Tomasulo. He's about to do us a favor, but I'm going to need you both to leave the room for a minute."

Farrah immediately understood what Detective Murray was going to do — play a little psychological warfare on their suspects. Seeing Tomasulo may cause one of them to crack, and Farrah guessed it would be Costello, who looked like he was on the verge of cracking anyway. Murray must have had the same hunch because he closed the curtain looking into The Cowboy's interview room.

"I need to use the bathroom anyway." Jimmy said.

Farrah got up to follow him. Her reasoning was twofold: She really had to go, and every time Jimmy went to the bathroom at a critical moment, something bad happened. Following him was her way of covering their asses.

With Farrah and Jimmy gone, Murray turned on the light inside the observation room, and "Fast" Eddie reacted quickly. He saw Tomasulo pointing directly at him, and the cracks in his armor shattered like glass.

"I want to give a statement," Eddie shouted.

"Piece of cake," Murray said to Terry. "I'll have my brother take your statement while I get Costello's."

Terry Tomasulo refused to break eye contact with the man whose prowling ruined the lives of so many women who came to Hollywood seeking fame. While Terry was no choir boy, he viewed his job in the Carbona Family as one of moral significance; people were obliged to pay their debts and his role was to make sure they did. Plus,

Terry only went after those who had wronged his boss — Costello ruined innocent lives. Terry vowed to bring those lives some justice.

"Actually," Terry said, "can I watch you talk to Costello? I've never seen a real interrogation before."

"Why not," Murray said. "This is the fun part."

The minute the lights came on in the observation room and Eddie saw the man who The Cowboy was supposed to have taken care of the evening before, he knew it was game over. When Detective Murray Nelson returned, the conversation was brief.

"Where's your brother?" Costello asked.

"He's about to have a similar chat with your cowboy friend. I wonder what he'll have to say about seeing the guy he almost murdered last night."

"I had nothing to do with that."

"What if your friend says he was acting on orders from you. You'd be an accessory to attempted murder."

"I was here last night," Costello said. "I drove Jenny Slade to the station and waited for her to come out."

"You must have been concerned when you saw her leave in an ambulance."

"She's a client of mine. Of course, I was concerned."

"Let's cut the shit, Costello. You have a choice: Do you want your life to get better, or worse?"

"You got nothing on me. If you did, you'd have formally charged me with something by now."

"Have it your way. I'm going to check in with my brother and see how his chat with The Cowboy is going. When I come back, I'll likely be able to grant your wish of being charged with something."

"Fuck!" Costello said. "What do you want to know?"

"Did Greg 'The Cowboy' Page kill Bernie Deville?"

"Yes."

"Why?"

"Because he's a big dumb fuck. I hired him to keep an eye out for Jenny, who was supposed to be recording a pilot for..."

"Fantasy First Dates, I know. Just get to why Bernie's dead."

"The Cowboy parked outside of Jenny's room and when he heard things get loud inside, he went in to make sure Jenny was okay. He takes his job really seriously."

"So Bernie's getting loud, why throw him off the balcony?"

"Cowboy isn't what you would call well adjusted. In his defense, he told me he aimed for the pool."

"He missed."

"No shit."

"Now all I need you to do is write this down for me and sign it. Then, we'll see about letting you go."

"Come on, man. Technically, I haven't broken any laws."

"I'm sure if we did enough digging into your background we'd find something."

"You'll need a warrant for that."

"You start writing everything you just told me and sign it," Murray said, tossing a pad and pen toward Costello, "and we won't need to worry about a warrant."

CHAPTER THIRTY-SIX

Mother

It was the first restful night of sleep Jimmy Doubts had in days. No longer being a murder suspect will do that. The fact that he and Farrah didn't get back from the police station until one-thirty didn't hurt either. The two met in the lobby then drove the fifteen miles east of Beverly Hills to Highland Park, where they were set to appear on SMH (Shaking My Head) with Drew Baron. Drew was so anal about sound quality that he refused to have guests call into the show and, since Farrah and Jimmy didn't plan on returning to LA anytime soon, it was now or never.

Baron was a stand-up comedian popular in the alternative comedy circuit of the 1990s. Considered a voice for the progressive left, he was offered a job hosting a left-wing radio show for an upstart liberal network called Air Guevara.

Unfortunately for Baron, the network couldn't come close to touching the dominance of right wing radio and went under shortly after launch. Down on his luck, Baron launched a podcast in which he interviewed fellow comedians about their lives, peeling back the curtain on what the life of a funny man (or woman) was really like. As the show steadily rose in popularity, he added actors, authors, and musicians to his list of subjects, and before long, he had one of the hottest podcasts in the US. The success of the podcast helped him relaunch his stand-up career. His shows now sold out in record time.

Farrah and Jimmy had listened to his show enough to know what they were in for, an autobiographical interview about how they grew up, what their home lives were like, how they got into podcasting, and what fame had done for them. It wasn't going to be as inappropriately personal as a Howard Stern interview, but both knew Baron wouldn't let them get away with skipping details.

Baron recorded most of his interviews in the studio he built in his garage, which is where Farrah and Jimmy found themselves that Sunday morning.

"So I understand we only have about an hour because you guys are going home, is that right?" Baron asked. He'd started recording without telling them. It was a tactic he often used. He liked kicking off his interviews with a little organic small talk.

"Yes," Farrah said. "We're flying back to New York this afternoon."

"Ah-choo!" Jimmy sneezed so loudly Farrah thought the walls would collapse.

"Hey there, buddy," Baron said, "you all right?"

"Do you have cats?" Jimmy asked. He was highly allergic and could feel his throat closing up.

"Four. Feral ones, too. They're on the other side of the house, though."

"Blah-chewie!" Jimmy sneezed again and reached for a

box of tissues Baron kept on his desk. As he brought his hands to his nose, he knocked over a coffee cup with the SMH logo on it.

"Awe shit, man!" Baron said, "President Obama drank out of that cup."

Jimmy looked mortified.

"I'm just fucking with you. You think I'd keep that cup on my desk? No, man, it's over there on my shelf along with a tissue he used to blow his nose."

"Ah...ah...ah-choo!" Jimmy sneezed again. Baron looked at Farrah and shook his head. She took the hint.

"Doubts, I think I'm going to have to do this one solo. We'll never get through it with your cat allergy in full swing. How about you wait in the car?"

Jimmy was devastated, but he knew Farrah was right. His throat was so scratchy he'd have a hard time speaking.

"Fine," Jimmy said. "But if you ever come to New York, I'd love to do an interview with you."

"Yeah, man, that'd be great," Baron said. Truthfully, he was much more interested in interviewing Farrah and much more comfortable in one-on-one settings.

Jimmy left through a door in the garage that led to the driveway; when Farrah and Drew heard a door to the car open and close, the interview began in earnest. Since Drew always recorded an extended intro to each interview after it was concluded, he didn't bother to start by introducing Farrah to his audience and dove right in.

"So I want to get to why you were out in California this week, Farrah, but first, tell me more about you. Where were you born?"

"I was born in a small town, Greenwich, Connecticut..."

"Ohh, father have some money?" Drew was always interested in what his interviewee's fathers did for a living. He knew Greenwich was a playground for the wealthy and assumed Farrah came from money.

"It wasn't like that. We were the poor people of Greenwich. My father was a greens keeper for a country club that provided housing for us."

"A man of the earth?" Baron asked.

"You could say that."

"And your mom, what did she do?"

"She was a social worker when she met my dad but put her career on hold after my brother and I were born."

"Is your brother in the entertainment business too? What does he do?"

"He's a man of the cloth," Farrah said. Her brother, Michael, was a priest in Greenwich. He was intimately involved with season three of Uncorking a Murder when a friend of his, a fellow priest, was poisoned while saying Mass in the resort town of Chatham on Cape Cod.

"Catholic?"

"And Irish," Farrah replied.

"So that's interesting. You still a good Catholic girl?"

"I don't know about good, but I do practice the faith. I've had my moments of doubt, but it brings me comfort."

"Now I'm a listener of your podcast and know that you recently ended a long-term relationship with another woman. How do you reconcile your personal life with your religious faith?"

While Farrah preferred to keep her personal life personal, she knew she couldn't avoid questions about her sexuality. And since becoming a celebrity, her life had become an open book. She couldn't dodge the question, so she answered it the best way she could. "I guess I don't see my sexuality as black and white. Nor do I see my religion as black and white. While there are of people who judge me for who I am and the choices I make, I've found there are circles within circles."

"What does that mean, circles within circles?"

"It means there are people within my faith who are very welcoming of diversity. I choose to surround myself with those people."

"Still, it must be hard knowing that a core tenant of the Church says homosexuality is a sin."

"Divorce is also a sin, but half of all marriages end in it. You should know, you've been divorced three times, and to the same woman twice."

"Don't remind me," Baron said with a laugh. "But I'm not Catholic, I'm Jewish. I can get divorced as many times as I want."

Farrah laughed. "The point is, I don't know anyone in my faith who is as perfect as our Church wants us to be, but as I experience life, I'm constantly trying to be a better person."

"Fair enough," Baron said. He then asked a series of questions about her education, how she wound up leaving a high-powered job as a partner in a New York City firm, and how she started the podcast as a hobby.

"I've listened to every season of your show, but I have to say my favorite is the second, with the vampire guy."

The second season of Uncorking a Murder focused on a man wrongfully imprisoned for the murder of his wife. Sonny Michaels worked for a large pharmaceutical company run by a narcissistic Romanian CEO who had delusions of being a vampire. That CEO, Adrian Tepes, went so far as to have a dentist file his teeth into fangs that he flashed during business negotiations. Tepes was serving a ten-year sentence in a Florida Federal Prison for a host of white collar crimes, including bribery, insider trading, and price fixing. Farrah and Jimmy's podcast was responsible for bringing him down.

"We have Jimmy Doubts to thank for that one. He was my intern at the time and convinced me to call back a retired Detective named Rodney Peters who was eager for me to look into one of his old cases."

"I wonder how sneezy is doing," Baron chuckled into the mic. He made a mental note to discuss Jimmy's sneezing fit in the intro, so his audience would understand where that comment came from.

"He's a piece of work," Farrah said.

"That whole thing, though, with the Romanian CEO, Bram Stoker could have written that."

Farrah had a puzzled look on her face, as if she were thinking of something but couldn't put her finger on it.

"What did you say?"

"Come on, an educated woman such as yourself must have read Bram Stoker's Dracula. I mean, the plot line is almost identical to season two of your podcast."

Bram Stoker? What was the name of Joe Feld's business partner? Bram Wallachia? Yes, Farrah thought, that's it.

"Where did you go just, Farrah? I know your mind left the room."

"How well do you know Bram Stoker?" she asked.

"I am dark mother fucker," Baron admitted. "I was obsessed by Stoker's work."

"Does the word Wallachia ring a bell?"

Now Baron was confused — the interview was taking

an odd turn.

"It was an area of Romania. It's believed that Stoker based his Dracula character on a prince of Wallachia named Vlad Tepes."

Tepes? Adrian's last name! Farrah had an epiphany; if Jimmy's cousin was so fueled by revenge, would he stoop so low as to seek help from a man of means who would likely do anything to get back at the people whose actions led to his demise? The more she thought about it, the likelier it seemed that Joe Feld's ultra-secretive investor was Adrian Tepes. He was a federal inmate, but Farrah knew he'd have access to the Internet, even a phone. While his assets were frozen, he almost definitely had funds stashed away in offshore accounts the government couldn't touch, most rich people did.

"Earth to Farrah," Baron said.

Farrah shook her head a few times to clear it. "Sorry," she said. "I just had a thought. I'm back."

"While it's been great getting to know you, Farrah, I believe we have some bigger matters to discuss."

While prepping for the interview, Farrah and Baron discussed weaving in the story about the patent troll then segueing into a pitch for help supporting their crowdfunding campaign. Farrah took the cue and dove into the peril facing podcasters and how they were planning to fight it. Baron then explained the incentives for different fundraising levels.

"For everyone who donates twenty-five bucks, I'll send you an SMH coffee cup like the one Jimmy broke earlier today. Fifty big ones gets you an autographed picture of me, Drew Baron. Big spenders who give a hundred bucks or more will get two free tickets to one of my upcoming shows. Come on people, this isn't a time to be bashful. The world as we know it is ending. My cats have to eat so show us a little love."

Baron then thanked Farrah for the interview and walked her to the door. She was eager to get back to the East Coast.

Jimmy sneezed his way back to the car then decided to use his newfound free time to call his mother — she'd be relieved to hear he was in the clear, and he was interested to see if anything had developed with her sister.

"Jimmy, I have been worried sick. I stayed after Mass this morning and lit a candle for you." Diane never missed Sunday mass and over the years she could have bought a used car with the amount of money she spent on votive candles.

"Everything's fine, mom. I'm clear." He went on to tell her about Joe's confession and that Bernie's killer was in custody.

"Thank you, Jesus," she said. "Your cousin is such a little shit."

That his mother went from praising the Lord to using profanity caught Jimmy by surprise.

"When are you coming home?"

"We're flying out this afternoon. We land just before midnight."

"Do you want to stay here tonight?"

Jimmy's mother lived in an apartment in Stamford. She sold the house she raised Jimmy in when he moved out the year before. The house was only a two-bedroom ranch, but she thought it was too large to live in all by herself.

"I'm going to stay at my place in the city tonight,"

Jimmy said. "You have to wake up early for work, and I don't want to disturb you by coming in after midnight. Why don't we have dinner tomorrow? I'll take the train in."

"Okay, but if I said it once, I'll say it again, I hate the thought of you living in New York City with all those weirdos."

After making big money through the podcast, Jimmy leased a 5th floor walkup on Irving Place, not far from Union Square.

"I'll tell you one thing, the people in LA make New Yorkers look like choir boys."

"Well, take an early train," Diane said. "We'll go to your favorite spot."

"Tequila Mockingbird?" Jimmy asked excitedly. It was a Mexican restaurant one town over from Stamford that Jimmy loved.

"Yep. But I want to get there by 5. If I eat any later, I'll have trouble sleeping."

"Early bird special?"

"Two for one margaritas before 5:30. Hey, I'm not making millions as a school secretary."

"If you're tight on money, mom, I can help you."

"Never mind that, James Peter Rella. I'm doing just fine but I have to save where I can."

Over the past year, Jimmy offered to buy his mother everything from a new car to a townhouse, but she refused to take his money.

"Anyway, if you want to give me something..." Diane began to say, "give me some grandchildren," Jimmy finished her thought for her.

"And what's wrong with that?" Diane asked. "You are

my only child and I'm not getting any younger."

"There's one problem with that mom," Jimmy said. "I'm not even dating anyone."

"Then get your butt out there and find a girl. I was just talking to Mrs. D'Onofrio at church this morning and her daughter Tara is back from graduate school for the next few weeks. Maybe you should see if she wants to grab dinner sometime this week."

As long as Jimmy could remember, his mother and her friend Angela D'Onofrio had been conspiring to get their children together. In truth, Jimmy was very attracted to Tara but thought she was way out of his league. Every time he tried to talk to her, he'd get tongue tied.

"Give me her number tomorrow night, maybe I'll call her this week."

"Really?"

"Yeah, mom."

"You wouldn't lie to your mother, would you?"

"No mom." And he wouldn't. Jimmy respected her too much to mislead her.

"Good. See you tomorrow night."

Jimmy hung up and rested his head against the window and closed his eyes for a minute.

Farrah walked out of Drew Baron's garage and found Jimmy napping in the car. She woke him up by rattling the window his head was leaning against.

"Bah!" he said, scared out of his mind.

"Wake up, Doubts. We got a plane to catch."

On the way to the airport, Farrah told Jimmy her theory about Adrian Tepes being his cousin's silent partner and Jimmy agreed that it made sense.

While Farrah drove, Jimmy called Greg Moore, the FBI agent who built the case against Tepes, to see if there was any way he could get Tepes' visitor log and email activity. The agent gave Jimmy some startling news—Tepes had been released from federal prison a few weeks earlier for good behavior. He was now confined to house arrest in his Ft. Lauderdale home.

"Shit," Jimmy said.

"What?" Farrah asked.

"The plot thickens. Tepes is out."

CHAPTER THIRTY-SEVEN

Twisted Sister

Diane Rella was relieved to hear from her son that he was no longer a suspect in Bernie Deville's murder, but she remained unsettled at the role her nephew played in the affair. It takes a special kind of jerk to do what Joe did.

It was the early evening and Diane decided to start prepping dinner; even though Jimmy moved out almost a year ago, she still had trouble cooking for only one — she either made too much or too little. Whenever this struggle came up in conversation, she referred to it as Project Goldilocks.

She took a chicken breast from the freezer and put it in a bowl of cold water to defrost; tonight was a shake-n-bake night and she had at least an hour before it would be ready to coat with Kraft's magical seasoning. As such, she decided to head to her bedroom and do some time on the stationary bike she'd purchased at a tag sale the previous summer but the journey to her bedroom was interrupted by a knock at the door. She wasn't expecting any company and was surprised by the interruption.

Diane looked through the peephole to see who her caller was and was surprised to see her sister Anne in the doorway.

"Anne, I've been trying to reach you all week. What are you doing here?"

"We need to talk," Anne said.

"That's an understatement," Diane said sarcastically and then motioned her inside. She followed her sister into the kitchen where Anne had taken a seat at Diane's small kitchen table.

"So what do you want to talk about?"

"Can you make some coffee?"

"Sure." Diane said, clearly aggravated that her sister wanted to be waited on hand and foot when she was the one who wanted to talk. Nevertheless, Diane's manners had her walking over to her single brew coffee machine where she made two cups and set them both down on the kitchen table.

She was about to sit down when Anne asked, "Have any cream?" Once Diane walked over to her refrigerator, Anne removed a vile of powder from her pocket and emptied it into Diane's coffee.

Diane offered the cream to her sister, sat down, and took a sip of her coffee. Her face winced at the bitter flavor.

"Remind me never to buy that brand again. So, what do you want to talk about?"

Anne didn't particularly like speaking with Diane, but knew she had at least twenty minutes before the tranquilizer she just slipped her sister kicked in. Prescription drugs were a staple of hedge fund ex-wives and Anne didn't have any trouble getting her hands on a powerful relaxant. "We haven't connected in a while and I thought it would be nice to catch up."

Diane sensed her sister was feeding her a pile of horseshit, particularly given everything her son had done to Jimmy this week.

"How's work going?"

"Fine," Diane obliged her sister. "Thinking about retiring soon."

This superficial game of twenty questions went on until Anne saw signs that the drug Diane had been ingesting through her coffee was taking effect.

"Cut the crap and tell me what you really came to talk about?" Diane was feeling nauseous, her eyelids heavy.

"How you and your son ruined my life."

Diane was confused. Did her sister just say what she thought she said?

"I don't understand," Diane's words were slurred and her vision was starting to get blurry. "I don't feel right." She tried to stand, but found that her legs wouldn't support her. Anne got up and supported her sister under the arms. They walked towards Diane's bedroom.

"Something's wrong," Diane said drowsily.

"No, everything's just right."

Farrah and Jimmy had an uneventful flight back to New York. Farrah had the ability to sleep anywhere and used the five-hour flight to catch up on some much needed rest; Jimmy, on the other hand, was a nervous flier. Even though he had his private pilot's license and logged hundreds of hours of solo flight time, commercial flights made him too nervous to sleep – he needed to be in control, so he used the time to catch up on movies. He was an interactive movie watcher, oblivious to the stares from his fellow first-class passengers. But he couldn't help himself — the critics universally panned *The Lone Ranger*, but Jimmy found it hysterical.

After landing, Jimmy and Farrah went their separate ways — Farrah to her townhouse in New Canaan, and Jimmy to his apartment in Manhattan. Farrah sold a house that she owned with her former partner, Melody, after their relationship ended the prior summer. Since she owned a large vacation home on Cape Cod, she decided to downsize her primary residence and opted for a place where she could just lock the door and leave whenever she wanted to.

Once Jimmy got back to his apartment, he dropped his bags in the hallway and got into bed without even taking his clothes off. He was out immediately and didn't wake up until his phone started ringing at 8:20 the following morning.

"Hello," Jimmy said groggily.

"Mr. D...Rella?" The caller barely caught himself. "This is Principal Pavia from Trinity High School."

Jimmy's pulse started to race – there was only one reason the principal would be calling.

"Have you heard from your mother? It's after 8, and she isn't in. She hasn't called, and she isn't picking up at home. She's never been late for a day of school in all the years she's worked here. She looked fine when I saw her on Saturday so I just wanted to make sure everything was fine."

Diane never married after her husband died, but she considered herself married to the school where she worked as the main office secretary for forty years.

Students past and present considered her the heart and soul of the school and, while Jimmy was her only biological child, she considered herself a surrogate mother to all of those who'd passed through Trinity's halls over her four-decade tenure. In Diane, they found more than just a friendly face — she was someone who actually took the time to listen to their teenage problems. As a result, she knew who everyone dated, hated, and slept with – this went for students and faculty. That she didn't show up for work made the principal nervous.

Jimmy felt an ache form in the pit of his stomach. He knew he was right to be nervous that Adrian Tepes had been released from prison; that his release happened so close to his framing by Joe couldn't have been a coincidence.

"I'll find out," he said to Principal Pavia and then got dressed and called Farrah as he ran out the door.

"Doubts, do you know what time it is?"

"8:25."

"It was rhetorical. I know what time it is. Why the hell are you calling so early? I only got home a few hours ago."

"My mother's missing." Farrah could hear the fear in his voice.

"What?" She was awake now. Wide awake.

"She didn't show up at work and there's no answer at home. I'm on my way there, but it'll take me an hour by train."

"What can I do?"

"Can you go over to her place and see if she's there?"

"Of course," Farrah said. She knew how close Jimmy and his mother were and didn't want him to worry. "I'm sure she's fine."

"I hope you're right," he said, then bolted down a flight of subway stairs to catch an uptown local subway train to Grand Central.

Diane woke at the sound of her house phone ringing and then the sound of her machine picking up. "Diane, this is Tony from school just wondering where you are. Please call back and let me know that you are okay."

Diane was confused, why was Principal Pavia calling her on a Sunday? She tried to move, but found that her arms and legs were tied to the bed.

"Sleep well?" Anne said rubbing her sister's cheek with the back of her hand. Diane winced at how cold it felt.

"You've been out for over ten hours." Having never "Roofied" anyone before, Anne overdid it on the tranquilizer.

"What are you doing?"

"Getting justice."

"Why am I tied to my bed?" Diane was groggy, whatever sedative Anne had slipped her was still at work.

"Be a good girl and I won't have to use this," Anne held up a pistol. "How sentimental of you to keep your husband's service revolver."

"You are insane," Diane said, waking up more by the second. "What's this about?"

"I believe there's a question that has been bothering you this week. Go ahead and ask it."

"Untie me!" Diane demanded.

"We can do this the easy way, or the hard way," Anne replied flashing the gun once again.

Diane acquiesced. "Why does Joe hate Jimmy so much?" Diane asked, heavy eyed.

"You really want to know?"

"Yes."

"Joe had every material thing a kid could have. When he was younger, his room looked like a toy store, and when he was older it was like an electronics shop. He wanted for nothing."

"I remember," Diane said groggily. Even in her haze, she remembered it well. On the rare occasions when Jimmy was invited to his cousin's house, he'd come home feeling awful because Joe had all this cool stuff that Jimmy wasn't allowed to touch.

"Despite all that, he wasn't a very happy kid. His father was tough on him, and no matter what, Joe couldn't live up to Roland's expectations."

It had been a long time since Diane thought of her sister's ex-husband. The two divorced after Roland decided to upgrade to a younger model. Anne did very well in the divorce settlement, but she never got over her husband's infidelities. That she offered herself so freely to the lead singer of The Beagles when she was still married was justified by the fact that she did it for her son.

"What does this have to do with Jimmy?"

"Don't you get it? Jimmy was always happy. Here's a kid whose father had died and whose mother had a low paying job in a high school, yet he was the happiest kid Joe knew. Do you know how hard that was on my son?"

Diane was thunderstruck. She worked her butt off to make ends meet and give her son a fighting chance at climbing out of life at the poverty level, and yet her nephew struggled with Jimmy's happiness? Joe would have liked her son more if he was miserable? As hard as it was to concentrate, Diane was eager to see where her sister's crazy train of thought was going.

"While Joe needed tutors and extra help, school came easy to Jimmy. When Joe couldn't make a varsity sports team, Jimmy lettered in three, even though compared to Joe your boy was a scrawny runt. When that podcast took off, I got an earful about how everything falls in Jimmy's lap, whereas Joe had to work twice as hard for anything."

"Are we talking about the same Joe who was number 1 in his class at MIT, launched a tech company, and is selling it for millions?" Diane's anger transcended her drowsiness.

"And?" Anne said defiantly.

"He could have anything money can buy, yet he's jealous of my son?"

"You'll never get it."

"Get what?"

"Money. You've never had any, so you don't know what it can do to a person."

"Pardon me while I play the world's tiniest violin." Diane rubbed her thumb and index finger together.

"No, really. I haven't had to worry about much in life because I married well, but my husband's obsession with money made me feel like I was just another asset. Once I declined in value, he pretty much sold me for something new and shiny."

Anne rarely spoke of her divorce. She wasn't one to admit failure.

"After he left, I thought I could spend my way out of pain, but it didn't help. In many ways, it made things worse. And then I see you happy as a clam living in that one-bedroom apartment and driving mom's 1988 Oldsmobile, content just to get by. I get how my son feels toward Jimmy because I feel the same way about you!"

Anne's life underscored something their grandmother taught Diane long ago — money can't buy happiness.

The sedative Anne administered earlier was starting to wear off. "Untie me!" Diane demanded.

"Not until Jimmy gets here. We are going to have a little family reunion."

Anne then walked to her sister and covered her mouth with a piece of tape.

Farrah pulled up to Diane's apartment building in Stamford and parked in the visitor lot. She walked into the main lobby where a security guard named Herschel was looking into a bank of monitors. He was an older guy with dyed red hair who took the job to stay busy after retiring from the Stamford police department.

"Can I help you?"

"I'm here to see Diane Rella."

"Is she expecting you?"

"No," Farrah said. "Have you seen her today?"

"No, but my shift only started at 8. She's usually gone by then."

"That's why I'm here. She didn't show up for work today and didn't call the school where she works. No one has heard from her and her son's concerned. He's on his way here from the city."

"Jimmy. He's a great kid, a little nervous, though."

"Tell me about it."

"Can I see your ID?"

Farrah handed her license to the security guard, who wrote her name on the visitor's log. Her's was the first name on there, given the hour of the day.

"Let me buzz her."

It was the policy of the condominium that all visitors had to be announced unless they were on a registered visitor's list. Since Farrah wasn't on it, Herschel picked up his phone and dialed Diane's number; while he was distracted, Farrah turned the page to the visitor's log and saw Anne Feld's name on it, having signed in at 6:30 the night before. Farrah knew she wouldn't be allowed up unless Diane answered, and was surprised to hear Herschel say, "Go on up," Ms. Graham.

A lightbulb flashed in her mind and she texted Jimmy from the elevator.

Anne Feld walked through her sister's apartment in disgust. How could someone live in such a squalor? The apartment was far from dirty, but it was small with just one bedroom, one bathroom, a tiny living area, and a kitchen. Anne's own master bedroom suite was bigger than her sister's entire living space.

She wondered who would show up first, her nephew or his business partner. Anne assumed the school called Jimmy when his mother failed to make it into work, but the fact that he lived in New York City meant he'd likely send Farrah to check on his mother while he made his way to Connecticut. In fact, she was counting on it.

Her suspicion was confirmed when she heard the guard's voice come across the intercom. "Mrs. Rella, there's a Farrah Graham here to see you."

While most new buildings used a phone line to buzz a resident's apartment, Diane's building was built in the 1960s and still used an old-fashioned intercom system.

"Send her up," Anne replied. She opened the front

door and left it ajar, and then looked over some graffiti she left on her sister's wall.

Farrah was outside of Diane Rella's door and saw that it was ajar. Before entering, she listened for any sign of activity in the apartment. Not hearing any, she walked in and was caught off guard by some writing on Diane's wall.

"The truth will set you free," Farrah read out loud.

It was a phrase that came into play during the second season of Uncorking a Murder. A retired detective, Rodney Peters, sent suspects taunting messages with that passage from scripture. Clearly, Anne was a fan.

Anne walked out from her sister's bedroom and pointed a gun at the podcaster, "Do not come any further or I'll shoot."

"How cliche," Farrah said. "Out of curiosity, what's your plan to get out of here?"

"Shut up," was the only answer Farrah received.

"The building has a record of you coming here, and with your sister and me as witnesses I bet you think your only play here is to kill us all. Am I right about that?"

Why was she so calm? Anne asked herself.

"Have you ever fired one of those before?" Farrah asked. "It's a lot harder than they make it look in the movies and on TV. Louder too. Cut your losses, why add murder to the inevitable kidnapping charge?"

"Shut up!"

"Have it your way." Farrah advanced and Anne pulled back the hammer of the revolver causing Farrah to stop in her tracks. This game of chicken was over and Anne had won.

* * *

Jimmy's fear had transformed itself into energy and he wanted off the train, pronto. Unfortunately, he still had two stops to go. He tried calling Farrah and was relieved when his call was answered on the second ring; however, he was surprised when it wasn't her voice at the end of the line, but that of his aunt's.

"Well, if it isn't the famous Jimmy Doubts. I bet you want to know how your mother is."

"Aunt Anne, what are you doing at my mother's place?"

"That's all entirely up to you."

"I don't understand, where's my mother?"

"I'm afraid she's not feeling so well."

"Is she okay?"

"Again, my dear boy, that's entirely up to you. Just come over to your mother's place and don't even think about bringing the police or everybody dies."

"What have you done?" Jimmy screamed, to the irritation of morning commuters.

When the train pulled into Stamford Station, Jimmy rushed out and sprinted for her building like a bat out of hell.

Farrah was bound to a chair in the kitchen. While she could have easily taken Anne under other circumstances, the gun changed everything.

"Good news," Anne said, "your little friend Jimmy Doubts is on his way and then we can all be together. It's going to be a blast."

"Do you really want to do this to your life?"

"My life?" Anne asked. "My life is over, and I fully intend to take everyone else down with me."

Farrah looked confused. "What's this really about?"

"My nephew has ruined my life," Anne said. "I took every penny I had left and invested in my son's company, which, based on the bomb he dropped on me last night, is no longer being sold to the Universal Products Company. Imagine the shock when he told me he was selling it to some private investor for next to nothing."

"So that's it," Farrah said, a lightbulb had gone off in her head. "You're Bram Wallachia."

"The mysterious silent investor in the flesh. I thought you might like that name."

"Creative," Farrah admitted.

Anne was wild eyed. In the course of the last twenty-four hours she'd gone from rich Connecticut divorcee about to get richer to almost homeless.

"I didn't just lose my shirt in Joe's company, I mortgaged my house to buy the patent we were going to use to end your podcast. Now we can't even afford to fight you and your fellow podcasters in court and it's only a matter of time before the bank forecloses on my home."

Jimmy ran into his mother's building out of breath and made it into the elevator before Herschel finished asking, "What's the rush Jimmy?" There's no time for pleasantries when lives are on the line.

Arriving on his mother's floor, Jimmy sprinted down the hallway and found that her door was open. He walked in and saw the inscription Anne had written on the wall and then followed the sound of her voice to the kitchen. When he saw Farrah bound to a chair, he walked towards his Aunt. She responded by raising the gun and pointing it directly at him.

"Doubts, don't!" Farrah said.

"I would advise against coming any closer," Anne said. "I was just telling your business partner about how you ruined my life."

"I don't understand," Jimmy was dumbfounded.

"Sure you do. Because of you, my son's company is no longer being sold and I've lost everything."

"You've lost everything. How?"

"Jimmy Doubts, meet Bram Wallachia."

"Wait, you're Bram Wallachia?"

"All I wanted to do was help my son and you had to ruin us!" Anne was incredulous. She couldn't even consider the possibility that the plan to ruin Jimmy's life and help her son fulfill his dream of becoming one of The Beagles was at the heart of why she found herself in her current predicament.

"So what, you're going to kill me?"

"Don't sound so dramatic. You'll just be the victim of another murder suicide committed by a poor woman who secretly hated living in the shadow of her ultra-successful younger sister."

So that was it, Anne was going to kill Farrah, Jimmy, his mother, and then finally herself; her plan had more plot holes than Iron Eagle, but of course that wouldn't matter when everyone was dead.

"And the spray paint in the hallway? The truth will set you free?"

"The first part of her suicide note. The rest of it is under her pillow."

"Why would you do this? Were you that jealous of her?"

"If I can't be happy, then why should she?"

"I want to see her," Jimmy said.

"No harm in that," Anne said, then positioned herself behind her nephew. "Walk." She pointed the gun at his back.

Jimmy walked into his mother's room knowing he was at a disadvantage, he had to think quickly and shouted, "Is this some kind of joke?"

"She's not dead," Anne said. "Not yet anyway, she's just resting."

"She's not here!" Jimmy screamed.

"What?" Anne pushed herself into the room and Jimmy stuck out his leg causing her to trip. When she hit the floor, Jimmy jumped on her back, reached for her wrist, and forced the gun from her hand.

He pointed it at his Aunt.

His mother, who was, of course, still in her bed, started to come to.

"Jimmy, is that you?"

"It's me, mom. Everything is going to be okay."

CHAPTER THIRTY-EIGHT

After the Rain

In the days that passed, Farrah and Jimmy debated whether to use Bernie Deville's death as the subject of the next season of Uncorking a Murder. On the one hand, it was perfect—a former children's musician turned outlaw country artist was thrown from a building and Jimmy Doubts was suspected in the murder. On the other hand, the story would humiliate his family.

In the end, though, they agreed it was too perfect a story to pass up. The fourth season of Uncorking a Murder would go on to break multiple records for downloads, audience engagement, and advertising revenue.

Of course, the fact that the show continued was largely because the lawsuit brought on by the patent troll, who turned out to be not one, but two people — Joe Feld and his mother — was dropped after Anne's arrest. By that point, the crowdfunding campaign that Farrah started with Baron and Tercel had raised over one million dollars. The three approached their fans with a survey on what to do with the fund and fans overwhelmingly agreed to have them donate it to charity, as long as all the incentives for donations were honored.

Farrah and Jimmy decided to forgo a west coast media tour for Season 4 and waited until Adam Kimmel came to New York for his annual week of East Coast shows. While they could have done the New York based late night shows, they stuck with Kimmel. After all, their appearance on his show is where the story for the fourth season actually began.

Jimmy took up Allison Hart on her offer to meet and discuss his idea for Reasonable Doubts. She came to New York to visit her brother, actor Blaze Hazelwood, and their father. She loved the idea and gave him a holding deal from UPC. Jimmy cut out the article that appeared in Variety and sent it to his mother, who immediately photocopied it and mailed it to her sister who was now living under house arrest in an efficiency apartment with her son. Joe had moved back to the east coast to make good on the deal he made with Anthony Carbona. Having used all of the proceeds from the sale of his place in Manhattan Beach to post his mother's bail, he could only afford a tiny apartment in Queens.

As Jimmy and Farrah waited in Kimmel's green room at the studio in Brooklyn, Doubts waved a production assistant over.

"Excuse me, who is the musical guest tonight?"

"The Eagles."

Jimmy's face went pale. "Excuse me?"

"Oh, you're kind of young. You may not have heard of them. You ever hear Tequila Sunrise, Peaceful Easy Feeling, Hotel California?"

"I know them well. Didn't their singer die last year?"

"Yes, Glenn Fry passed away. His son Deacon will be performing with Don Henley, Joe Walsh, and Timothy B. Schmidt tonight."

"Wasn't there another guy? Don Felder?"

"He's no longer in the band."

"Thank you," Jimmy said.

"5-minute warning," another production assistant called out.

"That's my cue," Jimmy said.

"For what?" Farrah asked.

"To go to the bathroom." Jimmy winked at Farrah.

"Some things never change."

Epilogue: And Justice for All

Joe Feld got into his limo and drove to the first address on his list of fares. Since selling his business to Anthony Carbona, he had worked twelve hours a day, seven days a week, driving a limo for one of the Carbona's livery companies. His first pickup was in Manhattan, and he made it from his small studio apartment in Queens in no time — Saturday traffic was light.

He pulled up to the address on the lower east side and was surprised when Glenn Beagle approached his car, acoustic guitar in hand. He wanted so badly to tell him about his alter ego, Max Ruby, but knew that it wouldn't get him anywhere. Besides, Glenn might not be too happy to meet him, given he was promised six figures to reunite with the rest of the band for a tour that Joe could no longer fund.

He then drove to Connecticut where he stopped to pick up none other than Donnie Beagle at his parent's home in Greenwich. He got out of the car to help Donnie with his drums; only a high hat, a snare, and a bass could fit in the trunk, but that was okay — Donnie had sold the rest of his kit for a bag of weed.

The last remaining member of The Beagles, Randy, remained at The Henley Center in Winslow, AZ after he relapsed back into sexual dysfunction just days after being released from the center. While being home for only forty-eight hours, Randy exposed himself to one of the bushes outside his home and attempted to have sex with it; unfortunately, it was one in the front yard. Had he chosen one in the back, a neighbor would never have recorded the incident and uploaded it to social media with the tag #worstsextapeever. Authorities promptly arrested Randy and sent him back to Winslow.

After Donnie was settled in the car, Joe drove to an address in New Canaan where, after passing through a security gate, they were met by Anthony Carbona himself.

"It's great that youse guys finally had a chance to meet."

Glenn and Donnie exchanged confused glances.

"What, your driver didn't tell yas who he is? Boys, let me introduce you to the one and only Max Ruby."

Joe looked at his passengers and saw the anger in their eyes.

"Don't be that way, fellas. If you aren't loose, you won't perform well for my granddaughter and you definitely don't wanna disappoint her, or me."

Joe helped Glenn and Donnie haul their equipment into Carbona's home, where they set up in a great room.

"I almost forgot, I got youse guys a little something."

Carbona handed Glenn, Donnie, and Joe yellow, purple, and red shirts, respectively, along with matching socks and cargo shorts. "Put on your uniforms, boys."

"He's not playing with us," Donnie protested.

Carbona got into the singer's face. "You wanna rethink

your position on that? Wait, where's the bass player anyway?"

Glenn attempted to explain where Randy was, "He, uh..."

"Don't beat around the bush!" Carbona demanded. Unfortunately, Carbona's words led Glenn and Donnie into a fit of hysterics.

"He's back at the Henley Center," Joe stepped in. "Relapse."

Carbona, Glenn, and Donnie all stared at Joe.

"What, I keep up to date with everything Beagle."

"Well, looks like you'll be a trio after all."

"I'm not playing with that mother fu..." Donnie didn't finish his sentence.

Carbona gave him a stare that suggested Donnie and Glenn had no choice but to accept Joe as a member of the band, for that day anyway.

"What I mean to say is, we don't have an extra guitar for him."

Carbona left the room for a minute and came back with an acoustic guitar in his hands. "Problem solved, fellas. Now go change and warm your fingers up. For every note you miss, I'm going to charge a finger."

Blood rushed from Joe's face. He hadn't picked up a guitar in months and imagined life without fingers.

"Relax, kid, I'm just fucking with ya. Youse think I would hurt anyone on my granddaughter's birthday? Waddya think I am, an animal?"

The trio went to change and returned to find forty or so kids sitting on the floor of the great room, awaiting the show. Each took their position on the makeshift stage.

"Hi everybody," Glenn said while putting the strap of

his guitar around his shoulder. "My name is Glenn Beagle, and these are my friends, Donnie and Max. Can we sing a few songs for you?"

"Yeah!" forty tiny voices said in unison.

"Great. We'd like to start out with a song to honor the memory of a good friend of ours. Bernie, wherever you are, this one is for you. One, two, three four..."

The trio then went into a rousing rendition of Humpty Dumpty.

Terry Tomasulo was a steady visitor of Jenny Slade's while she went through rehab in Pasadena. She now went by her birth name of Michelle and cut ties with all things Slade. As part of that, with Tommy's help, she started a charity called The Fallen Angels Foundation, which raised money to help women get out of the sex industry. She was amazed when an anonymous donation of over one million dollars was made to her foundation just a month after it launched.

Michelle stayed in Pasadena for a month after her treatment was over — she didn't feel ready to enter the outside world. After that, she decided to move back to Indiana and live with her parents while she continued to get her life together. She remained close with Terry but vowed not to start a romantic relationship until she was sober for at least one year. Eventually she would go to college, earn undergraduate and graduate degrees in psychology, and work tirelessly to counsel women who left the sex industry.

Terry, meanwhile, played no small part in helping future victims of LAs infamous sex industry when he confronted "Fast" Eddie Costello at the Greyhound station. He spotted Costello prowling for victims and interrupted a conversation the sleaze-ball was having with a young woman who'd just stepped off a bus from Iowa. She appeared to be buying his bullshit, hook, line, and (almost) sinker.

"Excuse me, Eddie?"

Costello turned around and his look of annoyance was quickly replaced with one of genuine fear once he realized who'd interrupted him.

Terry grabbed Costello by the lapels and directed his attention to the girl. "Do you want to be in porn?"

"What? No!"

"Then stay as far away from this creep as you can."

The girl ran away toward the queue for Taxis.

"What do you say you and I take a little walk. I got that warrant you were asking about at the station."

Terry led Costello to a large, blue Cadillac.

"What are you a pimp or something?" Costello asked. His question was answered by a punch to the stomach and another to the face.

"Consider your warrant served," Terry said, then popped the trunk and put Costello's unconscious body inside. If any law enforcement officers or station security guards saw this go down, none of them did anything about it.

Terry took the 405 to the 101 and tried to hit every pothole along the 45-minute drive. He got off in Agoura Hills and parked in the driveway of a former Major Leaguer known for his bad temper. Bob "Nasty Boy" Hagan opened his garage door and Terry pulled his Cadillac in and opened the trunk.

"I believe you two have some catching up to do," Terry

said to Costello as the former pitcher pulled him from the trunk. In the empty space next to the Terry's car was a chair, a bucket of water, a marine battery, and alligator clips.

"Payback time," Nasty Boy said.

After helping Nasty Boy secure Costello to the chair, and fitting a gag into Costello's mouth to muffle his imminent screams, Terry opened the bay his car was parked in and drove off into the cool LA night. He popped in a cassette of Kiss Alive II, rolled down his windows, and blasted Shock Me on his way back to the 101.

Those Nelson twins have a sick sense of humor, he thought and then merged onto the highway.

Acknowledgements

First off, I would like to thank the fans of the Farrah Graham series for your support. While writing these books takes a tremendous amount of time and work, it is also a guilty pleasure and the fact that you enjoy them so much fuels the passion I put into crafting each story.

My editors, Joe Gartrell and Ben Gibson at Word Mule, were invaluable during this process. Beyond the tweaks and trims they made to each line, their big picture suggestions (and questions) forced me to take another look at the overall story and make it the best it could be. I would (and have) recommended the Word Mule team to anyone in need of thoughtful editors interested in being part of a team.

My beta readers, Nicole Wilson, Sue Oates, Marc Siciliano, and Cecilia Cordova-Kling were also life savers as they pointed out typos that were invisible to me in the final draft. Thank you Nicole, Sue, Marc, and Cecilia for your feedback and continued support.

I want to give you all some insight into how this book came to be, as it marks a return to the quirkiness that was evident in the first Farrah Graham book, Uncorking a

Murder. People who know me well know how much I love music, particularly 80s hair metal. This story started with the idea of twin detectives who have a penchant for that genre. Growing up in Connecticut, I knew these identical twins who lived near me; Mike and Rhett Connelly. They wore their blond hair long and my brother and I nicknamed them the Tom Petty twins; though I'm sure we weren't the first to do so. Today, both are cops in Stamford, and Detectives Murray and Jeff Nelson are based loosely on them.

Speaking of Murray and Jeff, if you have kids around the same age as mine, you no doubt remember The Wiggles and Murray and Jeff were the guitarist and keyboardist of that outfit. That band brought a lot of joy to my kids when they were younger and I'll admit to having a rather unhealthy obsession with them myself (albeit not to the level of Joe Feld's obsession with The Beagles). The other members of the band were Greg and Anthony, whose names found their way into this story respectively as The Cowboy and the HGTV-loving crime boss.

I thought it would be a nice twist to have a real jerk like Bernie Deville play in a band like The Wiggles but wanted to pull back the curtain to let you know how The Beagles came about. After Glenn Fry of The Eagles passed away, my eighty-four-year-old mother told me that she and my father were going to a yacht club in Ft. Lauderdale to see The Eagles perform. Obviously, they were seeing a tribute band as the prospect of the remaining members getting together and performing for the grey-haired set at a private club seemed unlikely. Nevertheless, I made a joke on Facebook that perhaps my mother meant The Beagles, a band playing covers by both The Beatles and The Eagles. And thus, The Beagles were born.

Detectives Murray and Jeff Nelson loved to argue about heavy metal bands and kept themselves rooted in the 80s by keeping a cassette player in their car. Some of you may have recognized a running theme with each chapter title -- all are the names of songs or bands that I embrace in the body of my soul. Hey, to each their own. Don't judge. \m/ \m/

Lastly, this book is dedicated to a person who has played a very important role in my life. Diane O'Connell is the main office secretary of Trinity Catholic High School in Stamford. I, and many other students, formed a very special connection with Mrs. O'Connell during our four years at the school. For me, that relationship continued through college and, now that my triplets attend the school, remains strong to this day. Diane remains the heart and soul of TCHS and is a surrogate mother to anyone seeking her guidance. I love you, Diane, as do countless students, graduates, and staff at TCHS.

Also By Michael Carlon

All the F*cks I Cannot Give

The Last Homily

Winning Streak

Uncorking a Murder

Return to Casa Grande

Made in the USA
Columbia, SC
27 March 2018